Dancing with

Mark McKay

Dancing with Mortality

Table of Contents

Part One

The Politics of Violence

1981

Chapter 1

County Cork, Ireland

Once, when he was about eighteen, he'd been on a caving expedition in the South Island. They'd been underground for about half an hour, and in his enthusiasm to find the stalactite studded cavern he was looking for he forged ahead, leaving his sluggish mates a minute or so behind him. As he worked his way through a narrow gap in the rock he brushed his helmet against something, and the headlamp went out. The total blackness, devoid of even a promise of light, was so dense and cloying he thought it might smother him.

For a moment, when he'd turned off the engine and cut the Land Rover's lights on arrival here a few hours ago, he'd had the same sensation. The blank overcast sky and the absence of anything human or otherwise that might cast a light, had blotted out the world. After a while, when his eyes had adjusted, he could make out the shifting shapes of trees and a small stretch of road, but not much else. Now he waited.

The sound of automatic gunfire shattered the stillness. Harry looked towards the distant beach, and saw intermittent flashes of white light rip open the blackness. He stared out the window with a grim fascination, one hand tight on the steering wheel, his heart pounding. A minute later the firing stopped, and the echoes, then the sighing of the wind, reclaimed the darkness.

He was sure the noise must have been heard by the local residents, but then remembered there weren't any for at least two miles. He turned to look behind him, but there were no approaching headlights, or indeed any sign of life in the blackness. He sat very still in the Land Rover, his other hand holding the two way radio. He was in a layby in a lane off the main road to the beach, and now he waited for the call telling him he could safely drive down there.

What the hell had happened? O'Riordan had warned him that these men wouldn't come quietly. They'd made a fight of it. Should he drive to the beach? Better wait for the signal first. He realised how tense he was, and he relaxed his grip on the steering wheel and took a few slow deep breaths. Then he checked his watch – 5am and still pitch black outside.

He'd been parked since 1am, and although he knew there was a team of SAS men nearby, he'd heard and seen nothing. The only things discernible were the salty tang of the sea and the soft breeze rising and falling.

Then, around 2:30am, just as he'd started to doze fitfully, he was jerked into wakefulness by the sound of an engine on the main road. Nothing to be seen, whoever it was had dispensed with the headlights. The engine faded as the vehicle – a truck he guessed, wound its way down the incline to the beach.

Then everything was quiet again, until the gunfire just now. But now he thought he could hear a new sound through the darkness,

5

like a distant staccato drumbeat. It was getting louder all the time. Suddenly the sound changed it's timbre, and he recognised the sound of a galloping horse coming off the sand and onto the road. He sat mesmerised as the sound came ever closer. He saw the shadow of the horse as it raced past his parking place, and he had just enough time to make out the shape of a man on its back, then all he could do was listen as the hoofbeats faded into the distance. He doubted very much that it was an SAS man riding. Now what?

The radio spluttered into life and he nearly dropped it in alarm. Hanson's voice:

'Operation successful. It was definitely an arms shipment. Tell Litchfield that we've secured both the boat and the arms. I haven't counted, but there are hundreds of Armalites and Kalashnikovs. And several thousand rounds of ammunition. Tell Litchfield I'll be in touch tomorrow. And we don't need you down here now. There were fatal casualties, on their side that is.'

'You shot all of them dead? How many?'

'Eight men in all. One got away though. They had two bloody horses in the back of their truck. One man managed to ride out before we could stop him. He was lucky. If we hadn't been surprised you'd have nine casualties. Did you see him?'

'Heard him. Do you know who it was?'

'Not yet. Once we've identified this lot it might give us a clue, but don't count on it.'

'Ok.' Harry felt numb. 'You shot them all, Jesus Christ.'

'That's right. Sorry about that. Stay there for half an hour then go home lad.'

Harry sat quietly collecting his thoughts. He'd come all this way as a supposed observer in the arrest of the men who'd been shot dead on the beach. He hadn't expected the fatalities, and he knew it shouldn't have happened. He'd been told the SAS were trigger happy when it came to the IRA though. That hardly excused their tactics in his opinion.

It was his birthday tomorrow – well today actually. A great place to start your 26th year of existence. A Land Rover in the middle of nowhere. Natalie wouldn't be pleased at his sudden absence either. His wife had something planned for later in the day. He didn't know exactly what, but he knew he wanted to be back in Dublin for it just as soon as he could. He checked his watch – 20 minutes had passed. Still no sign of life from the beach. What the hell, he thought, I'm getting out of here.

He took his time driving back. He couldn't quite believe he'd been involved in the events of this morning, however peripheral that involvement might have been. Working part time for the Secret Intelligence Service had never been on the agenda when he and Natalie left their quiet little house in the Western Suburbs of Auckland to come to Ireland. He knew Natalie wouldn't be happy about what had happened tonight, so of course he couldn't tell her. He'd already lied by saying there was an urgent parcel of documents he had to collect personally in Cork. His lips pursed as he contemplated the ramifications - once you start lying, where does it stop?

There had been very little time to prepare for this operation. He thought back to the phone call that had set this whole train of events in motion. He'd returned from Trinity College, where he was studying Irish, to the one bedroom flat that he and Natalie rented in Harcourt Street. It was about 5pm and she was already there, making dinner. She walked through to the hall to greet him.

She smiled that vivacious smile that had got his attention and kept it the first time he saw her.

'Good day at Uni?'

'As ever. What about you?'

'Fine. I'll tell you later, dinner will burn.' She kissed him and he just had time to stroke her long black hair before she turned away and ran back to the kitchen. 'It's fish tonight, as it's Friday and we're both good Catholics.'

'Only by birth,' he replied. 'I'm agnostic, I like to keep my options open. Let's go with tradition though.'

Ten minutes later they were sat down and eating, when the phone rang.

'Great timing, I'd better get it Nat. Won't be long'. He moved into the hall and picked up the phone.

'Sorry to disturb you Harry.' O'Riordan's deep Belfast brogue filled the earpiece. Harry could feel the urgency in the man's voice.

O'Riordan was their SIS intelligence source inside the IRA. His information on their movements and upcoming activities in the North had been valuable on several occasions.

'What is it Sean? I didn't know you had my number.'

'No one is answering your office phone, Harry. Mr Litchfield gave me your number as a last resort. Is this line secure?'

'Yes, we can talk. There should be someone in the office, perhaps he popped out for a minute.'

'Never mind that now. You need to get information to Litchfield right away. Tonight, or should I say tomorrow morning around 3am, there'll be a large arms shipment coming in on a fishing boat to Ballyrisode beach near Goleen in Cork. It's too late to get the Navy out to intercept them. If you want them you'll need to get some military lads down there in the next few hours. Understood?'

Harry took a deep breath. Goleen was at least 4 hours away by car.

'You sure about this, Sean?'

'Christ, man, do you think I'd be calling if I wasn't? I'd like it if we got off the phone and you found your Mr. Litchfield right away.'

'How many people are we dealing with?'

'On the boat, I don't know, but I expect no more than 4 or 5. On the beach I only have one name – Michael O'Reilly. He'll probably have 3 or 4 men with him to unload the boat. O'Reilly's a dedicated Republican, Harry. He'll shoot in preference to surrendering, so tell your men to watch themselves.'

'Thanks Sean, leave it with me, I'll find Litchfield straight away.'

'Good luck, Harry'. The line went dead.

Harry returned to the dining room. Natalie was looking at him anxiously.

'Who was that?' she asked.

'You know I can't say, Nat. He shouldn't even be calling me here. Listen, I need to go out for a while, sorry. Just to pass on this message, I'll be back in an hour.'

'I wish you'd never agreed to work for these people. I thought they just needed you to do some Irish language translations. That didn't sound like translation work to me.'

'That is all they need me for. Unfortunately my caller couldn't get through to anyone else. But I need to pass this on. Put my dinner in the oven will you? I'll be back in plenty of time to eat it. Just need to phone Litchfield first and set up a quick meeting.'

He met Kevin Litchfield at the offices of Downey's Accountancy Services, only five minutes walk from the flat. Mr. Downey was a myth, as was his accountancy business. Any potential customer walking in off the street would be met with a notice on the door proclaiming Mr Downey's unfortunate indisposition due to illness, which precluded his acceptance of any new business. An unmarked door further down the corridor was a second entrance to the same office, which was in fact SIS headquarters, Dublin branch.

Litchfield sat behind the absent Mr Downey's desk. It was a large wooden desk with a green leather inlaid top, populated by two black telephones and a green shaded desk lamp. Papers of any sort were conspicuous by their absence, until you glanced at the heavy

10

Chubb safe on the floor behind Litchfield. Nothing written stayed in plain sight after office hours.

The office had two smaller and less impressive examples of the Downey desk, with three more telephones, two typewriters, and a telex machine. Jack Hudson, who had been the absent man at the time of O'Riordan's first phone call, sat next to the telex looking slightly sheepish.

'Sorry Harry, I literally popped out for a packet of fags,' said Jack. 'Can't have been more than 5 minutes.'

Harry said nothing. Judging by the smell of alcohol that accompanied the words, he thought that 5 minutes might have been stretched a little further by a visit to the Bleeding Horse around the corner. No time to dwell on that now.

'Spit it out then Harry, what did Sean O'Riordan want?' Kevin Litchfield was the SIS chief of station in Dublin. A public school educated Englishman of about 45, he exuded confidence and charm in his public persona of successful businessman about town. In his SIS incarnation however, he showed a calculated cold bloodedness that Harry found a little disconcerting. He had become progressively larger during his Dublin stint, as evidenced by the tightness of his suit jacket around the shoulders and the paunch overriding his belt buckle. His face had developed a florid complexion, and his razor thin lips, slightly flattened nose and squinting gaze put Harry in mind of a heavyweight boxer who'd taken one punch too many. But the man's mind was sharp, and there was a noticeable absence of charm in his manner this evening.

Harry repeated Sean's message, watching Litchfield's eyes as they opened fully and focused intently on him. Just as he was about to ask why O'Riordan had his home number, Litchfield sat up ramrod straight and swore profusely.

'No bloody way of verifying this, and no bloody time either. O'Riordan's not been wrong yet though.' Litchfield picked up the phone and dialled quickly. Harry walked to the window on the far side of the office and gazed over the lit street below. He felt a dim annoyance at being dragged into operational matters. He'd been employed more in an academic capacity in his opinion. He was supposed to stay away from the rough end of the business.

He turned to the sound of the receiver being slammed back onto the phone.

'Alright Harry, this is how it is,' said Litchfield. 'There's a small team of SAS men who can be in place undetected by 2am. They will wait until the cargo is unloaded, then they'll arrest everyone involved. There will be an interrogation on the spot, then the team will quietly transport these men to Belfast, where the law will deal with them. The guns will be taken somewhere safe.'

'Good,' replied Harry. 'I'm going back to my dinner now, glad to know it's all in hand.'

'Not so fast, Harry. I've given a Captain Hanson your name as a contact. You'll drive to Cork and meet him at this hotel,' he said, passing Harry a folded sheet of paper, 'where you will identify yourself and act as an impartial observer until these men are arrested.

I want you present at their interrogation. It's more than likely that they'll speak Irish amongst each other, knowing full well that we won't have a clue what they're on about. But you will. You may pick up something of interest. Take the Land Rover outside and you'd better leave now.'

'Hang on sir, I'm only here to translate any suspicious Irish language communications that we intercept. I've no training in the field. Send Jack for God's sake.'

'Jack doesn't speak the language. It's perfectly safe Harry, they know full well you're only there to confirm the success of the op and to be present at the interrogation. There's no time to waste, so get going.'

'How will this Hanson know who I am?'

'He's looking for the Land Rover, and if it isn't you driving it they'll be shot. So use the code word 'Sterling' when you meet him if you want to avoid that. That's it, go now. I'll call Natalie and say you're doing some overtime.'

'No sir, I'll call her.' He returned Litchfield's challenging gaze with a quiet fury, and picked up the phone.

Harry had driven as fast as he could to Cork, arriving at the hotel just after midnight. Hanson had been in the car park waiting for him. Dressed in civvies, he was a tall powerfully built man in his mid thirties, with a solid well sculpted face sporting an equally well sculpted Roman nose and steady brown eyes. After verifying Harry's identity he'd briefed him in short clipped tones. Hanson had 10 men, they were on their way (from where God only knew), and that they would be quite invisible to anyone near the beach by 1am.

'Where's that accent from?' said Hanson, abruptly changing the subject.

'New Zealand, why?'

'What's a Kiwi doing in this line of work then?'

'My parents are English. I got into this more by accident than anything else. The locals hear the accent and assume I'm a harmless student, which is what I tell them. Studying Irish at Trinity, which is true enough most of the time. They assume I have no sympathies on either side, Unionist or Republican. I don't contradict them.'

'But you speak Irish fluently I'm told.'

'Fluently enough.'

'I hope so. Enough chit chat then.'

He handed the radio to Harry and told him to park in the layby and await confirmation of success, which Harry had gratefully done. It was unlikely that anyone would approach from this direction. If they did spot him and get curious he intended to say he'd had a few too many and was sleeping it off. He took the flask of whiskey from his coat pocket and had a small sip. Would need some alcohol on the breath to back that story up. But it was a flimsy story and he felt a surge of anger towards Litchfield for dropping him in the deep end. And he was scared. He wasn't armed and he had no military training. He felt exposed and defenceless.

Now, after the lethal conclusion of the SAS ambush, he wondered how the hell he'd allowed himself to be put in this situation. And where was the man on the horse?

Harry had been in Ireland for almost two years. Auckland was a long way from 'the troubles', and although the IRA got some media coverage, the struggle in Northern Ireland seemed remote and slightly surreal. He couldn't see it impacting on his decision to take some time to travel and study abroad. He'd done exceptionally well in his modern languages studies, with a BA and MA under his belt, and was recognised as a talented German and French linguist. Irish presented a quite different challenge, as it was so grammatically and conceptually different. Seeing it written, and looking nothing like the languages he already knew, made him wonder just how ancient in origin it must be. When his tutor had mentioned a scholarship at Trinity College his interest had been aroused, and he'd been pleasantly surprised to find out his application had been accepted.

The plan was to do the post grad degree, travel around Europe, and then return home. Natalie, who had recently finished her own MA in clinical psychology, had bagged a contract through the Irish consulate in Auckland to work as a psychologist assistant at St. Patrick's hospital. And it was an opportunity to travel regularly. They'd only been married 6 months, and it seemed an ideal opportunity to get out and see some of the world before settling down.

The first year they had taken the chance to discover Europe, spending that Summer in France and Germany. They'd travelled between one cheap hostel and another on their limited budget, using the rail links wherever they could to find their way round the popular destinations.

One evening shortly after their return and the resumption of his studies, and just as he was leaving class for the day, he'd been approached by Jack Hudson. Harry had noticed Hudson sitting in on lectures, and wondered what the older man, who took no notes and seemed anomalous in comparison to Harry's studious and mostly twenty-something contemporaries, was actually doing in an Irish lecture.

Hudson was a lean man with a long thin face that had delicately defined features. He sported very long feminine eyelashes, and was immaculately dressed in a three piece pinstripe suit. He introduced himself to Harry and proffered a card with a slender well manicured hand.

'I work in security Mr Ellis. We may have a vacancy for an Irish speaker here in Dublin, if you're interested. Part time of course, we know you need to study. But the extra money will boost your income, and you might find the work interesting too. Phone that number if you want to take it further. Any time during office hours.'

Then, before Harry had a chance to respond, Hudson had smiled and walked away. So more out of curiosity than anything Harry had phoned the number, and a few days later he found himself talking to Litchfield in a local pub.

Litchfield had donned his charming persona for the occasion.

They were sitting in a booth away from the other customers.

16

'Harry, must confess we've got you here under slightly false pretences. Oh the job is real enough, but if you do decide to take it there are certain undertakings we'll need from you first.'

'Such as?'

'Well, firstly we'll need a signature from you confirming that any knowledge you acquire here is not to be disclosed to anyone outside the office. Standard confidentiality stuff. And secondly, even though your involvement will be limited to translating certain documents, there is some risk involved in your being employed by us at all in Ireland just at this time. Am I making myself clear?'

'Not entirely, no.'

'This is shall we say, confidential work. I've taken the liberty of checking you out. I know that both your parents are English, which takes care of the main eligibility requirement. We also made some discreet enquiries in Auckland. I think you'll be an asset to us, as the fact you're neither English nor Irish means you won't arouse certain suspicions. And that your language abilities are first rate.'

'What sort of suspicions are you talking about?'

'Let's just say that if certain people with Republican sympathies got to know you were working for us, they might not take it too kindly.'

'And how real is that risk?'

'Minimal. We have a small office here. No one knows about us, I can assure you. But protocol means I need to point out the pros and cons, that's all.'

'What do I tell my wife?'

'You tell her you're doing translation work for a security firm. And that there may be some anti-social hours involved. That's all true enough.'

'Security firm - who are you really then? You've taken a lot of trouble over me already.'

Litchfield smiled enigmatically. 'I've told you about the work and stated our conditions. You'll be needed on a part time basis, some afternoons and evenings to fit in with your studies here. I think you'll find our financial terms more than adequate. If you accept you'll get a full briefing then. Go away and consider it for a few days, then call me at this number when you've made up your mind.' He handed Harry his card.

He discussed it with Natalie, leaving out the bit about miffed Republicans and the consequent risk. God knew they needed the extra money. The exchange rate against the Kiwi dollar meant that the money they'd brought with them was being spent a little too fast for comfort. He decided to accept Litchfield's offer, even when he found out later that the 'security' firm was in fact SIS. He weighed the extra income against the perceived risk and concluded he'd be here studying one more year then they'd leave Ireland, and any risk of incurring the wrath of anyone would disappear.

After tonight's little party at the beach he wasn't so sure.

Chapter 2

The sky was lightening and the grey cloud cover was dispersing to reveal patches of blue overhead. The intermittent showers of rain that had punctuated Michael's frantic last two hours of riding looked like they might die away completely. There was even the odd ray of sunshine forcing its way between the retreating clouds.

He wasn't sure where he was. An hour ago he'd taken his leave of the road and turned his horse into the fields and up into higher country. Visibility was still poor and it was slow going. All he could do was urge the horse forward at a walk, hoping that the direction they were taking was leading them to the North, away from the beach and his possible pursuers. Now that daylight had arrived he reined his mount in and stopped to take stock of his surroundings.

He'd climbed higher than he thought. Behind him the sea was clearly visible, he reckoned he must have put only ten miles between him and the beach in the last two hours. The horse had found its way onto a track through the rocky ridges that bordered the narrow fields in this area. He needed to strike North East to get away from these ridges and into the forested land where he wouldn't be so easy to spot.

He dismounted, tying the reins to an outcrop of rock. The horse gave a soft snort and nuzzled his shoulder gently. He brushed its long neck in automatic response.

'Glad to have me off your back are you? You look as exhausted as I feel.'

He sat down heavily on the pebbly surface. His legs felt rubbery, and he realised just how tired he was. He gave a long exhalation, and then as he allowed himself to relax a little, the import of what had transpired just a few hours previously hit him hard, like a punch to the stomach. He put his head in his hands, taking long rasping breaths, waiting for his body to find some equilibrium again.

After five or so minutes, when his breathing became more regular, he stood up and went over to his horse. He stroked its neck and head softly, whispering calming words in its ear.

'Listen with me.'

Horse and man stood stock still, sensing their environment. Michael could see the track by which they'd negotiated their way, winding through the fields down to the road, which was no longer visible. His eyes and ears were sharp with the aftermath of adrenalin. The green of the countryside below him and the birdsong of the morning were crystal clear. He knew that the horse was more sensitive to disturbances than he was, but the animal seemed calm enough. He relaxed a little more.

He started to try and piece it all together. Someone must have informed on them. That was always a danger, but he thought this particular event had been kept well under wraps. Obviously not. Then he thought of the men who to the best of his knowledge must all be either dead or captured. He knew three of them personally, but the men on the boat had to be taken on trust. Could one of them have been an informer?

Once the arms were unloaded the plan had been to transport them to arms dumps in the South Armagh region, but he'd intended to hold a dozen rifles and ammunition back. He and Tom O'Brien were to load up the two horses and ride to a deserted farmhouse further South, the theory being that it was always useful to have a private stash available just in case.

Now Tom was lying dead on the beach. They'd known each other since primary school, and lived on the same street in West Belfast. Their friendship had jelled and grown as they rode shotgun for each other to and from school. The sectarian divide was literal enough, you knew where you could and couldn't go. But at times there were trespassers from the Protestant side, and it was best to see them first, then fade into a side street.

As adolescents, and having witnessed some savage attacks instigated by both factions, they'd stopped avoiding trouble and actively gone looking for it. Everyone knew someone or had a friend who'd suffered from the unpredictable violence. People would get shot on a whim. There was both fear and anger in Michael, and he directed it back at the bastards who'd been grinding the Catholic population of Belfast down since before Cromwell's arrival in Ulster. And relentlessly ever since.

He was a well built lad even at 16, and wasn't afraid to fight. But sometimes his anger would predominate over a rational assessment of the odds in these encounters. Tom, who was just as angry but more level headed, had helped him out of some nasty confrontations simply by calming him down. Had saved his life effectively.

He remembered 1968 when the Civil Rights movement came to Belfast, with its demands for fairer Catholic treatment. And what had happened? Just an appalling escalation in violence, especially in the following year when houses were burned, and people were killed or driven out of their homes. Shortly after that the British troops arrived. And we were grateful for them too, he thought ruefully. How that changed.

At the same time the Provisional IRA came into being, as a result of a split in Republican ranks over participation in the political process. The faction that became the Provos had been embarrassed at how unprepared they were to actively defend Catholics during the Belfast and Derry riots. Now they intended to redress that error by resorting to more traditional tactics.

Michael hadn't thought about joining the IRA in '69, because they weren't seen as an influential force at that point. Although his daily life could be punctuated by violence, his plan to cope with it was to do well at secondary school, go to Queens University, then find a way out of Belfast.

Then on Bloody Sunday, January 30, 1972, everything changed. When he heard the news that 26 unarmed civil rights marchers had been shot by British troops in Derry, he knew he no longer wanted to run away from the problem, he wanted to do something to fix it. Catholics should not allow themselves to be shot in the street. They needed to fight more tangibly for their rights and their own

22

protection. Marches and politics were achieving nothing. The only person he confided in about this change of heart was Tom O'Brien. Tom felt the same way he did, and they weren't the only ones. After Bloody Sunday there was a sudden influx of young men wanting to join the IRA, and along with Tom, he became one of them. In 1972, aged 18, he stopped being an uncommitted spectator, and embraced the politics of violence. He'd maintained that embrace wholeheartedly ever since.

Those bastards didn't give us any chance to surrender, he thought bitterly. They just opened fire and didn't stop. The first intimation of trouble came when two searchlights suddenly appeared from the direction of the dunes, illuminating the men on the beach clear as day. With yells and curses Tom and the others tried to evade the light, and then the firing started. He doubted if any of his men even had the chance to return it.

If he hadn't been in the back of the truck preparing to lead out the horses he'd be dead now. He'd quickly mounted his terrified horse and jumped it straight out onto the sand. He saw Tom face down with blood streaming from his head as he kicked hard at the horse's flanks. The animal needed no encouragement to gallop like hell away from the bloody melee. He was damn lucky the road away from the beach had no one on it, they must all have been in the surrounding dunes. Obviously not expecting a man on horseback to come out of there so fast. But given the amount of automatic fire raining down, both he and the horse had been fortunate to escape unscathed.

He exhaled long and slowly, shock and sadness mingling together. With that level of gunfire it seemed unlikely that anyone else on the beach would have survived. He'd not be drinking another pint anywhere with Tom O'Brien again. His sadness began to be tempered with anger. He needed to stay alive, get further away from here, and work out what came next. The first thing to do was to seek more cover. He suddenly realised that his clothes were damp, and he shivered. He needed to get moving. He listened again intently to the sounds of the day around him, and could hear nothing to suggest anyone else was nearby. Not that I'd hear them coming anyway, if they're any good, he reflected.

He looked back once more to the distant sea, then mounted his horse and urged it onward. He would find somewhere secluded where he could lay low for a few hours. Then maybe he could ditch the horse and risk taking a bus back to Dublin. He moved his hand up to his chest, to seek out the reassuring presence of the Browning semi automatic pistol in the inside jacket pocket. He had one spare magazine in the other pocket. An instrument of last resort, the only time he carried it was during an operation. Unless he was stopped and searched by the army or Garda men it would stay just where it was.

The sun warmed his back as he flicked the reins. The horse picked up the pace a little, though on this uneven terrain it would be tough getting it to trot, let alone canter. After twenty minutes the slope began to even out, the rocky path gave way to a grassy track, and he could see the forest looming ever closer. Ten minutes later he was swallowed by the trees.

Siobhan O'Reilly shuffled impatiently through her bag and found the house keys. She'd walked for twenty minutes from the Harcourt hotel where she worked as personnel manager, to the small terraced house she rented off Fitzwilliam Street. The dusk of early evening was rapidly deepening into darkness as she opened the door and stepped into the hall. After removing her coat she walked through to the narrow kitchen and filled the kettle. She retrieved the teapot from the draining board where it had languished since breakfast, and after quickly rinsing it added two teaspoons of tea. Stifling a yawn, she switched on the radio and waited for the kettle to boil.

She ran a hand through her wavy red hair. It needed brushing. God knew at the best of times it was difficult to bring any semblance of order to her flowing but unruly locks, which seemed to have a mind of their own. She walked back to the hall and looked at herself in the mirror, picking up the hairbrush she kept on the hall table for bad hair moments. Should just cut it short she thought, as the brush found its way through the tangles. But she was proud of her long auburn hair. Someone had once told her she reminded him of a Pre Raphaelite painting, and after she'd browsed through a number of illustrated art books on the movement in the local library, she could see why. She could easily have substituted for one of Rosetti's models. She was 25, and had the full lips and pale skin to complement the hair, with a pair of pale blue eyes, and a well

proportioned figure. Born in the wrong age she thought wistfully –
sure his models didn't come from Belfast either.

Her reverie was interrupted by a soft knock at the front door. She
paused her brushing, slightly surprised. Not many people knew
where she lived, so callers at this hour were rare.

'Who is it?'

'It's Michael sis, let me in.'

She dropped the brush back on the table and walked quickly to the
door and opened it. 'I didn't know you were in Dublin,' she began.
The smile on her lips and the surge of happiness she felt on hearing
her brother's voice were extinguished by the deadly intensity etched
on his face. He looked bedraggled, tired and on edge. He saw the
effect his appearance had produced and tried to smile.

'Siobhan, good to see you.' He came through into the hall and
wrapped her in a bear hug, lifting her off her feet. At a shade over
six feet he was a powerfully built man and she felt the breath go out
of her.

'Put me down,' she gasped, and he laughed as he released her. His
laugh brought back some of the light to his equally pale blue eyes,
and his face relaxed for a moment. She felt a stab of relief at seeing a
flash of the big brother she knew and loved. Then his face turned
serious again. She knew something bad must have happened, but
decided to say nothing on that score.

'I'm making some tea, want some?'

'Yes, that would be grand. You alone?'

'Just me and the radio.' She tried to smile but his mood had infected her and it died prematurely. 'Go into the living room, I'll be there in a minute.'

She returned to the kitchen and found another cup. As she filled the teapot the radio intruded on her thoughts:

'Unconfirmed reports are coming in of a shooting involving the Provisional IRA and British Army units in Cork earlier today. We're told there have been fatalities, but of whom and how many exactly is still unknown ..'

Siobhan switched it off, her heart sinking. She took a deep breath and poured the tea. She took it through to the living room, where Michael sat quietly staring out the window.

'Thanks,' he said, wrapping his hands around the cup and taking a sip. 'That's good, you always make good tea.'

He looked around the room. It wasn't a large room and Siobhan hadn't cluttered it with too many ornaments. There was a Victorian style fireplace with a mantelpiece sporting a few half used candles in saucers. Above those hung a poster of the Lady of Shallot, a redhead in a flowing white dress, sitting in her boat prior to drifting down to Camelot.

'Don't remember that being here last time.'

'That's me in my fantasy life, Michael. When I get tired of managing the staff at the Harcourt I pretend I'm in a boat on a river far away, chasing gallant knights.'

He raised his eyebrows. 'Such imagination. I see the resemblance, sure enough. Have you read the poem? She was cursed.'

'I know, but she died for love.'

His lips formed a harsh straight line, then he sighed. She sat down beside him on the sofa, which apart from the coffee table and a bookcase was the only other item of furniture in the room. She placed her hand on his shoulder.

'What happened? What are you doing in Dublin? You never said anything about coming down.'

'I heard the radio from here, while you were making the tea. That's what happened.'

Siobhan put her tea down on the coffee table. She noticed a slight tremble in her hands, and her heart began to race.

'Jesus Michael, it said people had died. How many?'

'Don't know for sure – I'm pretty sure I'm the only one who got out though.' He decided not to upset her more by mentioning Tom. 'I had a horse. You don't need to know about it Siobhan, the less you know the better.'

She looked at him, her eyes widening. Suddenly she had both hands on his shoulders and was shaking him and shouting. 'No I don't want to know what you do. And I don't want to be the one identifying your dead body on a slab somewhere. I don't!' She burst into tears and put her arms around him, holding him as tight as she could. She felt the shape of the Browning in his jacket pressing into her breast.

They stayed in that embrace, and Michael stroked her back. 'I know girl, I know. I'm sorry.'

28

She finally released him and stood up, wiping away the tears and regaining some composure. 'I'm finished now. I'm making bolognese, want some?'

'Sure. I need to stay a night or two.'

'Who knows you're here?'

'A couple of people in Belfast know I went to Cork. They know nothing about you.'

'Stay as long as you need.' She went back into the kitchen and opened the fridge.

'Turn on the radio Siobhan, there might be more news.'

'No.' She took a deep breath, her heart still racing. 'I've had enough news thank you.' She found the mince in the freezer compartment. Without thinking she suddenly blurted out 'Where's your horse?'

He joined her and they looked at each other for a moment. Then they were both laughing, and some of the tension of the past half hour receded.

'You got anything stronger than tea?' he said.

'No, I don't keep much booze in the house.'

'I'll go out and see what I can find.'

She gave him a swift glance. 'No Michael, you stay right here. I'll go out and get a bottle of wine in a minute.' She smiled and threw a playful punch at his shoulder. 'It's good to see you. Tell me how they all are up North these days.' She put her worry and shock to one side and began preparing dinner. 'How's Tom?'

Chapter 3

Harry eased the Land Rover into a parking space and looked up at the windows of Downey's Accountancy Services. Impossible to know if anyone was there without going up, and normally neither Jack nor Litchfield arrived before 10. He locked the vehicle and went up to the office. Nobody around. He left a note to the effect that he would be in later, after catching up on some sleep. He wondered if Litchfield knew yet just what had transpired last night. Surely he must. Harry decided not to dwell on it. He left the Land Rover keys on Litchfield's desk and then walked back to the flat.

He expected Natalie to be on her way to work, so was surprised to find her sitting in the dining room, obviously waiting for him. She was dressed for work, in a dark knee length skirt and a light blue button up blouse, but she hadn't put on any make up as yet. Her dark hair, which she usually put into a ponytail before leaving the house, hung loose around her shoulders. She was looking stern and worried as he joined her on the sofa.

'He called twice, first at 6 O'Clock then again at 7. Wanted to know where you were. I said he knew where you were, because he'd sent you to Cork to pick up some papers, but all he said was that you should call him as soon as you got back. Then I heard on the radio just now that there was a shooting last night, and I thought something might have happened to you, but that's ridiculous isn't it? You only went to get some papers.' Her eyes were wide and misty, yet they bored into his with a steely intensity. 'But I couldn't get it out of my head. Why was that horrible man calling you? So I've been sitting here waiting and worrying, and inventing all sorts of stories about what could have happened, and ..' Suddenly she came to a dead stop, her eyes narrowing, anger distorting her features. Then she slapped him hard across the face.

'Shit!' Harry put his hand to his reddening cheek, shocked by the blow. 'Nat, there was nothing to worry about, really ..'

She looked back at him cynically, then her face softened marginally, though here eyes still blazed. Her voice was flat but clear. 'I don't believe you. Now I'm going to work.'

With that she rose from the sofa, retrieving her jacket from the back of the dining room chair as she walked through to the hall. She quickly adjusted her hair. 'See you later.' She slung her bag over her shoulder, opened the front door, and was gone.

Harry sat, head in hands, stunned. A tiredness both mental and physical started seeping through him. He couldn't think, and his body became heavier with each passing second. Through the fog in his brain he registered irritation at Litchfield's lack of foresight with his bloody phone calls. This was not how it was supposed to be at all, he reflected. Damn it, I need sleep. He dragged his body from the sofa to the bedroom, stripped down to his underwear, and got into bed. But even though he was tired, he found himself thinking back to earlier days, to his first meeting with Nat.

It was his second year at Uni. There was a concert on campus one evening, he couldn't even remember who was playing now. It had been packed though, standing room only. A girl had brushed past him, knocking his drink from his hand as she did so.

'Oh My God, I'm so sorry,' she said.

He looked at his beer stained arm, and then at her. There was a split second where something passed between them, like a flash of recognition, though he'd never seen her before. Then she smiled.

'Can I get you another one?'

And that was it, they clicked. They started seeing each other. She was vivacious and sporty, and had just been chosen for the New Zealand under 21 Netball team. Her enthusiasm for her sport and her sheer love of competition fascinated him, sporty was the last thing he was. He loved his rugby, but strictly as a spectator, he knew he wouldn't last five minutes on a rugby field. She teased him about his relative inactivity and he told her he burnt more calories thinking than she ever could playing Netball. She was sharp witted too, and she wanted to know why people acted the way they did, hence her study of psychology.

It very quickly became serious. They didn't need anyone else for company, they were entirely wrapped up in each other. In the summer of that year he remembered a camping trip they took. It was to one of the more isolated West Coast beaches in Auckland, and it was approached via a steep pathway through the bush. They parked the car and took two large packs consisting of a tent and two days supply of food and water, then found their way down.

In the midday sun the black sand, which glittered silver with iron filings, was too hot to walk on barefooted. The beach formed a

32

kind of natural amphitheatre which swelled the sound of the waves into a constant muffled roar, and the place seemed so elemental and primordial that you could be forgiven for thinking you were the last remaining inhabitants on the planet. Nobody came along in the two days they were there to dispel that illusion.

They spent those days and nights swimming, walking, reading, making love, and most of all talking. Nat wanted a family but she also wanted a career, her own intellectual space as she put it. She loved New Zealand, but no matter how beautiful it was it existed in isolation from everywhere else. On the Southern edge of nowhere. She wasn't going to settle down until she'd done some travelling and seen how the other half lived.

Harry had no problem with that. No point in being a language student if you didn't at least visit the countries whose languages you so assiduously studied. Even live there for a while if you could.

And so it had unfolded. Perhaps not quite as foreseen, they had come to Ireland rather than France or Germany, but it had proven nonetheless interesting. SIS was certainly unforeseen.

That thought dragged Harry firmly back to the present. His mind drifted between annoyance with Litchfield, and guilt at how his lying had provoked such a violent response from Natalie. The image of her aggrieved face was the last thing he was conscious of, before drifting into a troubled sleep.

It was late afternoon, and already the light was fading in an overcast sky. A chilly wind whipped Harry's face as he walked briskly from the flat to the office. His intention was to give his report on the previous evening's events to Litchfield, and then head home to make peace with Nat. He was searching his mind for a diplomatic way to convey his displeasure about the unnecessary phone calls, when he realised someone was calling his name. He looked quickly behind him. It was Jack Hudson.

'Harry, good thing I caught you first. He's in a foul mood. He was expecting you hours ago.'

'Didn't you get my note? I needed some sleep.'

'Yes, we got it. Didn't cut much ice with the boss though. What happened last night? No, don't tell me here. We'll be there in a minute.'

They walked on in silence. A few minutes later they entered the office. Litchfield was sat in his customary place, his face a picture of absorption as he studied a file laid on the desk. Harry took off his coat and glanced across the room, gauging Litchfield's mood. Jack was filling the kettle at a sink on the far side of the office, his back to both of them.

'Tea, Harry?'

'No thanks Jack.'

Litchfield looked up, and glared at Harry. Then he glanced briefly at Jack's back.

'I'll have some, Jack.'

'Right you are boss.'

Litchfield turned his attention back to Harry, gesturing with an outstretched hand.

34

'Take a seat Harry.'

Harry did as he was told. He sensed the other man's irritation, and decided to check his own annoyance until Litchfield had vented whatever he wanted to vent. It wasn't long in coming.

'It would have been bloody useful if you'd been here earlier and I'd got your report on what happened last night. I've waited most of the day to get anything out of Hanson, who frankly was reluctant to say a great deal. I do however have this preliminary report now, which tells me that eight IRA men were shot dead resisting arrest, and not much else. Oh yes, and one escaped. Anything you can add? What the hell happened out there?'

Harry recounted the events as he'd witnessed them. Litchfield's eyebrows rose as he mentioned the man on the horse, but otherwise he showed little reaction.

'I was too far away to know what went on sir,' finished Harry. 'All I know is they got all the arms and they shot everyone – except the one. In my opinion those men weren't given the chance to resist arrest. It was all over pretty quickly.'

Litchfield leaned back in his chair and said nothing. He took a sip of tea, closed his eyes, and stayed immobile, thinking.

Harry was about to continue, but Jack raised a warning hand, and he held his tongue.

Then Litchfield returned to the room, eyes fixed once more on the file on his desk. He addressed Harry without looking up.

'They're still identifying these casualties. If Hanson's mob was trigger happy then our escapee will no doubt relay that to his superiors. I would expect some retaliatory action as a result. Of course we don't know who your horseman was, but we'll put the Garda on high alert for known IRA men in Dublin. Not that it will help much, there are plenty of them around. However you cut it, we've inflicted a serious blow. And we've pissed off certain people more than we needed to. It was one thing to arrest them, another to cold bloodedly massacre them. Yes, we'll need to keep our wits about us for a bit.' He closed the file, and gently thumped the desk.

Harry felt a tinge of unease. 'I thought nobody knew about SIS in Dublin.'

Litchfield smiled, his glum mood seeming to dissipate. The charmer returns, thought Harry. He looked Harry full in the face.

'Nobody does, Harry. Let's keep it that way, shall we?'

Harry spent the next two hours translating a statement of IRA political aims and methods, supposedly for new recruits. Some of whom would no doubt need to improve their Irish before reading it, he thought. The language had been in decline since English rule in the 17th century, but it was enjoying a revival in Republican circles.

'Surely there must be an English version of this in circulation,' he muttered to no one in particular.

'Yes, there is,' replied Hudson. 'When you've finished your translation we'll compare them and see if there was anything deliberately left out of the English version. Sometimes you glean some small difference in expression, and that can lead to an insight you might otherwise miss.'

Harry grunted and continued writing. He hadn't expressed his displeasure to Litchfield on the subject of early morning phone calls. He was disturbed that the man hadn't stopped to think what conclusions Natalie might draw, given the fact Litchfield knew that she thought Harry was running a harmless errand. It didn't give him a lot of confidence in the security of the operation, and that added to his worry. He checked his watch, almost 7pm. He needed to speak to his wife, though just right now he had no idea what he was going to tell her.

'I'll finish this tomorrow Jack,' He placed the papers carefully into a manilla folder and carried it over to Hudson's desk. Bidding both men a good evening, he donned his overcoat and set off for home.

She was in the kitchen when he arrived, slicing onions.

'Still mad at me?'

She looked at him calmly but coolly. 'Yes, I am.' She followed his gaze to the knife she was holding, and smiled. 'Not that mad.' She put the knife on the worktop and proceeded to rinse her hands. 'Tell me what's going on, Harry.' She put one of her wet hands to his cheek. 'I'm sorry about that.'

He took her hand and they moved to the living room sofa.

'I wasn't collecting documents, I got drawn into operational stuff. The shooting you heard about on the radio – I was nearby.'

'So much for translation work then.'

Natalie placed her hands in her lap and gazed steadily at them, saying nothing more. After a long minute of silence, Harry decided to come clean. He gave her the edited version of his evening at the beach, sticking to his role as translator and observer. He left out his sighting of the escaping horseman, and his initial meeting with Hanson.

'I wasn't needed in the end, so I left. Simple really.'

'You weren't needed because there was no one left to interview. That's not simple, that just scares me. You can't get involved in that kind of thing. I want you to stop working for them.' Her face wore a determined look.

'We need the money Nat. My scholarship grant is minimal, savings are running low, and if you didn't work we certainly wouldn't last long.'

'We could if we had to.'

She wasn't going to change her mind. He sighed. 'Ok. If I can't agree that my duties are limited to just translating documents, then I'll tell Litchfield what he can do with his job. I'll discuss it with him tomorrow.'

Chapter 4

Michael hadn't slept well. He'd woken twice, once from a dream of being surrounded by hooded men pointing machine guns at him. He'd fired at them, but his gun had no bullets and all he could hear were repeated loud clicks as he desperately pulled the trigger again and again. Then the second time he'd opened his eyes from a dreamless sleep, and not known where he was. It took a few seconds to remember he was in Siobhan's spare room. Thoughts of the beach crowded his mind, but eventually he'd drifted off again.

He got up around 7:30, and found Siobhan had already gone to work. She'd left a note though: 'On early shift, help yourself to everything.' He rummaged through the fridge and kitchen cupboards, eventually settling for fried eggs on toast and a large mug of tea.

The previous evening had been difficult after he'd told Siobhan that Tom was on the beach with him.

'So he's dead then. Another wasted life. Or do you not see it that way Michael?' She didn't look at him, busying herself with the cooking. She slammed the frying pan on to the hob and filled it with mince. 'Jesus, we all grew up together.'

He had no words of comfort to offer her. He muttered something about everyone knowing the risks.

She looked up, her face a mixture of grief and anger. 'It's madness. Sure I want the Brits out just as much as anyone, but not like this. We kill them, they kill us and everything stays the same. Except it doesn't, does it? People I care about die.'

They'd eaten in silence. Siobhan didn't want the TV or the radio on. After dinner they sat quietly in the dining room, working their way through the wine she'd bought. Siobhan alternated between staring out the front window and trying to read a book. Michael decided not to initiate any conversation. Siobhan was convinced of the futility of the armed struggle, and he knew that if he started any kind of dialogue she would simply steer the conversation back to that issue before long. It wasn't something he wanted to discuss that evening. He could have done with a bottle of whiskey to dull his thoughts.

About 10ish Siobhan closed the book and got up.

'I can't concentrate. And I'm up early tomorrow. Good night.' She turned to him and planted a kiss on his forehead. 'Sleep well.' She went upstairs.

Soon after, he did the same.

He finished his tea, and turned on the television. He caught the morning news. There was a report on the 'Beach incident' as they had dubbed it. The eight casualties were mentioned, but nothing about the one who'd got away. He switched the set off.

He needed to report the 'Beach Incident' to his battalion commander in Belfast. Doubtless the word had already reached them up there. But they wouldn't know who, if anyone, had survived or eluded capture. And they wouldn't be at all pleased to have lost such a large weapons shipment. He anticipated an awkward conversation. Not wanting to use Siobhan's phone, he decided to find a public phone box. Taking the spare key from its hook in the kitchen, he slipped on his jacket and walked out the door.

The day was cold but bright, with little wind and a cloudless sky. Michael paused at the top of the small flight of stairs leading to the street, looking carefully to right and left. A few men in suits and overcoats were walking briskly to what he imagined must be their office jobs. A trio of binmen were emptying bins into a rubbish truck about twenty yards away. Nothing felt out of place – a normal Dublin morning as far as he could tell. Being constantly vigilant had become second nature to him though, and his senses were tuned in to the environment as he descended the steps. He turned left, and walked swiftly past the rubbish truck and onwards toward the main road.

Maybe I'm overdoing it, he thought. No one should know of his presence in Dublin, and theoretically not many people even inside the IRA knew how active he was operationally. He'd tried to keep a low profile over the years, and to a certain extent he thought he'd succeeded. But he knew allegiances in his organisation could change, and it was never wise to assume the intelligence services were ignorant of his identity either. So far, he'd not been detained or arrested, and he wanted to keep it that way. He continued to scan the street as he walked, but could see nothing to alarm him. Of course, they could be observing him from a window or from a passing car.

He sighed, - paranoia must be the price of freedom after all. Lighten up, man.

A few minutes later and he stood in a phone box, feeding loose change into the slot. He dialled a Belfast number and waited, still scanning the area for anything unusual. The call was answered after three rings.

'Fitzpatrick Carpentry, how can I help you?'

Michael knew the voice, but before acknowledging it there was a ritual to be followed.

'I need a custom made bookcase for a specialised book collection,' he began.

'What's your specialised subject then?'

'The Easter Uprising, 1916.'

'A fascinating period of Irish history. Are you wanting to place an order now?'

Michael concluded the coded exchange 'Yes, that would be grand.'

'I know that voice. What happened to you then, Michael?'

'Hello Colin, all well with you I trust?' Colin Fitzpatrick was his immediate superior, and the commander of the battalion to which he belonged.

'Fine, thank you. We were wondering if anyone got out. Tell me what happened.'

Michael recounted the events on the beach and his horseback escape.

42

'And you had no idea you were being ambushed?' Fitzpatrick's voice was calm and level, but Michael detected an undertone of doubt. He answered promptly, with a touch of indignation.

'Of course not. Do you think I'd have got myself into any such situation?'

'Ok Michael. We lost good people, not to mention valuable arms. I thought security was tight on this one. I wonder where it slipped up. Where are you now?'

'Dublin. I'll wait a couple of days and then be on my way back to see you.'

'You at a hotel?'

'No, I ..' He paused for a split second. 'I mean yes, just off O'Connell Street.'

He wondered if the pause had gone unnoticed. He thought it best to keep his sister's house out of the conversation. She wasn't affiliated to the IRA in any way, and she wouldn't be amused by him giving her address to his colleagues.

'Call me when you get back to Belfast. We'll have a talk then.' The phone went dead.

Michael felt mildly surprised. Fitzpatrick hadn't asked many questions. Just waiting till I show up I guess, then it will be a full debrief. He was also probably angry that all the organisation, planning and expense lavished on the arms shipment had been wasted. Understandable.

He zipped up his jacket, stepping out of the phone box. Reflecting on the brevity and the content of the conversation, he neglected his usual vigilance as he retraced his steps back to the house.

Siobhan came home late afternoon. She seemed in better spirits, but he could see the anxiety in her eyes when she looked at him. He tried to distract her by suggesting they go out for dinner.

'It's my last night with you. I'm getting the bus back up North in the morning. Let's go to the Italian round the corner, I've got money.'

'We had bolognese last night, Michael. Should you be going out after what's happened?'

'It's fine, Sis. Stop worrying. And I'm sure there's more to Italian cuisine than bolognese. Come on.'

'Alright then. I'm having a long soak in the bath first though. You can entertain yourself until I've finished.' She grinned at him.

That's an improvement, he thought.

It was quiet at Gennaro's. The proprietor knew Siobhan from previous visits.

'Ah, pleasure to see you again Signorina. Not many people tonight, so you can choose your table.'

'Hello Stefano – this is my brother. Be nice to him.'

'Your brother! But he doesn't have your beautiful red hair. He has your eyes though. Please, take a seat.'

'No, you're right Stefano,' she laughed. 'What happened to your beautiful red hair, brother?' She reached up a hand and ruffled Michael's jet black locks.

'You're the only redhead in the O'Reilly family. You're a freak of nature, Sis. Either that or the milkman's got some explaining to do.'

They settled on a corner table, and after perusing the menu decided on Ravioli and a bottle of Chianti. Michael felt himself beginning to unwind, only now recognising how tense he'd been for the last two days. After the second glass of wine Siobhan started to loosen up too. She began telling him her plans for the future.

'When I've saved enough I'm going to buy somewhere by the sea, and manage a hotel. Somewhere that gets the tourist trade in the Summer. You can come and visit of course.'

'Mmm, sounds good. Suppose I should stop doing building work and find something more lucrative to do. Never did go to University in the end. And I'm nearly 30. I thought you wanted to go to America.'

'Yes, that's an option too. I haven't really worked it all out yet Michael. When I do I'll be sure to let you know.'

The talk continued over a second bottle of Chianti and an ice cream dessert. For a few hours Republicanism and dead friends, if not forgotten, were temporarily relegated to the backroom of memory. Around 10.30 they said goodbye to Stefano and returned to the house. Siobhan was a little unsteady on her feet. She put her arm through Michael's and they weaved ever so slightly to the front door.

'I'll make some tea,' she said, heading for the kitchen.

'Ok, I'll be next door.' Michael walked into the living room, switching on the light. He stopped dead in his tracks. The room was occupied. A man wearing a balaclava stood next to the fireplace, pointing a pistol at his midsection. He had one finger to his lips. Michael stood immobile in shock as the visitor motioned him to sit on the sofa. He forced his legs to move, then sat down, his brain racing. The man once again raised his finger to his lips and moved quietly to the door, waiting. Michael did as he was bid, and said nothing.

The gunman was behind the door when Siobhan arrived, holding two mugs of tea. She saw Michael's grim expression first.

'What is it?' she began, then as she closed the door, saw for herself.

To her credit she stifled a scream when she saw the raised finger. She exhaled with a long moaning sound as the mugs left her hands and shattered on the bare wooden floor, then she took an involuntary step backwards.

'Sorry to alarm you,' came a voice from behind the balaclava. 'I need a word with your brother. Why don't you sit down next to him?'

Siobhan moved to the sofa, her breath coming in quick gasps. For a minute everyone was silent. Michael was inwardly cursing the fact that he'd relaxed his customary vigilance, and wondering who the hell this man was and for what purpose he'd been sent. Siobhan was willing herself to calm down. She took a few slow breaths, waiting for her heart to stop thumping.

46

'How the hell did you get into my house?'

Michael put a hand on her arm. 'Don't get angry, Siobhan.' He looked at their visitor. 'What do you want?'

The man stayed by the door, gun levelled at both of them. 'The business of an arms shipment in Cork, Michael. After your phone call this morning it was discussed long and hard. Certain conclusions were reached.' His voice was clear and calm. He's done this before, thought Michael. An executioner. He tried to place the accent. It wasn't Irish, maybe Northern England. Certainly nobody he'd ever met.

'What conclusions?'

'Eight men shot dead, allegedly resisting arrest. But one miraculously escapes, riding a horse no less. In an operation that was supposed to be watertight. And you simply rode away. That's a little too convenient for the high command to stomach, Michael. You sold us to the enemy.'

Michael found himself feeling very clear headed and focused, but certainly not relaxed. His body felt wound up like a spring. Ready to uncoil, should that be an option. The effect of the wine he'd consumed was no longer clouding his perception, adrenalin had overpowered alcohol. Still, the situation was on a knife edge.

'That is ridiculous. I'm owed the chance to tell my side of it in person.'

'Those aren't my orders. You know what happens to informers.' He turned the gun directly on Michael.

Then everything happened at once. The assassin fired as Michael threw himself to the left. He felt the bullet rip through his jacket and into his shoulder, then he hit the floor.

The man's aim had been distracted by Siobhan, who leapt from the sofa and threw herself directly at him, screaming abuse and clawing at his eyes. He stumbled back in surprise, his gun arm momentarily dropping to his side. Then he recovered himself, delivering an uppercut with his left that sent her reeling backwards. He lifted the gun and fired one silenced shot into her stomach. She collapsed with a loud sigh, back onto the sofa.

But the diversion had given Michael enough time to draw the Browning from his jacket pocket. He aimed and squeezed the trigger, drilling a neat hole straight through his assailant's forehead. The man was dead as he crashed backwards on to the wall, and slid down it to the floor.

The Browning wasn't silenced, and the echo of the shot reverberated. It seemed to come off the walls like waves, and he knew it must have been heard. His shoulder had gone numb, but that didn't matter. He rolled off the floor and knelt next to his sister.

She sat with her head bowed, both hands clasped to her stomach. Her breath was coming in sobs as he stroked her hair. He put his palm under her chin and gently lifted her head. They looked at each other, and time seemed to stand still.

'It doesn't hurt Michael, it doesn't …' There were tears in her eyes, and in his.

48

'Don't move, Sis. Keep your hands there. I'm phoning for help.'
He saw the blood seeping through the bars of her hands. 'Why did
you do that, Jesus ...'

He rushed out into the hall, picked up the phone and dialled for an
ambulance.

'It's a gunshot wound, I need them now,' he told the operator.

'Fifteen minutes sir, address please.'

Michael swiftly finished the call and rushed back to the living
room. Siobhan was as he'd left her. He knew that the first hour after
being shot was critical. She was losing blood. He ran to the
bathroom, returning with a towel.

'Need to put pressure on it now,' he whispered. He held the towel
over her hands and gently applied pressure. 'Breathe, just breathe for
me.'

She managed to look up at him and almost smiled. He could see
the far away look in her eyes, and knew she was going into shock.

'Love you,' she whispered.

'Shh, don't talk.' He kissed her forehead. 'They'll be here soon.'
Nothing more to do now but wait.

Fifteen minutes later he heard the sound of an approaching siren,
swiftly followed by a loud knocking on the front door. He opened it
to two burly ambulance men, who marched in with a stretcher. They
glanced briefly at his bloodstained hands, then looked at each other.

'Where's the victim? Is it you?' asked one.

'Living room. Follow me.'

'He's dead,' said Michael as ambulance man number two looked at the balaclava clad gunman stretched out on the floor.

'So I see.' With no further conversation the two men proceeded to get Siobhan off the sofa and on to the stretcher, while keeping pressure on her wound.

'We'll stabilise her as best we can in the ambulance,' said one. 'You coming with us son? You need attention too.'

'No, not right now. Where are you taking her?'

'St. James's.' The first ambulance attendant, a stocky man in his forties with a weathered face and curly graying hair, gave Michael a direct but not unkindly stare.

'Listen Son, I don't know what's gone on here, but I can assure you of two things: the Garda are right behind us, and you need treatment for that wound. I suggest you get it looked at by A&E before you do anything else.'

'I know someone who can help. Please, get my sister out of here.'

Without further ado Siobhan was placed in the ambulance, which pulled away at speed with its siren blaring.

Michael acted quickly. He found a small pack that he knew Siobhan kept in her room. He filled two empty wine bottles with water, and fishing the corks from the rubbish bin sealed them as best he could. He found a pair of scissors in the kitchen drawer. All this he stuffed into the pack. He then proceeded to the bathroom, where he took two towels and added them to his haul. He looked into the mirror. His jacket was bloodstained around the right shoulder, but he had nothing else to wear. He'd lost some blood, but as far as he could tell it wasn't affecting him too much – yet.

He ran upstairs to the spare room. In the wardrobe there was a bundle of cash, which had been destined for the men on the boat delivering the arms. The weapons themselves had already been paid for, but he'd brought several thousand pounds to the beach as a delivery payment. He stuffed the notes under the towels.

He went back to the living room. Placing one hand under the dead man's head, he peeled off the balaclava with the other. The man looked to have been in his mid thirties, with an inch long scar running vertically from his left eye. His prone body wasn't carrying any extra weight and he looked strong and fit. Ex army maybe. It wasn't a face Michael knew from anywhere. He quickly extinguished the lights and grabbed the pack.

It was only after he'd left the house and been walking for ten minutes that his shoulder started to hurt. The throb accompanied his footsteps like a metronome as he walked into the cold Dublin night.

Chapter 5

It was nearing midnight. In the South Dublin suburb of Blackrock, James O'Donnell was considering one last nightcap, before retiring and surrendering to a whiskey inspired slumber. He lifted his middle aged frame from the chair, and deposited the book he'd been reading on the little table he kept close by. It formed a convenient receptacle for both book and whiskey glass, but not the bottle. He deliberately kept that on the far side of the room. In that way he resisted temptation for long enough to constitute what he considered to be a respectable period of abstinence. Not that he'd ever actually defined a 'respectable' period of abstinence. But whatever it was, he'd noticed it shortening recently.

'James bloody Joyce, stream of consciousness rambling,' he muttered, crossing the room. 'Need to be lubricated just to keep up with it.' He found the bottle and poured himself a generous measure. Then he sat down again and resumed his reading of *Ulysses*. This was his second attempt to get through the entire book without discarding it halfway. Well, he'd passed the halfway point this time, he thought with a twinge of satisfaction. But it was never going to be the easiest read as far as he was concerned.

He was jolted out of his musings by a sharp knock at the front door. Rather late for an unscheduled visit. He once more discarded book and whiskey glass, and moved across the room to the window. Pushing the curtain to one side, he looked out.

The house was on the seafront. The living room window when fully uncurtained admitted a pleasant sea view. And if you stood where he was now, you could also look left and see whoever might be knocking at your front door. Unfortunately at this time of night only the street lighting could assist in illuminating his visitor. O'Donnell saw a well built man around six feet tall, with a pack on his back. And he had his left hand pressed to his right shoulder. The face was turned toward the front door, and the light wasn't revealing much beyond the silhouette of a youngish man, he thought.

He tapped on the sash window to attract the young man's attention, then slid it down from the top. A chilly sea breeze swept through the gap.

'The practice is closed. If you need a doctor I can give you a number for the person on call tonight. Or go to the local hospital.'

'Doctor O'Donnell, I'm from Fitzpatrick Carpentry. I was here a while ago with a friend who needed treatment. Do you remember?'

O'Donnell took a long look at the face now fully turned towards him. He grunted in the affirmative. 'That's different lad. Stay there, I'm coming to let you in.' He slid up the window and went to the door.

Michael came inside. O'Donnell noticed his pale and drawn expression. He saw what looked like padding under the right shoulder of Michael's jacket. And the bloodstains on the outside.

'I cut up some towels and wrapped them around the wound,' said Michael. 'There's no exit wound, so the bullet's still in there, but I'm not bleeding too much. Just tired. It's cold out there.'

'Follow me to the consulting room.' O'Donnell led him down the hall and opened a door halfway along. He switched on the light. 'Lie on that bench. Take your jacket and shirt off first. Leave the padding on for now.'

Michael did as he was told. In the meantime O'Donnell manoeuvred a spotlight into position. He wheeled over a stainless steel trolley containing various surgical instruments and disinfectants.

'Right, I'm going to unwind these towels. Just stay as still as possible, and we'll take a look at you.'

'Sure you're up to it Doc? Seems you've had a few this evening.'

O'Donnell held up a hand for inspection. 'See this? Rock steady. It's when I'm stone cold sober you can start to worry. Now don't talk.'

Michael's shoulder was now revealed. There was coagulation around the bullet's entry point, and O'Donnell gave a snort of satisfaction.

'You're not losing any more blood, which is obviously good. And it means no arteries were involved, or you'd not be here with me now. I'm going to give you a local, then I need to take a look around.'

He administered the local anaesthetic and waited a few minutes. Then he prised open the entry point, and inserted a small pair of forceps. After about a minute of poking around he withdrew them.

'Nice clean hole, but I can't feel the bullet. I think it's lodged in the muscle. If I go deep enough I will probably be able to get it

54

out for you, but I think that might start a haemorrhage, and I don't want to take that risk here, so I'll disinfect it and stitch you up.'

'Whatever you think best.'

'As long as you have mobility in that arm you'll be ok. You'll need a surgical procedure in hospital if you want the bullet out though. And I take it that isn't an option.'

'It's not.'

O'Donnell did as promised. He suggested that Michael stay the night to recuperate. The offer was gratefully accepted.

Early the following morning the doctor walked into his kitchen to find his patient sitting at the table with a glass of water.

'How's the arm?'

'Stiff, but I can move it.'

'Good. I'll give you some bandages and antiseptics to take with you. Change them every day for the next week. But you should really rest for at least another twenty four hours. You can stay here one more day, if you don't mind being shut up in my back room while I go about my business.'

'Thanks Doc, but I need to see someone. I can't hang about.'

'In that case, let's get some breakfast organised. And by the way, where do I send the bill?'

'I thought you helped people like me out of political conviction, not for money.'

'Political conviction is expensive.'

Michael laughed. 'Where did you send it last time?'

'To the Belfast address. Fitzpatrick Carpentry.'

'Sure, that will be fine.'

Eammon McKenzie was the General Manager at the Harcourt. And this morning, sitting in his office, he was concerned. His personnel manager was missing, and as a consequence he felt that his high standards of customer service were being eroded. It was Siobhan's job to roster bar staff and chambermaids, ensuring they turned up and performed as required. And to find replacements when they didn't. She was so good at it that he never had cause to interfere. So in her unscheduled and most unusual absence, he would need to do it himself. And he was just plain worried. He'd dialled her number to no avail. What could have happened?

Well, it was now almost 11am, so if she wasn't coming in he needed to check the roster, which she normally kept in her office. As he stood up from his desk to do just that, the internal phone rang. Ah, he thought, perhaps she's arrived. He picked up the receiver.

'McKenzie speaking.'

'Eammon, It's Aoife at reception. I've got Siobhan's brother with me. He would like a word.'

There was a moment's silence. McKenzie remembered a snippet of conversation he'd had with Siobhan at a staff drinks evening some time ago about their respective families. After what was probably one drink too many, she'd mentioned that her older brother was 'a political activist'. The euphemism had not been entirely lost on him, and he didn't press her for more detail.

'I'll come down Aoife.'

He left the office, and descended a flight of stairs leading to reception. Apart from Aoife there was only one other person present. He walked up to Michael, offering his hand.

'I'm Eammon McKenzie, the general manager here. It's Michael, if I remember correctly. Am I right?'

Michael smiled back. 'So she mentioned me.' He took the offered hand. The smile was replaced with a wince as they shook. 'Sorry, sore arm.'

McKenzie withdrew his hand. 'You've injured yourself?'

'It's nothing.' O'Donnell had found him a replacement jacket, a similar zip up model in black, with convenient inside pockets for weaponry. With no telltale bloodstains.

'Is Siobhan alright?'

Michael's lips narrowed for a moment. 'Is there somewhere private we can talk?'

McKenzie didn't reply immediately. He took a few seconds just to size Michael up. Yes, they have the same eyes. He noticed Aoife gawking at both of them with undisguised curiosity, not that he wasn't just the least bit curious too.

'We can use my office. Follow me.'

Back upstairs, McKenzie motioned Michael to the chair facing his desk, then sat down himself. Looks like he could use a good night's sleep, thought McKenzie.

'What's happened to Siobhan, then?' He tried to keep the tone light, in contrast to his rising sense of foreboding.

Michael looked directly into his eyes. 'She was shot last night.'
He saw the eyes widen in disbelief, but before the man could
interrupt, he raised his hand. 'Sorry to come right out with it. I need
your help. They took her to St. James's with a stomach wound, and
I need to find out just where she is now, and what her condition is.'

McKenzie stared at him. Now it was his turn to raise his hand.

'Wait, wait just a moment.' He lowered his eyes, staring at the
desktop. He wanted a little time to digest this. After a few seconds of
rapid thought he looked up. 'You can't ask them yourself?'

'No. Look Mr McKenzie, I feel responsible.' He noted the alarm
on the other man's face. 'Don't think that - I didn't shoot her. But
the man who did was after me. That's all I can tell you. And I can't
go to the hospital and ask directly. I don't want to phone them either.
It will put me at risk, and Siobhan at further risk. Do you
understand?'

'Not entirely. But I appreciate your position. What can I do?'

'I'd like you to phone the hospital as her employer, and inquire
about her condition, the ward she's on, and visiting hours. Will you
do that?'

'Alright. But they'll wonder why I'm calling out of the blue.'

'Let's invent a reason then.'

After further discussion it was decided that on not being able to
raise his most reliable employee on the phone, McKenzie had
concluded something must have happened to her. And as a
concerned boss he was checking all the medical facilities in town.

He found the number and made the call. A few minutes passed as he asked the questions Michael had primed him with. Then he hung up, and turned to Michael.

'They confirmed that she'd been admitted, but because I'm not family they won't say why or tell me what her condition is. They did say however that she's in a private room on Alexander ward. No visitors allowed for the time being, though. They wouldn't give me more than that.'

'That will do. Thank you. And when she is allowed visitors, don't forget to go and see her.'

'I intend to, Michael.'

'I'm indebted to you, Mr. McKenzie. If anyone asks, and they probably will, you made the call under duress.'

'I'll be sure to remember that.'

Michael reached across the desk and shook hands once more. Then he rose from his seat, and walked swiftly to the door. McKenzie heard his rapid footsteps descending the stairs, and he was gone.

Michael had found a cheap hotel on the Drumcondra Road on his return from Blackrock. He didn't intend staying more than one night though. He would change hotels for a few more nights, then decide what to do next. He couldn't stay in Dublin. The Garda might or might not know what he looked like, but they knew that Siobhan O'Reilly had a brother who was at the scene of a fatal shooting. And

Fitzpatrick's boys would certainly have a good description of him.

He was in the privacy of his room, changing the bandage on his shoulder. He tried to concentrate on that immediate task, but his mind wandered. He was struggling to come to terms with the fact that he was now considered an informer. He'd been left in no doubt as to what his superiors thought that meant. Not even a court martial.

How had they found him? Either he'd been careless, or they knew Siobhan now lived in Dublin, and just stuck to her till he showed up. And he'd thought her whereabouts was a well kept secret. He sighed - it was irrelevant now. He'd been found. And Siobhan had suffered for it. Guilt about exposing his sister to a danger he hadn't anticipated mingled with the emptiness of knowing his career with the Provos was essentially over. The one thing he couldn't understand was how quickly someone had been despatched to deal with him. Suspected informers were normally brought in for questioning before sentence was passed. Why hadn't they extended him that dubious courtesy?

He pinned the bandage into place, then donned his shirt. He stood up and looked in the cheap mirror on the wall adjacent the equally cheap single bed he'd be sleeping in later. A tired and somewhat bemused reflection stared back at him.

'Not a care in the world,' he muttered 'And I have no idea what to do next.' He reached for his jacket. What he did know was that he wasn't leaving Dublin before finding out how Siobhan was doing. And to hell with the risk. He checked his watch. If he left now, he should be in plenty of time for afternoon visiting hours.

60

A hospital is the easiest place in the world to walk into unchallenged and unnoticed. Nevertheless, he couldn't rule out that possibility, and he took a long look around the reception area before turning to the board listing the various wards and departments. There was a middle aged couple at the desk talking to the receptionist. A group of nurses were passing through, laughing amongst themselves. They were oblivious of his presence. And two doctors in white coats stood avidly discussing something on the far side of the room. There was a family – parents and two young children, who seemed to know where they were going. They strode off down the corridor into the hospital proper. Alexander Ward was on the second floor. He followed the family, looking for a stairway.

On the second floor, still following the family, he walked down yet another corridor. He passed the haematology department, then took a left turn. He could see about 20 yards further on that the corridor opened into a hexagonal space, and beyond that, above a pair of swing doors, there was a sign reading: 'Welcome to Alexander Ward'.

And in that hexagonal area, outside the door of one of the two private rooms that occupied that space, sat a Garda officer. With his nose in a book.

Michael looked around quickly. He was partially obscured by the family in front of him. On his immediate right there was a recessed seating area under a bay window. On the left a theatre trolley stood unattended against the wall. In one swift movement he wheeled the trolley from left wall to right, and sat down. Now he had a vantage point with extra cover, hopefully. He was just in time. The Garda man looked up as the family came in, gave them a cursory glance, and returned to his book. No doubt where Siobhan was. But unless that man took a break at some point, this was as far as he went. He decided to wait.

Half an hour passed and nothing had changed. Michael felt conspicuous as he sat there with no apparent purpose whatsoever. The Garda man must go for a cup of tea or a toilet break at some point. It was just a question of patience.

Suddenly the door opened. A nurse emerged, quietly shutting it behind her. She said something to the Garda man, who just smiled and nodded. Then she began walking towards Michael. He leaned back in his seat, trying to adopt a relaxed posture. As she passed by she turned her head and smiled. He smiled back, trying to appear nonchalant. At the same time he took a good look. Her light grey uniform made her look rather shapeless. It consisted of a calf length dress and a starched white cap. No belt, and she wore white flat heeled shoes. She was slim however, that much he could tell. And quite young, no more than twenty. Her straight black hair was swept up into a bun, and she wore no make up that he was aware of. He just had time to notice her hazel eyes and well defined mouth before she turned her head back and continued on her way.

He watched her go. He gave her a ten second start, then followed right behind, keeping a discreet distance. She went up a flight of stairs and then into the canteen. He stopped just outside the door and watched as she ordered a cup of tea, which she took to a table by a window overlooking the road. She sat quietly, sipping tea and contemplating the view.

Michael considered the situation. She was in a private spot. The six other people in the room were at tables some distance away, and there was one woman serving behind the counter, who had her back to him. This could go badly wrong, but his options were limited, so he decided to risk it. He entered the canteen, walking casually in her direction. He sat at a table next to hers, in a position that put her diagonally in his line of sight. Then he waited for her to look at him.

Their eyes met, and he saw the flash of recognition.

'Are you following me?' She spoke with a European accent, but he couldn't place it.

Now that they were no more than six feet apart, he had a much better opportunity to look at her. She was smiling again, and he couldn't help but return it. Her smile was infectious. Her eyes had an openness and clarity that he found attractive and disconcerting all at once. Her hands lay palm down on the table, long elegant fingers outstretched. She sat very still, but he could sense a latent energy in that stillness. It was an arresting combination. She saw him looking at her hands, but she left them where they were.

'Are my hands that interesting?'

'Sorry. I didn't mean to stare. And I'm not really following you. But I would like to ask you how your patient is.'

The smile faded. She moved her hands into her lap, and looked at him curiously.

'Why do you want to know? Are you a relative?'

'I'm her brother.'

'I see. You are the reason I have a policeman outside the door. I don't think I should be talking to you, really.'

Michael gave an inward sigh of relief. She hadn't panicked or screamed. In fact she was ice cool.

'You don't need to tell anyone. Just tell me how she is. I can't enquire so easily you see.'

She considered this for a moment. 'Alright. Your sister – Siobhan, was shot in the stomach. But you must know this. She went straight into theatre when she came in. The bullet is gone, but there was internal damage. The surgeon has tidied that up, and she is now stable, but still critical. And under heavy sedation. She is under constant observation for now. There is someone in there with her while I take a break.'

Michael stared at the table. It was as much as he could have hoped for. 'Thank you.'

'I must get back now.' She made a move to get up.

'Just give me five minutes to get out of here before you tell our friend on the door who you've been talking to.'

'I won't mention it. And yes, you should leave first.'

They exchanged a long look. He was trying to read her, would she or wouldn't she? His gut told him she was telling the truth. But he asked anyway.

'Why not?'

'Perhaps they will shoot you. I don't want that on my conscience.'

He stood up. 'I'm sure that won't happen, but thanks anyway.' He hesitated for a moment. 'I'm Michael.'

'Sabine. Is it nice to meet you?'

He laughed. 'Where are you from, Sabine?'

'Germany, a place called Heidelberg. It's in the South. You know it?'

'No I don't. I'd like to talk to you again, Sabine, just to know how Siobhan's doing. Is that possible?'

'So. You're going to follow me again. Well, you know where I am.'

'I do. Goodbye then.' He hesitated. He wanted to stay longer and find out more about this woman. But this was not a time to be distracted. He contented himself with a last look, then abruptly turned around and walked swiftly away.

Chapter 6

'There is news,' Jack Hudson pronounced as Harry entered the office.

'You mean the shooting of that girl? It wasn't far from here either. I saw the TV report. You know who she was? They haven't named her yet.'

'And they won't for the moment. It's been 48 hours though, and we can't keep a lid on it for much longer. But yes, that's the news I'm talking about. Her name is Siobhan O'Reilly, mean anything?'

Harry shrugged. 'No, should it?' Then it hit him. 'You mean, as in Michael O'Reilly?'

Jack smiled. 'His sister. What the TV didn't tell you is that there were three people at the scene when the ambulance crew arrived. Siobhan and two men, one of whom was dead. The other referred to Siobhan as his sister, so by a simple process of elimination ...'

'The man on the horse then, must have been.' Harry pulled up a chair and sat opposite Jack. 'But who shot his sister? And why?'

Jack began to speak, then thought better of it. He punctuated the pause by clearing his throat. 'Actually, we don't know the answer to that one. Wasn't us though.'

'Where's O'Reilly now then?'

'Don't know that either. His sister is in hospital, alive but critical. Perhaps O'Reilly will go there at some point, though that would be unwise in my opinion. Apparently he was shot too. In the shoulder.'

Harry leaned back in his chair. From his perspective, none of this was making him any happier.

'Look Jack, all of this shooting and me getting involved in things I had no idea I'd get involved in, is making me very uncomfortable.' He leaned forward to make his point. 'I think if you continue to ask me to do things I didn't sign up to do, then I have to quit. Natalie is scared, and actually, so am I.'

Jack's face hardened. 'You told your wife what you've been doing?' He almost spat the words.

Harry felt his temper rising. 'I didn't need to. Mr. Litchfield's phone calls asking where the hell I was scared her half to death. She's not stupid.'

Jack stared fixedly at him. When he spoke again the vitriol had gone. 'Alright Harry. Calm down, point taken.' He got up and walked over to the sink in the corner, opening the cupboard directly underneath. When he came back it was with two glasses and a half bottle of Jamesons. Harry raised his hand in protest and opened his mouth to refuse, but Jack cut in before he could say anything.

'I'm about to tell you the facts of life, Harry. I suggest you might like to keep your options open on the drink.'

He poured a half measure into both glasses, taking a small sip from his own, and handing the other to Harry.

'As Litchfield isn't here, I can speak freely. Yes, you were brought in to do Irish translations, but what you weren't told – what goes without saying as far as Litchfield is concerned, is that you will do anything within reason that we ask you to do.' He paused to gauge the effect of his words so far. Harry was looking back at him with a mixture of astonishment and anger, but he remained silent. Jack continued.

'You don't quit SIS, Harry. You can walk out of course, and we can't stop you doing that. But if at any time we need you again for anything – be it ten days or ten years from now, we won't hesitate to let you know. And I can assure you it will be in your best interests to co-operate.'

Harry stared in disbelief. He took a drink.

'Fuck you Hudson.'

Unperturbed, Jack ploughed on. 'Speech over. What will happen in all probability is that you'll finish up here, go back to where you came from, and never hear from us again. There are no guarantees though.'

'Jesus,' breathed Harry. 'Well let me assure you, that as long as I'm stuck in this office with you I will refuse to do anything from now on that doesn't involve Irish translations. Understood?'

Jack sighed. 'Fine. You have holidays coming up, don't you?'

Harry was thrown. 'What? Yes, there's the Christmas break coming up, why?'

Jack gently placed his empty glass on the desk. 'The boss and I are just as concerned as you about the way things are going. The way the arms shipment was handled, and now this shooting of O'Reilly's sister. It's all getting rather messy.'

Harry drained his own glass. He was glad someone else shared his anxiety about the situation. His anger abated slightly. 'So what do you suggest, and what does that have to do with holidays?'

'We're closing the office for the festive season, starting early. As of next week, being second week of December, we're all on holiday. Till further notice.'

Harry felt that sense of unease again. 'What are you worried about?'

'Just keen to preserve our anonymity, that's all.'

'Christ, this is just great. The more I work here the safer I feel.'

His sarcasm went unregistered. 'I suggest you take a trip out of Dublin,' said Jack. 'See a bit of Ireland, it's lovely.'

'And freezing in December. Especially without a car.'

'We've thought of that. You can borrow the Land Rover. All you need to do is fill it with petrol. What could be better?'

'Alright, I'll do that. Thanks. I wonder where O'Reilly is now.'

Jack pursed his lips. 'Difficult to say. Away from here I should think. We don't actually know what he looks like, but that's being rectified. Someone in Belfast is sending us a photograph. Should be here tomorrow. In the meantime, if you should run into him, let me know.' Jack snorted at this witticism, and reached for the whiskey.

'Pour me one while you're at it,' said Harry.

Michael stamped his feet, warding off the cold. He stood by a bus stop about fifty yards from the hospital entrance, waiting. He'd worked as a hospital porter one summer before he finished secondary school, and he remembered the shift pattern. Either on at 7am and off at 3pm, or on at 2pm and off at 10pm. So he figured if he was in the vicinity at the right time, he'd catch Sabine on her way out.

He'd seen plenty of women exiting the reception area around 3.30pm, some in uniform and some not, but she wasn't among them, so he'd retreated to the hotel. Now at 10pm he'd returned, and had been watching for her for ten minutes or so. He had good sight of the reception area from the bus stop, and it gave him a reason to be standing around.

Five minutes later he spotted her. She was out of uniform, in jeans and an overcoat, and her hair was loose. But it was unmistakeably her. She was carrying a case that he realised contained some sort of musical instrument. And he wouldn't need to chase her, because it looked like she was heading right towards the bus stop.

He stood back in the shadows, letting her get closer. When she still had ten yards left to cover he stepped forward into the light of the shelter. He saw the brief hesitation when she realised who he was, then she was in front of him.

'I wondered if I would see you again,' she said. No smile this time.

'Can we talk for a minute?'

'Yes, if you want, I ..' she looked behind her at an approaching bus. 'I must catch this bus. Coming?'

They boarded the bus and took the wide back seat. She lay the case next to her.

'Sit there please,' she said, pointing to the space adjacent the case. He did as instructed. 'I'm not here to hurt you.'

'If you try you will regret it. You want to know about Siobhan? There is no change from yesterday. She is conscious some of the time, but because of the drugs she isn't speaking clearly. Actually, there is something you can tell me.'

'What's that?' He rested his hand on the barrier between them, and tried to ignore her look of disapproval.

'We have no details for next of kin. You are not suitable exactly. Where are your parents?'

He looked away from her, directing his gaze at his reflection in the side window. 'I phoned them this afternoon. They will be here tomorrow.'

The tone of his voice had not gone unnoticed.

'So, it was not an easy conversation then?'

'It wasn't. They blame me for going to see her in the first place. I couldn't really disagree with that.'

Sabine's mood changed to one of concern and she reached across, covering his hand with hers. 'What will you do?'

He tried to hide his surprise at her sudden gesture. 'Can't stay in Dublin much longer. In fact, I'm not sure what the next move is. Now that my parents know about Siobhan ..'

They sat in silence. She made no effort to remove her hand. For him, it was simply good to be touched.

'What's in the case?'

'Oh, it's a saxophone.'

'Doesn't look very big.'

'It's an alto sax. I have a tenor too, but I didn't bring it with me from Germany.'

'And where are you going with this alto sax?'

She finally lifted her hand. She seemed more relaxed now. 'There is a bar I go to some nights. I sit in with a trio, on the last set of the evening.'

'I see. Are you good?'

She smiled then. 'Good enough. Come and listen if you like. I can hardly stop you. It's a free country.'

He found himself grinning. 'I'm afraid you were misinformed about that. But yes, I'll listen for a while.'

She was good. Not that he was a connoisseur of jazz by any stretch of the imagination, but he'd heard a bit. The trio consisted of piano, bass and drums. The only thing he recognised was 'Take Five', by Dave Brubeck. She played the sax part very well he thought, and the drummer delivered a great solo to back it up.

The bar was in a side street off Temple Bar. For a Wednesday and so late the place was well frequented, with a mixture of Irish, Europeans and Americans. When they entered she'd immediately gone across to greet the band, and he'd warily found his way to a small corner table next to the kitchen. He knew it was stupid to be in a public place, but right now it seemed preferable to the four walls of his cheap hotel. The lighting was dim, the room was smoky and humming, and no one showed the least interest in him. He wouldn't stay long.

One hour and two beers later, she joined him, glass of wine in hand.

'Hardly traditional Irish,' he said.

'Not tonight. Did you like it?' Her earlier reserve had gone. She seemed quietly exhilarated by the music she'd helped create.

'I liked you.'

She didn't reply immediately. She took a sip of wine, then stared at the table for a while. When she looked up at him her face seemed determined and sad.

'I want to explain something. I had an older sister, Monika. She was ten years older. She called me the 'Mauer Mädchen', which means the 'Wall Maiden', because I was born the day they started the Berlin Wall. And also because I used to stand in her way when I thought she was going to do something crazy. I was younger, but I always thought it was my job to look after her. She was always doing crazy things.' She stared into the space over his shoulder.

'Go on.' He sensed her distress, but she obviously needed to say this.

'She became a communist when she was 20. Always going to protests, and writing for some underground magazine. Anyway, in 1972 Baader Meinhof put a bomb in the US Army barracks in Heidelberg. It killed a lot of people. Monika was arrested. They knew about her from the communist stuff, but she wasn't involved. The police beat her up badly. She was released later on. We thought she was ok, but a few days after we got her home she died. It was a blood clot in her brain. The police would not take responsibility.'

She picked up the wine glass and took a long drink. Michael sat in stunned silence.

'Since then I don't care for the police very much. I still miss my sister. But I'm telling you this because I want you to understand why I said nothing about you. Not that I approve of what you do either, if what they tell me about you is correct.'

'I'm sorry about your sister. I don't know what they told you, but I fight for a cause.'

'I hope your conscience is clear then.'

She stood up and went to the bar. A minute later she returned with wine for her and a beer for him. Neither of them ventured another word. The pianist was doing a slow solo number while the bass player and drummer chatted over a drink nearby. Whirls of smoke drifted in and out of the stage lighting. The bar was starting to empty, and Michael realised it was well past midnight.

Sabine finished her wine. She had her chair turned away from him with its back against the wall. She turned her head towards him.

'I'm working a late shift tomorrow. Will you take me home please?'

He gazed into the cool hazel eyes, then drained his glass. 'Alright. Let's go.'

They took a taxi. On the journey she leaned her body against him, head on his shoulder. Her free arm cradled the saxophone case,

74

and she closed her eyes. He looked at her face in repose, wondering how she managed to shift so easily between the distress he'd seen in the bar, and the serene stillness he saw now. She was a conundrum, one minute distant and disapproving, and then the next unexpectedly vulnerable and intimate. He looked out the window at the houses rushing by, and let his mind wander.

'Will you come in for a while?' she asked as the taxi drew to a halt.

He didn't need to deliberate. 'Yes, ok.'

She lived in a tiny one bedroom flat, right under a dental surgery.

'It's very small, but I like it,' she said, leading him down the hall and into the living room. She dumped her overcoat on the sofa. 'It's quiet at night too. Are you tired?'

'No. Are you?'

They looked at each other. Then she stepped forward and kissed him. He wrapped his arms around her and she buried her face in his chest.

'I'm sorry,' she murmured. 'Do you mind?'

'No, not at all.'

She took his hand and led him to the bedroom, turning on a lamp next to the bed. He sat down and took off his shoes and socks.

'Wait,' she said. 'Let me get undressed first.'

He watched as she took her clothes off. She stood in front of him and smiled. Then she knelt down and unbuttoned his shirt. When she saw the bandaged shoulder she stopped.

'They said you were shot. I forgot. Does it hurt?'

'Sometimes. I'm getting used to it.'

She carefully removed the shirt and flung it to one side.

'I will look at if for you later. Now, lie down.'

He surrendered to her lips and her hands and the caress of her body, and for a while the events of the past few days left his mind completely. Afterwards she lay on top of him, her head on his chest, catching her breath.

'Das war schön,' she gasped. 'Sorry, that was beautiful. I'm tired now.'

He turned off the bedside lamp. 'Yes, that was beautiful. Sleep now.'

She was already asleep, in the same position. Michael lay staring at the ceiling. He'd disentangle himself later. For now he quietly stroked her hair and listened to her breathe.

Chapter 7

The temperature had dropped below zero in Dublin, and there were occasional snow flurries, but nothing that settled for long. Harry walked up Grafton Street on his way back from Trinity. He wore an overcoat, scarf and gloves, and a woolly hat. It made the temperature bearable, until the wind blew. Then his heavy woollen overcoat became chiffon. The icy breeze went right through it, and right through him. Every time it happened he involuntarily hugged himself as he walked, trying to restore some warmth. He noticed that no one else seemed to be engaged in this ritual. They must know something I don't, he reflected, they seem immune to it.

Christmas lights and decorations were strung the length and breadth of Grafton Street. A bright smiling reindeer pulled a sleigh full of presents overhead. Just beyond that the Irish name for Dublin - 'Baile Átha Cliath', stood illuminated in ten foot high sparkling letters. Numerous neon Christmas trees clung to the buildings on either side, winking on and off in unison. And the street was thronged with shoppers. He wound his way through the buzzing crowd, wondering what he could buy for Natalie on his limited budget.

The Trinity term had finished for the year, and he had a lecture free month till mid January. Natalie had one more week of work, then they could spend some uninterrupted time together till just after New Year. He just wished it wasn't so cold. On the other side of the world in Auckland they'd be looking forward to a hot Christmas day and a visit to the beach. This time next year that's exactly where he intended to be. Not that Dublin was without charm, it was just the weather that left something to be desired.

With two clear weeks together they needed a plan. SIS was shutting down in a couple of days, and Harry was mindful of Jack's recommendation to leave Dublin for a bit. He decided to call in on the travel agent at the far end of the street, and see if they had any ideas for a cheap week somewhere in the Emerald Isle. He could pick up some brochures at least.

Half an hour later he sat studying possible Christmas retreats in various 'stunningly scenic' locations in the Republic. Hotels in Wexford, cottages on the Dingle peninsula. Would there be any availability at this time of year? He really should have thought this out much earlier.

He heard the door open, and a moment later Natalie appeared in the living room doorway, still attired in overcoat and reinforcing layers.

'So cold out there. What are you looking at?' She began unravelling her scarf.

'Holiday brochures. I need you to help me to decide where we should go. And when.'

'Alright. I'll just get this lot off first.'

A minute later they sat absorbed in the options.

'There are plenty of hotels and cottages on the Dingle peninsula,' said Natalie. 'Maybe we'll get lucky with the weather. I'm told it's beautiful at any time of year.'

They decided to call a few numbers and see if anyone could accommodate them the week following boxing day.

'You can do that Harry. I'm going to Netball training tonight. I need the exercise.'

She was still an avid Netball player, though not at the level she'd once enjoyed. She still liked to stay competitive though, and she'd found a local team to join not long after their arrival to ensure that she did.

'You sure Nat? You look a bit tired actually.'

'I spent most of the day trying to sell the benefits of cognitive therapy to a group of depressed patients. It was hard work. This will perk me up a bit.'

'Tell them to exercise more, how's that for a therapy?'

She grinned. 'Works for me. Maybe I should start a hospital team.'

Harry took a chair into the hall and started dialling numbers. A few minutes later Natalie passed him on her way out.

'Can I take the Land Rover?' she mouthed, while he asked about the facilities on offer at the third hotel on his list.

He picked up the keys on the hall table and handed them to her. She planted a quick kiss on his cheek, and was gone.

Eventually Harry made a booking at a hotel on the shore of Dingle Bay. They could leave Dublin on the 27th and take in the New

Year overlooking the sea. In the meantime perhaps he should think about getting a Christmas tree. And a present for his wife. But before that he needed to make his last call of the year on Litchfield and Hudson.

Litchfield slid a folder across the desk.

'Read this, Harry.'

Harry opened the file. The first thing to meet his eye was a photograph of a man who looked roughly his own age. It was a black and white image, taken from the shoulders up. The face wore a half smile, and was broad and well defined. There was a certain softness around the eyes that didn't quite fit Harry's pre-conceptions of a hardened terrorist.

'Is this O'Reilly? Looks harmless enough.'

'Well he's not. Read on.'

There were a few typed A4 pages under the photo, summarising what was known or guessed about the man. Harry read out the salient parts.

'Known to have been a member of the Provisional IRA in excess of five years … Suspected participant in bomb attack on Army barracks near Crosmaglen … Alleged to have been the gunman responsible for the deaths of two off duty soldiers in a Belfast pub in 1978 … Involved in cross border arms smuggling in 1979, not apprehended as his appearance unknown, but seized documents mention him by name …' He closed the file, and sat staring at the photo. 'Lots of allegations here. If they don't know what he looks like, where did this come from?'

'Courtesy of O'Riordan. Where he got if from I don't know, but he assures me it's recent and genuine. We'll check it with the ambulance crew, just to be sure. Then we'll let the Garda have it.'

'Can I keep this?'

'Yes. I have copies. Leave the typed pages here.' Litchfield leaned back in his chair, folding his arms. 'I've decided to close the office tomorrow, once I have confirmation of this photo. Jack is on his way back to England for Christmas, and I'm right behind him.'

'London, is it?'

'For me it is. I think Jack is going to a sister in Cornwall. Take the spare keys with you Harry. I'm not anticipating any activity, but you're our man on site, so to speak.'

'I'll be out of Dublin from the 27th. Nat and I are taking a trip to Dingle. I want to use the Land Rover while we have it.'

Litchfield yawned. 'Good. Glad to see you took Jack up on his suggestion. Anything else you need?'

'I'd just like to use the office phone to call home on Christmas Eve. It'll be Christmas morning there. Do you mind?'

A smile of magnanimity lit up his chief's face. 'Of course not, Harry. I'm sure Her Majesty's Government can stand the cost. And have a Merry Christmas.'

When Michael opened his eyes the next morning the bed was empty. He could hear signs of life in the next room, and he swung himself out of bed and into trousers and shirt.

Sabine stood in the small kitchen adjoining the living room, barefooted but wearing her coat.

'I'm cold,' she explained. 'And I can't find socks. The heating will come on soon, it's on a timer.'

'Perhaps I should go out and get something for breakfast.'

'I'm boiling some eggs, I made two for you. And there's toast.'

She turned to face him, holding the coat tight around her. 'I was a little drunk last night. But I don't regret bringing you here, or what we did.'

He stepped forward to hug her, and felt her melt into him. 'Me neither. You did surprise me a little though.'

She seemed satisfied with his response. 'Let me finish the eggs. Then I'm going to look at your shoulder, and after that we need to talk.'

He stroked her back. 'Fine. What are you wearing under this coat?'

'Nothing at the moment. You just concentrate on breakfast please. Go and sit down.'

They ate mostly in silence. She looked at him almost shyly once or twice, which he found ironic given her confidence in the bedroom only hours earlier.

She finished her tea. The determined look was back. 'I don't know what your plans are. The doctors think Siobhan will be fine if

82

there are no complications in the next 48 hours. Do you want to stay here until then?'

'Why are you doing this, Sabine? You know the Garda want me. The longer I stay, the riskier it is.'

'I will know that before you do, I think. And I know you will only find me again until you know Siobhan is well. It's better if you stay here. Then in a couple of days you can go back to your people.'

'Ah, that's exactly what I can't do.'

'I don't understand, why not?'

He explained the events that had culminated in the situation he now found himself in, from the beach to the shooting at Siobhan's.

'They think I betrayed them, so now I have everyone looking for me.'

'What will you do?'

'Disappear. Exactly how at the moment, I don't know.'

'So you aren't a terrorist anymore. Good.'

He gave her a sharp look of rebuke. 'I was never a terrorist. I told you, I fight for a cause.'

She held his gaze. 'Yes, well I'm glad you have to stop.' Then changed the subject. 'Let me see your shoulder now.'

'I left the spare bandages at the hotel.'

'I have some things here, I just want to make sure it is clean.'

After looking at the wound, which appeared to be healing, they agreed that Michael would retrieve his belongings from the hotel and return to the flat. And then, once Siobhan was out of the woods, he could decide on his next move.

'Are you staying in Dublin for Christmas?' he asked.

'Yes, I will go to my Aunt for Christmas day, but otherwise I'm working.'

'What brought you here in the first place?'

'My mother is Irish. I had never met my Irish relatives, so I thought I'd come here and work. Just for a short while. That was six months ago.'

'What do you think of us, then?'

'Everyone has been very nice to me. You have some strange customs though.' Her eyes crinkled mischievously.

'What do you mean?'

'Constantly following women until they agree to do whatever you want. We Germans would never behave like that.'

'I see. Let me assure you we only do that in exceptional circumstances. I wouldn't want you getting the wrong impression.'

She grinned and stood up. 'That's a relief.' Her arms stretched overhead as she yawned. 'It's warming up in here now. I don't need this anymore.' The overcoat came off. 'We have two hours before I leave for work. Come back to bed.'

That afternoon he left Sabine's flat and walked for ten minutes. Then he used a taxi to go back to the hotel. It was a safer option than public transport, or walking any more than necessary. The proprietor looked at him without interest when he explained he was going back to Belfast earlier than planned. He wrote out a receipt and wished

Michael a good journey.

On the return journey he sat in the back seat of the taxi, trying to formulate some sort of plan. He wasn't helped by the driver's views on Dublin's chances against Kerry in their forthcoming Gaelic Football encounter. The man's commentary didn't seem to require much in the way of a response, so he half listened and tried to think.

Dublin, if not the whole of Ireland, was now too hazardous for him to remain. If he could get across the Irish Sea to Liverpool he could at least regroup. He had a passport in a false name he could use, but retrieving that would mean going back to Belfast. And he was putting Sabine at risk just the way he had with Siobhan. If anything happened to her he couldn't live with himself. Whatever he decided in the long term, he would definitely leave Dublin the day after tomorrow.

'Natalie, move it, we're going to be late.'

It was Christmas Eve. The tree stood glittering with silver and gold baubles in one corner of the living room. The presents had been bought and laid beneath it. With only the two of them the pile was hardly impressive, thought Harry. Still, the spirit of Christmas had permeated at last, and he felt almost festive.

'They're expecting our call in five minutes, where are you?'

Natalie emerged from the bathroom. 'Don't panic. Just applying the finishing touches.'

She wore a clinging backless black dress. His eyes widened appreciatively.

'You look great. If you don't freeze to death before we get there.'

'Roisin's place isn't far. I should be ok for ten minutes in the car with my coat on.'

They'd been invited for a Christmas Eve drink by one of Natalie's colleagues. But first they needed to phone both his and her parents downunder to wish them a Merry Christmas. They both wrapped up and headed for the Land Rover.

They reached the office in two minutes. Harry felt a rare helping of goodwill towards Litchfield for allowing him the use of the office phone. Purely seasonal, he reasoned. He placed the first call with the International operator and spoke to his folks. The line was mostly clear, with the occasional echo that resulted from the 12,000 mile connection time. It was a warm morning in Auckland, and a barbecue was planned for later in the day.

The same ritual was repeated for Natalie, then they moved on to Roisin's house.

It was a convivial evening. There were several couples from the hospital. They all knew Natalie, but Harry had been only a name to them until tonight. To them he was Natalie's husband, the Irish scholar. Two of the men spoke fluently, and he found himself sharing whiskey and conversation while alternating between both languages.

'Are you writing a dissertation Harry?' asked one of the Irish speakers.

'Yes. The subject is The relevance of the Irish language in 20th Century Ireland"

'Plenty of bloody relevance in my opinion.'

'It depends on your politics it seems. I have some catching up to do on that score.'

'Speak English, boys,' said Roisin, a bubbly 30 year old paediatric nurse. 'You're being rude to Natalie, and I'm losing you too.'

Around 11pm it was time to go. They stood in the hall, thanking their hostess and wrapping up once more against the cold.

'I'll drive, Harry,' said Natalie. 'You've had far too much whiskey. Give me the keys.'

He handed them over. 'I think I left my gloves in the kitchen. I'll grab them.'

He was back in a minute. He thanked Roisin as he adjusted his gloves and scarf.

'Is Nat in the car already?'

'Yes, she wanted to get out there and get the heater going.'

He closed the door and began walking down the path leading through the small front garden. The Land Rover was parked right ahead of him. He could see Natalie smiling through the driver's window.

As he stepped forward it was as though suddenly his senses had gone out of tune, like a radio dial stuck on static. He heard a loud thump, which was followed a split second later by a huge whoosh of air that lifted him off his feet and hurled his body backwards, slamming it into the front door. All he registered before losing consciousness was the sight of a roofless, doorless, flame filled Land

Rover, along with a burning wave of heat searing his eyes. Of Natalie he saw nothing.

Chapter 8

It was a cloudless day, with a bright blue gleaming sky. They sat in a dinghy, floating across a long, broad, winding lake. Its still and even surface could have been blue Venetian glass. The only movement came from the ripples fanning into ever larger circles as the prow of the boat glided through the water. Its clarity was such that white stones and smooth large boulders were visible on the lake floor, easily twenty feet below.

On either side jagged green mountains observed their silent progress, broken intermittently by the call of an unseen bittern or heron. There was no other human being in evidence.

Natalie was standing near the prow with her back to him, wearing a long white cotton dress. The breeze pressed it against her long body, exaggerating her height. Her hair cut a ravine of black that flowed halfway down her back. She was quite still.

For some reason he didn't need oars, the boat moved perfectly without them. He willed her to turn around. She complied with his unspoken request, turning completely to face him.

But he couldn't see her face. There was nothing but a dark impenetrable oval. Then as he watched she began to dissolve into thousands of tiny sparkling blue crystals tumbling into the water, merging with that blue Venetian stillness. He tried to tell her to stop, but his vocal chords wouldn't respond, and he shouted silently as she slipped away. The boat glided on, and he remained sitting - transfixed and impotent.

His eyes snapped open. Such a vivid dream, it had unnerved him. But now he couldn't figure out where he was, or why he was lying in a bed with a needle in his arm. He was aware of a dull throbbing in his leg, was it left or right? Otherwise his body felt very light, as if he were suspended in space. He thought he'd like to sit up, but when he tried nothing happened. So frustrating. But being frustrated was too much effort. He'd try again later. Still, there was something at the back of his mind which was just tantalisingly out of reach. He wanted to know what it was. Then he heard voices.

'Doctor, he's awake.'

'Ah, good.' The voice came closer, then a face came into view. 'I'm Dr. Fitzgerald, Harry. You're in St. James's hospital.' A white coated figure with a bearded face and dark eyes leaned over him. 'The femoral artery in your leg was severed. We've operated successfully, and you've had a blood transfusion. You're getting lots of morphine too, so you're probably feeling quite relaxed right now.'

Harry tried to respond, and something resembling English must have issued from his mouth. He was drifting away again as the doctor answered.

'What happened? There was an explosion. Don't think about that now, Harry, just rest.'

No further encouragement was needed. Harry had exchanged the world of severed arteries for the oblivion of dreamless sleep.

When he woke the next day he knew she'd gone. The pain of it gnawed at his stomach and taunted his mind, telling him one moment that it was just another dream, and the next that he wasn't asleep, his wife was dead. The morphine played with him, taking him far away from the hospital bed to a place where nothing existed but pure and clear mind, uncluttered by thought. Then something would click in his head, and the image of the burning Land Rover would rush in to fill that space, making him relive that split second again and again.

A day later, with his morphine dose reduced, he could distinguish fact from fantasy. He remembered the explosion clearly, and now he sat up in his bed in a state of emotional numbness, trying to accept that Nat just wasn't here anymore. And wondering what he would tell her parents.

Apart from his leg injury, he'd suffered nothing more than bruising and concussion. Dr. Fitzgerald informed him that he should be home in a few days, and if all went well, walking normally in a month or two. Someone from the Garda arrived to let him know that no one else at Roisin's, or nearby, had suffered more than a few minor cuts, all due to flying glass from shattered windows.

'And Natalie?'

The Garda man looked grim. 'Car bombs aren't kind to the human body, Mr. Ellis.'

'No.'

'We will be able to make an identification, I can tell you that much. Perhaps you could tell me why someone would want to put a bomb in your vehicle?'

'No idea.'

The man gave Harry a quizzical look. 'We'll talk again later Mr. Ellis, once you're out of here. Meanwhile I'll need details of Natalie's next of kin. They'll need to be informed.'

Harry gave him the address and phone number of Natalie's parents. The Garda man told him that someone from the Irish Consulate in Auckland would give them the news personally. A part of Harry felt relieved. How could he possibly tell Nat's mother and father that his involvement with British Intelligence had got their daughter murdered?

Then the same evening, Litchfield arrived. An expression of sympathetic concern had replaced his customary irascibility, but not his brusque delivery.

'Harry, don't know what to say, this is an appalling situation. You have my sincere

condolences.'

Harry made no reply. The sight of Litchfield had triggered him rapidly out of his emotional numbness into a state of mounting anger. He didn't trust himself to speak.

Litchfield, taken aback by the silence, looked slightly embarrassed. He blinked furiously for a moment or two, then ploughed on. 'Of course, we will take care of everything – any expenses you incur in your recovery, funeral costs, anything at all.'

'How did they know?' asked Harry, his voice low and furious.

'Know? I can't answer that at the moment, some breach of security, they must have

found out about our Dublin operation. We weren't as anonymous as we thought.'

'Yes, I'd figured that out already. Was O'Reilly involved?'

Litchfield hesitated for a moment, as though debating something with himself. When he replied he'd regained his composure.

'Yes, I believe he was. I should know more in the next day or two. In the meantime

we need to discuss what we're going to do about your continued safety.'

'How can you possibly know it was him?'

'He certainly has motive, don't you think? If it wasn't him, then it was someone from

the Republican Brotherhood. I certainly intend to do my best to pinpoint that person.'

'I want to know when that happens.' Harry stared out the window, thoughts of

retribution clouding his grief. He missed Litchfield's little nod of satisfaction.

'Alright Harry. Let me tell you what we need to do.'

He went on to advise Harry on the measures required once he left hospital. Removal to a safe house while he convalesced. A suspension to his studies if at all possible.

'And we'll arm you too. If you haven't used a gun before Jack will be able to help with instruction. As soon as you're walking properly again you should get out of Ireland. We'll sort out the details later.'

Then, once again expressing his sympathy, he left. Harry lay back in bed replaying the visit. Not once had Litchfield mentioned Natalie's name.

He was discharged a few days later. Jack Hudson collected him and drove him to his new address. It was a semi detached two bedroom house about 15 minutes drive South of Dublin. Harry offered no conversation during the drive, and Jack took the opportunity to explain his new situation.

'We moved all your belongings from the Harcourt Street flat.' He registered Harry's sharp glance. 'Don't worry, no damage was done getting in. We can do some things efficiently.'

They arrived, and Harry noted that Jack was as good as his word. Nothing seemed to have been left behind. Almost nothing. The unopened Christmas presents were on the living room table – the tree was missing.

'Someone will look in on you every evening. A Mrs. Meehan. She's totally reliable.'

'The Garda wanted to speak to me again,' began Harry, remembering that his official visitor had promised to get the terrible news to Nat's parents.

'We've spoken to them,' Jack replied. 'They won't bother you any more. But I think both Natalie's and your parents need you to contact them as soon as you can.'

'God, I don't know what I'm going to tell them.'

'Actually, we can discuss that later. I'm so sorry Harry, about all of this. You need to take it one day at a time for the foreseeable future. I will do my utmost to help you.'

'Sure, Jack. Thanks.'

And so Harry's convalescence began. He had no desire to return to his studies, and asked Jack to communicate his decision to Trinity. His left leg was sore and would continue to be for a few weeks. The house had a garden backing onto a small wood, and he walked there every day with the help of crutches, allowing a little more weight to be borne on the leg as he began to heal.

He made the calls that he'd dreaded to both sets of parents. The event had been reported in the New Zealand media. A statement issued by the IRA had claimed that the bomb was the unauthorised work of a 'rogue individual'. To Harry's mind that could only mean one person.

Jack had advised him that for the moment he should say it must have been a case of mistaken identity, unless he wanted to reveal details of his work for SIS. Which neither they nor Harry wanted. Natalie's remains were to be buried in Dublin, and Harry assured his father that he would be on the way home very soon.

There was the funeral itself, which was attended by Roisin and her colleagues. Harry couldn't stop thinking that the whole event was too surreal to be true. They'd come from the other side of the world, been married so briefly, and suddenly in a country far away from home one of them had simply ceased to exist. The pain he experienced in the certain knowledge of Nat's death was mixed with this sense of the surreal as he worked to regain his fitness. Getting back to full strength was all he could focus on, the longer term future had no shape at all.

The New Year arrived. He spent it alone in the house, though Mrs. Meehan, who was a middle aged robust and practical woman, tried to engage him in conversation for an hour or two. She brought Sherry with her to facilitate this exercise, and although Harry partook of a couple of glasses, it still proved hard to get beyond small talk. Alone or in company, the pain was the same.

One morning that week Jack arrived. He found Harry in the kitchen, staring out the back window with a mug of tea in hand.

'Brought this for you,' said Jack. Harry turned to see him place a handgun on the kitchen table. 'It's for self defence only of course.'

'The only thing I've ever shot at was a deer on a hunting trip years ago. That was with a rifle of course.'

'Did you hit it?'

'Yes, I did.'

'This is a handgun. You shoot people with this, preferably at close range. We're going for a drive in the country now, to do some practice.'

96

An hour later they were deep in Irish countryside, looking for somewhere secluded and preferably private. They found a wooded area down a side road, parked the car, and proceeded into the shelter of the trees. When they reached an open area, Jack stopped.

'This will do.' He'd brought a cardboard target, complete with bullseye. He taped it against a tree and they both stood back about 30 feet.

'Right Harry. This is a Walther PPK, very popular with the Ulster Defence Regiment right now. You load the bullets into the magazine like so ..' Once he'd done it he made Harry repeat the exercise, then the magazine was slotted into the gun.

'It's semi automatic. Shoot once and you have a reloaded barrel. Try it. Use both hands to steady it.'

Harry did as instructed. He spent 15 minutes shooting at the target until Jack was satisfied he knew what he was doing. Then they returned to the cottage.

'If you feel like doing more practice, then Mrs M will take you out,' offered Jack, as they sat at the kitchen table drinking tea. He smiled at Harry's startled expression. 'In her youth she was something of a crack shot, so you'll definitely improve.'

'Might just do that,' replied Harry.

'When you leave the house take it with you, safety on of course. It's licensed in your name.' He rummaged in the small holdall he'd brought with him, and extracted the paperwork. 'And check any vehicle you intend to drive from now on. Under the bonnet and under the chassis. Got it?'

'You're making me nervous.'

'You're safe here, Harry. Just take precautions anyway. And we won't be operating from our former office in future. As far as we're concerned you're out of the picture, but I'll look in on you until you're fit again. You have my number.' Jack stood and prepared to leave.

'Any news on O'Reilly's whereabouts?' asked Harry.

'Not yet. But now we know what he looks like it won't be too long before we find him. Remember that he might not actually be the man responsible.'

'As far as I'm concerned, he's totally responsible.' Harry's face had assumed a stony determination. 'I'd like to meet that bastard.'

Jack gave him a hard stare, then laid a reassuring hand on his shoulder. 'Concentrate on getting yourself well again, and leave O'Reilly to us. Can you do that?'

'Sure, I'll do my best.'

Jack nodded, picked up his holdall, and left.

Pre-Christmas, Michael's decision to leave Dublin was still on hold. First he wanted his passport, and to make that happen he called his father and asked him to retrieve it from a PO box in Belfast. When Michael Senior had digested the implications of his son's situation and realised the limited to non-existent options on offer, he agreed. He had never taken the militant path his son had chosen, but he understood the temptation.

'I'll post you the key today, Dad.'

98

'Fine. We'll be back in Dublin on the 19th, to see Siobhan. I'm told she's sitting up now, and making good progress.'

'Put the passport in an envelope and address it to Sabine Maier, Alexander Ward.' He spelled out her name. 'Then leave it at the reception desk and she'll pick it up for me.'

'Who on earth is she?'

'Just a friend. She'll be working that day. You might even meet her. I won't be here, I'm leaving Dublin tonight. I need to find a safe passage across the sea to England. Once I've arranged that I'll be back to pick up the passport.'

'Keep in touch, Michael. Your mother will be worried sick.'

'I'll call you from a phone box once I'm settled. You might have to accept the charges though.'

He ended the call shortly afterwards, dropping the letter containing the key in a nearby mail box on his route back to Sabine's flat. She was getting ready for a late shift when he arrived.

She turned from her contemplation of the nearly boiled kettle as he came into the tiny kitchen.

'Is it done?'

'They'll be here on Saturday. My Dad will leave an envelope addressed to you at reception.'

She looked both annoyed and confused. 'Why can't you just meet him? Isn't that easier? I thought that was the arrangement.'

He put both hands on her shoulders. 'I can't wait around here till Saturday. Me being here puts you in danger, and I've already been here longer than I should have. I'm leaving later today.'

She twisted away from him, turning back to the steaming kettle, busying herself with making tea. When she'd poured two cups she turned back to face him.

'Where will you go?'

'To find a way out of here. That's all you should know, Sabine.'

'Alright. And won't you need a passport for that?'

'Well, I'll be back in a week, and then maybe we can celebrate Christmas together.'

She smiled. 'Good. Come and drink tea with me then.'

She gave him a quick kiss. In the living room, she leaned up against him on the sofa, and he drew her to him with an encircling arm. They said nothing, enjoying their tea and their closeness, till it was time for her to leave for work.

When she'd gone Michael went into the bedroom searching for his rucksack. He emptied the contents on to the bed. Some spare underwear, t-shirts and a jersey, all purchased by Sabine when she realised how little he had to wear. The bottles and towels he'd taken on his flight from Siobhan's had long been disposed of. And there was the money. He checked it – still in excess of two thousand pounds.

How much would an opportunist fisherman demand in exchange for a no questions asked passage across the Irish Sea? Assuming he could find said fisherman. He'd know soon enough. If he could get no positive response from a discreet enquiry in two or three harbour pubs, then it would be time for plan B, whatever that might be. The only alternative to leaving by sea was staying, and he'd need to come up with something far better than that.

Howth was a busy fishing port not far from Dublin. He would spend the next week in a cheap hotel and get to know a few of the locals in the popular drinking haunts. If the timing and the price was right, he should be able to strike a deal.

He repacked everything, put on his jacket, and took one last look around. Nothing forgotten. The Browning was in its familiar place, and the money was at the bottom of the pack. Apart from warm clothes, he didn't really need anything else. He set off to find a taxi.

It proved much easier than anticipated. He checked into a place about ten minutes walk from the port itself, saying he was looking for work on a trawler as a fishing hand. He was a big man and looked physically capable, and initially no one questioned his authenticity.

The proprietor of the hotel was an ex fisherman himself, and partial to a drop of whiskey of an evening. Fergus O'Malley had spent the best part of his adult life at sea, and knew plenty of people still on the boats. He sat with Michael in the hotel's little bar late one evening, a few days after Michael's arrival. The other residents had an early start and had retired for the night. They sat in two comfortable leather armchairs set in front of a roaring log fire, glasses in hand.

Fergus was in late middle age, his weatherbeaten face lined by years of exposure to biting sea spray and bitter gusting wind. His

101

eyes wore a permanent squint, as though he stood forever on a trawler deck, ducking the elements. Looking at Michael he saw none of the same signs of a seagoing man, and he was curious.

'If you don't mind me saying Michael, you don't look like you've much experience of the fishing game. What brings you to it now?'

Michael glanced across at Fergus, trying to read his expression.

'I need a job, that's all.'

Fergus grunted. 'This is hard work. Must be something else a young man can turn his hand to that doesn't involve being battered by the elements every day, and coming home smelling like a halibut.'

Michael decided to test the water. 'You're right, of course, it isn't my first choice. I have a job lined up as an HGV driver in Liverpool. But because of a little local difficulty I can't travel using the normal routes. So I'm stuck here, for now.'

Fergus looked at the contents of his glass, his squint suddenly liberated by the raising of his eyebrows. 'I see. So of course you came to a fishing port. Well you wouldn't be the first.' He drained his glass. 'Another?'

Michael nodded. Fergus retreated behind the bar, then reappeared with refills. He handed one to Michael. 'Slainche.' They raised glasses and drank.

'Let's say Michael, that there are people who might help you discreetly across the sea from here. But it will cost you. Five hundred pounds. Do you have that sort of money?'

'I do,' replied Michael.

'I hope so. I don't want to make enquiries on your behalf for nothing. I doubt that anything can be arranged before January now. But leave it with me, I'll see what can be done.'

Fergus was as good as his word. He found a man willing to make the run in the second week of January. Michael advanced £150 as a goodwill gesture, and the deal was done. All he had to do was turn up on the day.

He knew Sabine would be with her Aunt on Christmas Day, so he decided to stay where he was and travel back on Boxing Day. At the hotel it was business as usual on the 25th, with slightly better food and plenty of drink. He was sat in the bar when a news flash interrupted an ad break on the television. It was a report of a car bomb explosion in Dublin the previous evening. The victim, a young New Zealand woman. The IRA had issued a statement denying direct responsibility. Instead the action had been attributed to a 'rogue individual' acting without authorisation. The Garda were pursuing 'active leads.'

He was in momentary shock. He quickly looked around to see if anyone had noticed. Fergus was looking directly at him, his face expressionless. Then he turned to serve someone at the bar. The afternoon became evening and there was no sign of any further interest in the matter from Fergus. Feeling relieved, Michael made ready to leave the next day. He realised just how much he wanted to see Sabine again. He was sorry that their reunion would be tempered with the knowledge that soon he would leave Ireland for good.

At first she seemed quite sanguine about his impending departure. When he got back and told her about his travel arrangements her only comment was 'Yes, well now you have a definite date then.'

He couldn't help but feel disappointed.

Her actions, however, were more eloquent. In the days that followed her lovemaking became more frantic and demanding, as though she wanted to ingest the very essence of him. When she left him to go to work he felt a foretaste of the pain of their approaching separation. Would he ever see her again? The thought only made him want her more, intensifying their union when she returned from whatever shift she was on.

Sabine had collected the passport without incident, but had not met his parents. They debated about whether she should smuggle in written notes to Siobhan, but deemed it too dangerous. Sabine would deliver a letter from Michael once he'd left the country.

'I don't see her that often now she is getting better, anyway,' explained Sabine. 'She will be discharged soon I think.'

They made a plan to break cover on New Years Eve. Sabine would be playing saxophone with the trio again at a small jazz club to usher in 1982. He wanted a last chance to hear her and be out together before he left. The risk seemed worth it.

It was a risk he didn't take. The preceding evening Sabine returned, around 10.30. He took one look at her and knew something bad had happened.

'Is it Siobhan? It can't be, surely.' His look implored her to tell him no.

She began to cry. 'Oh, Michael, she was fine. Then a few hours ago she began to haemorrhage internally. They took her to theatre but they couldn't stop it. She died on the operating table. I'm so sorry.'

She embraced him tightly, sobbing for his loss and the pain she'd brought home with her. For a minute he stared into space, unable and unwilling to accept it. Then he felt his own tears hot on his cheeks, and he began to cry as he hadn't done since he was ten years old.

Chapter 9

Harry was reading a book, with limited success. His eyes were on the page but his mind wouldn't focus. He would turn a page and then realise he'd absorbed nothing of the previous one. Fleeting snapshots of Nat in earlier times came unbidden into consciousness, and he found himself chasing her image down a labyrinth of memory that had only one exit on Christmas Eve.

He closed the book, looking out the living room window at the grey shrouds of cloud. It wasn't raining at least. He would take the opportunity to navigate the woods with as little reliance as possible on his crutches. He could walk around the house unassisted for minutes at a time, but his left leg ached too much to try the same thing for extended periods outside the house.

He stood up, making his way to the hall. As he reached for his overcoat from the coat rack he heard the key in the front door. It opened to admit the stout and smiling figure of Mrs Meehan.

'Harry, off somewhere interesting?'

He smiled in spite of himself. 'Just to the bottom of the garden I'm afraid. Need the exercise. A thought struck him. 'Unless you'd help me with some target practice that is.'

'Target practice?' She was momentarily surprised. 'Ah, that Jack Hudson has been overstating my expertise again, has he?' She didn't wait for a reply. 'Get your gun and plenty of ammo and let's see what you can do then.'

They drove in her battered Morris 1100 to an isolated farm property, then down a one lane track that was little more than a tractor furrow to an empty barn.

'They know me here, we won't be disturbed.'

The barn was almost fifty feet long. At the far end bales of hay were stacked against the wall, and in front of them stood what looked like two archery targets.

'Let's see how you go from a distance then,' said Mrs M. She moved to a line scoured into the dirt about forty feet away. 'Take the one on the left, and aim for the bullseye.'

Harry discarded his crutches and stepped up to the line, trying to distribute his weight as equally as possible without too much discomfort. He took careful aim and fired six shots at the target. 'How did I do?'

'Just a minute, let me have a go.' He handed her the gun and watched as she steadied it in both hands, then fired smoothly at the right hand target. 'Let's have a look.'

They checked the results. Harry had put one in the bullseye and the others within a six inch radius. Mrs. Meehan on the other hand had landed three bullseyes and drilled a triangle with the other three directly around it.

'Where did you learn to shoot like that?' asked Harry.

'I served as a Greenfinch in the Ulster Defence Regiment for a few years. We didn't carry weapons on duty but we were trained to use them. I had my own for personal protection.'

He looked at her with interest. He really couldn't picture the forty something slightly overweight woman in front of him as a soldier. She read his thoughts.

'It was almost ten years ago, Harry. I was younger, slimmer and a lot fitter then.'

They spent another half hour in the barn and she helped him with sighting and correct handling of the weapon. Then it was time to go. The evening was drawing in as she manoeuvred the car back up the tractor furrow and on the road towards home.

'You heard about the O'Reilly girl of course, did you not?' she asked him as the Morris 1100, whose suspension had seen better days, sped less than gracefully through the dusk.

'No, heard what?' In fact he hadn't thought about Siobhan O'Reilly at all recently. She'd been erased from his memory until this moment.

'She died before New Year, in hospital. The same hospital you were in. You were practically neighbours. Do you never watch the news?'

In fact he very rarely switched on the TV or radio, and admitted to this shortcoming. 'To be honest I'd forgotten all about her.'

Mrs. Meehan gave him a sideways glance. 'Well it's her funeral tomorrow. No doubt the O'Reilly family will turn out. Might even see our man Michael there.' Her face betrayed nothing.

Harry was incredulous. 'You're joking, that's exactly what the Garda and anyone else looking for him will be counting on. He'd be mad to go. Where will it be?'

'St. Patrick's Church In Belfast. He has more chance of evading capture there if he decides to go. And in Ireland we don't always do the sane thing Harry. Runs against the grain sometimes.'

Harry said nothing. She was right about that. Based on his experience of the last few weeks, he could only conclude that sanity had become a rather scarce commodity.

It was dark early the following morning, and raining steadily. The taxi Harry had ordered drew up outside. He lay his crutches across the back seat and watched while the driver adjusted the front passenger seat as far back as it would go, so he could straighten his leg when he wanted to.

He climbed in and they drove off. The windscreen wipers beat a steady rhythm against the intensifying downpour, and the driver flicked the headlights on to full beam as often as possible. It could have been midnight and not 7am.

'How long to Belfast?'

'In this weather, between 2 and 3 hours.' His driver looked disconsolately at the road ahead.

'Take your time.'

The rain stopped shortly after and they made good time, arriving at St Patrick's around 9.30. The service was at 11.00, and although the church was open there was nobody inside. He gave the place a quick inspection. It was spacious and light, the pews arranged in a shallow semi-circle around an ornate marble altar. He wondered how many people would come. A notice pinned by the door on his way out confirmed that the service for Siobhan O'Reilly would indeed take place as scheduled. He decided to retreat for an hour, somewhere he could sit down. He found a café close by. Sitting at a table by the window he had a clear view of the church 100 yards away. He ordered tea and a bacon sandwich, and waited. If there was anyone else waiting for a sighting of O'Reilly at his sister's funeral, he couldn't spot them.

People began to arrive. It was difficult to make out faces at this distance. O'Reilly's photo was on the table in front of him, but Harry was doubtful of matching it with the man himself. Still, had he not come all this way in the hope of doing exactly that?

Then the funeral cortege pulled up, and the coffin was carried inside. If one of the pallbearers was O'Reilly he certainly couldn't tell from this vantage point. He waited till everyone had gone in, then he quietly slipped in himself and positioned himself in a seat towards the rear of the church.

When the readings were done and a few hymns sung it was over. The pallbearers once again shouldered Siobhan and bore her out. They were followed by what he assumed were her parents, and various relations. A few mildly curious looks were cast his way. Then the church was empty. Among all these assorted people he'd seen no one resembling the man in the photograph.

Just as he prepared to go he detected some movement on the far side of the room. Someone who had been partially obscured by a pillar had just stood up. It was just the two of them left in the church, the officiating priest had disappeared.

The man behind the pillar began walking towards the altar, and Harry realised he was heading towards a door located just to the right of it. As he stood up to get a clearer view his pew scraped loudly against the stone floor, and the man stopped. He turned to face Harry.

They were some distance apart, but there was no doubt. It was O'Reilly. Harry had one crutch supporting his left side, and he quickly drew his gun from his coat with his right hand, aiming it square at Michael's chest.

'Who are you?' asked Michael, staring in slight bemusement at the armed and apparently lame man in front of him.

'I'm the man whose wife you murdered. Christmas Eve.'

'Your wife?' Michael stayed as still as he could, hands by his side. 'The New Zealand girl? That wasn't me.'

'You or your friends, it's all the same.' Harry felt his leg beginning to throb. He sat down, and that freed up his other hand to steady the gun. He couldn't miss.

'I'm sorry about your wife.' Michael looked haggard. 'I buried my sister today. Have you thought about what that might mean?'

There was no reply. Now that Harry finally had O'Reilly in his sights it was proving difficult to pull the trigger. He'd never shot a man. Michael sensed his hesitation.

'Are you going to fire a gun in a church?' Still no reply. Michael took a measured breath. 'I'm going to walk out that door now. You do as you see fit.'

He turned and walked away. Harry's hands were trembling. He wanted to fire, but his body refused to co-operate . As the door closed behind Michael he lowered his gun, placing it on the pew next to him. He sat there with his head in his hands, feeling nothing but despair.

Part Two

Dancing with Mortality

2001

Chapter 10

Tunbridge Wells, England.

He eased the Mercedes smoothly into the vacant space, right outside the restaurant.

'That was good luck,' said Sophie.

'Perfect timing actually,' answered Harry, grinning across at his wife.

He'd reserved their usual table, in a private room made for dining à deux. The place was run by Alain, an ex Parisian who specialised in distinctive French cuisine, with an eclectic selection of stunning wines from lesser known vineyards all over France. And the better known ones.

'Any more of that Cheval Blanc we had last time?' enquired Harry, after Alain had seated them and asked them how they both were.

'The '71? Yes, I think so. Shall I bring a bottle?'

The room was oak panelled, with a polished oak table and darkly upholstered leather dining chairs. A small skylight admitted the dark blue of a clear summer evening. Discreet lighting on the walls behind both of them emitted a soft glow, complemented by the flickering flame of a candle stood centre table, in a simple brass holder.

'I've always liked this place,' said Sophie. 'Very private, no distractions.'

Alain returned with the wine. After tasting it and making the appropriate noises, they ordered a starter, then settled back to wait, just feeling the easy ambience of the place.

She looked good. Dark luxuriant black hair brushed right back and loose, smooth skinned face with a generous mouth and well shaped nose. She was ten years younger than him, with an easy assurity of manner and intelligence that had been honed by an expensive education, backed by an upbringing with all the material advantages one could wish for.

'What's the occasion?' she asked, with a hint of irony.

'Do I need a reason?'

'Not at all, I just thought we might be celebrating something.'

'They've renewed my contract at the bank, with a rate rise. I thought that might be a cause for celebration.'

'Honestly Harry.' She raised her eyes. 'You think of nothing but money.'

He said nothing. Sophie was beautiful and expensive. She'd studied fine art at the Royal College, and was now something of a Picasso prints and ceramics expert with one of the London auction houses. Although this paid a reasonable salary, it was an unspoken understanding that Harry's income was the driver keeping them both in in the style she was accustomed to.

She raised her glass. 'This wine is gorgeous. Let's drink to renewed contracts.'

The wine went down easily, and Harry ordered a second bottle. Sophie was chatting about a catalogue she was putting together for a European ceramics auction scheduled for the following week. It was an important sale event, and she was enthusiastic about the prospective bidders and potentially record prices that might be achieved.

Harry knew very little about the subject. He was content to listen and drink, and didn't interrupt her flow. The main course came and went. He poured himself another glass of wine, and found the bottle was almost empty.

'You're putting it away tonight,' said Sophie. 'I've only had two glasses.'

'Good, you can drive then.'

She sighed. 'I wish you wouldn't drink so much.'

'I don't drink so much,' he shot back, his annoyance showing. This was becoming a familiar refrain, on both their parts.

She looked disconsolate for a moment, then regained some composure. 'Let's not argue about it. Why don't we order some coffee?'

'Yes, sure.' The waiter appeared shortly afterwards and took the order. 'Actually, I meant to tell you something,' said Harry. 'I gave blood last month, and I had a letter this morning from the Blood people. Only opened it on the way to work.'

'Why would they write to you?'

'It appears I have some antibodies – hepatitis of some kind. I should be tested to see if I've still got it.'

116

'I doubt it, Harry. You'd feel lousy if you did. Tom picked it up in India a few years ago and felt miserable for months as I remember. It went away in time.'

Tom was Sophie's older brother. She'd met Harry when he'd worked with Tom at a fund management company.

He smiled reassuringly. 'I'm sure you're right. Still, I'll go to my GP and arrange something. Then I can assure them my blood is just fine.'

The coffee arrived. He drank half a cup to pacify Sophie. What he really wanted was another bottle.

Sophie drove home. Once out of the town if was a fifteen minute trip along a winding country road, finishing at the 1930's three bedroom art deco style house they had bought two years ago. It was a detached property in a private location that backed on to farm land, with no neighbours for at least 200 metres. The village primary school was within easy driving distance too. Sophie had decorated one room as a nursery, but despite their efforts it remained unoccupied.

'Up early tomorrow,' muttered Harry. 'You coming to bed?'

'Soon. Just want to finish this.' She sat on the living room sofa studying a magazine.

Harry retired upstairs. The wine was an effective anaesthetic and he was asleep within ten minutes. Downstairs Sophie discarded the magazine and stared wistfully into space. At least he doesn't snore, she thought.

'When was the last time I saw you then, Mr. Ellis?' asked his GP the following Saturday morning.

'Not sure. Think I was here for a travel vaccination last year.'

Dr. Finch, a young man with an earnest disposition, studied the letter Harry handed him. 'We'll take some blood and send it off. The antibodies they mention relate to hepatitis c. You may have cleared it early on, but we'll know soon enough. Make an appointment for next week and I'll have the results.'

A blood sample was taken. Harry thanked Dr. Finch and left. He knew nothing about hepatitis c, but he felt well enough. At 46 he was in good shape, not carrying any extra weight. His hair was thinning a little on top and greying at the temples, which was only to be expected really. He'd worn reasonably well in his estimation since arriving in England some twenty years ago. A little hepatitis, if he still had it, wouldn't change that.

Sophie was waiting for him in the car. They were driving up to London to have lunch with his in laws, a tedious duty from Harry's perspective, only relieved by the fact that his father in law had a capacity for wine that matched his own, and a well stocked cellar to indulge it. Harry was capable enough of being civil on these occasions, but he'd never felt particularly comfortable with his in laws. They were very different people from his own parents. His father was a carpenter and his mother had stayed home to bring up the children. Sophie's father was a partner at a top management consultancy, and her mother something of a Sloane Ranger, who'd never done anything much except socialize with other Sloane Rangers. He sometimes detected an air of perplexity about them when they saw him, as though they couldn't quite figure out how their beautiful daughter had chosen such an incongruous husband. At times he wondered that himself.

'Everything alright?' asked Sophie.

'They've taken a blood sample. I'll know more in a week or so.'

'I think I might stay up in London for the weekend, if you don't mind. I can get into the office early on Monday. There's still an awful lot of work to do before the auction.'

He was turning out of the surgery car park into busy Saturday morning traffic. 'Sure, if that's what you want to do. I'll amuse myself around the house on Sunday.'

They arrived in Fulham an hour and a half later, only marginally late. The house was an Edwardian five bedroom detached, with a large well landscaped garden. A Mercedes convertible and a Bentley graced the driveway, still leaving plenty of room for Harry to park his own Mercedes without obstructing anyone.

The door was opened by his father in law, Clive Sutherland. He was a tall and portly man in his mid sixties, dressed as ever in a well cut suit, without tie. Harry couldn't recall seeing him in anything else. He had a florid complexion, complemented by slightly bloodshot eyes that could have been the result of some pre-existing medical condition, or just too much booze. Harry's money was on the latter. He hugged Sophie and extended his hand to Harry.

'Lovely to see you both. Come on in, just time for an aperitif before lunch I think.'

Susanna, Sophie's mother, appeared as they walked inside. 'It's pheasant darling, needs another half hour or so though. Come and help me in the kitchen Sophie.' She took Sophie's arm and steered her away, flashing a brief smile of welcome in Harry's direction. She was a fifty something senior version of Sophie, well groomed and attractive, with a trim figure. She began chatting away to her daughter, who wasn't getting a chance to get a word in, as they retreated to the kitchen.

'Let's leave them to it, Harry. Come and have a glass of something. I've got a nice malt you might appreciate.'

Lunch was eventually served. The conversation turned to Clive's interest in rare coins, moved on to the upcoming auction, and then to the refurbishment of a second home in Italy. Susanna shared Sophie's interest in art, and painted herself. They were thinking of turning the old stable on the property into an artist's studio. Harry was finding Italy mildly interesting, when Clive changed course completely.

'Going to Dublin next week. Pitching for a project with Allied Irish Bank, Harry. It will be my first time in Ireland. How did you find it?'

'It was a long time ago now,' replied Harry. He didn't think about Ireland very much, not in his waking hours. Of course Clive knew that Harry had been married before, but the circumstances of

Natalie's death had never been revealed to him or Susanna. And they'd never shown much curiosity about it.

Sophie, who knew everything, looked apprehensive. After a few drinks on Harry's part, she knew that Ireland was a subject best left unmentioned.

'Let's talk about something else,' she ventured.

Harry had a far away look. He sat slowly twirling the stem of his wine glass. She wondered how many malts they'd had before lunch, and it did nothing to alleviate her anxiety.

'I never did tell you about Ireland.' He looked up and smiled at Clive, who reached for the wine bottle and refilled Harry's glass. Harry took a generous sip. 'We were there for about two years, I was studying Irish and had a little part time job with a security firm.' He laughed. Clive and Susanna caught the edge to his voice. Clive tried to retrieve the situation.

'Sorry Harry, let's change the subject. I forgot you lost your first wife back then.'

'Yes, that was careless of me. I left her alone for five minutes, and when I turned around she'd been blown to bits by a car bomb. Very careless, wouldn't you agree?'

For a few moments there was a stunned silence. Susanna was the first to react.

'My God, Harry. I'm so sorry, we had no idea.'

'No, you didn't.' Harry got up. 'I shouldn't have mentioned it really. If you'll excuse me, I think I might drive home.'

'Have a coffee first.' Sophie was at his side.

'I'll be fine. Thanks for lunch.' She knew he wouldn't change his mind. He kissed her, and when he moved away she saw the anguish in his eyes.

She touched his arm. 'I'll walk you to the car.'

Both Clive and Susanna were lost for words. They watched as their daughter linked arms with her husband and walked him out of the dining room. A few minutes later they heard the sound of a car traversing the gravel of the driveway.

Sophie reappeared. 'Well done, Daddy.' She held up her hand as Clive began to speak. 'You had to know sometime, I'm surprised it's taken this long.'

Harry slept badly. A part of him retained a peripheral awareness of the room, even with his eyes closed, and just as he began to sink into unconsciousness he would mysteriously snap back to a state of semi wakefulness, as though a mild electric current had been passed through his brain, forbidding him to sleep. After some time he stopped trying. He got up with the sunrise and the dawn chorus, feeling disturbed and unrested.

He didn't feel like eating right away. He decided to wait till mid morning, and once the supermarket opened he'd get fresh croissants for breakfast. Right now it was that time just after dawn when the world felt new again. There was a light mist over the field behind the house, dissolving as he watched in the warmth of the new day's sunlight. He pulled on his jeans, jersey and Wellingtons and headed to the bottom of the garden, unlatched the wooden gate and stepped on to the damp green grass.

He was quite alone as he walked across the field. He didn't want to think, and perhaps because he was tired his mind decided to co-operate, turning down the volume on the usual chatter of thought to an unobtrusive level. He passed through pockets of mist, aiming for the fence dividing this field from the next, about 100 yards ahead. Right by the fence he could see two large Copper Beech trees, their auburn colour contrasting sharply with the other predominantly green trees around him. As he looked, the morning sun bathed them in bright light, turning the auburn leaves to a shimmering gold. For a long moment he stood there, completely absorbed by the beauty of this unexpected spectacle, and totally one with the view in front of him. Nothing else existed.

He snapped out of it, after how long he wasn't sure. I must have seen that view a thousand times he thought, but never like that. He walked back to the house, feeling unusually serene. It was still far too early to go croissant hunting, so he returned to bed, and this time there were no electric currents. He slept until Sophie called four hours later.

She asked him how he was feeling.

'Better now. Though I didn't sleep well last night. Sorry if I upset your parents, by the way.'

'Well, they were certainly shocked. Daddy apologises for upsetting you too.'

'After all this time I'm surprised it still gets to me. Just feels like unfinished business.'

There was a short silence while she digested this. 'I don't understand. What do you mean – 'unfinished business'?'

He yawned. 'I'm not sure I know the answer to that one. Don't know why I said it. Can you come back today? I miss you.'

'Pick me up from the station later. I'll call you when I'm on the way.'

He smiled. 'Ok, will do. Now I need some breakfast.'

The following week a letter arrived from the surgery, informing Harry that his blood test had come back positive. An appointment had been made for him with a specialist at Thomas's hospital in London, so a few days later he found himself attending a morning clinic. After a long wait while several other people preceded him, he was finally called in to the consultant's office.

'Have a seat, Mr. Ellis.' His consultant sat studying the notes in front of him. 'I'm Dr. Ashe.'

Harry did as asked, and waited. Shortly afterwards the doctor looked up at him.

'Hepatitis C, what do you know about it?'

Harry had to admit his ignorance on the subject. Dr Ashe nodded, leaned back and contemplated the ceiling.

'It's a blood borne virus, which attacks the liver. Left untreated it can do enough damage to precipitate cirrhosis and possible liver failure.' He didn't register Harry's look of alarm. 'We can't say how long you may have had it. Have you ever injected hard drugs, had a blood transfusion before 1989 ..'

'Bingo,' chimed in Harry. 'Blood transfusion, 1981.'

'That could well be the event. How much do you drink by the way?'

'I don't count,' replied Harry. 'Is it important?'

'Alcohol speeds progression. Avoid it.'

Wonderful. 'Anything else I should know?'

He was told of the treatment on offer – a chemical cocktail with possible adverse side effects and a 50% success rate, that the disease progressed at different rates in different people but was often fatal, and sometimes a liver transplant was the only option left if nothing else worked. He felt slightly overwhelmed by the extent and nature of this new information.

'How long does it take to kill you then?'

'You may die of old age first. Or not. But I think treatment is the best course of action. Liver failure isn't a pleasant experience, so think about it and make a follow up appointment in any case. We like to monitor people.'

He left the hospital, reflecting on what he'd been told as he walked across Westminster Bridge. He couldn't absorb the implications all at once – an hour ago he was as healthy as ever and now he was about to meet the Reaper. He needed a drink. He stopped at the next pub he encountered and ordered a whisky. Sitting nursing the drink, he wouldn't accept that his diagnosis might mean a premature death. On the other hand, why be surprised? Death could come at any time. All he had to do was think of Natalie to know that.

After twenty years the pain of Nat's death was still with him. Occasionally he dreamed about the explosion, and would wake up sweating. No one had been arrested, and Litchfield had kept insisting that O'Reilly was the man responsible. Harry was still inclined to agree, even in the face of Michael's denial, which he'd never mentioned to Litchfield. He had stayed quiet about their meeting at Siobhan's funeral. Harry had left Ireland shortly afterwards, and Michael O'Reilly had effectively disappeared.

Harry had arrived in London, intending to stay a short time and then return home to New Zealand. That didn't happen. He rented a small flat in Notting Hill Gate, financed by the payments SIS continued to make him – blood money. The money was still going into his account now, though he hadn't seen anyone from SIS since Dublin. It was easier back then to pretend he preferred living in Europe, rather than face the condemnation of Nat's family back home. And after a while he stopped thinking about it. He took a course in computer programming and began working in financial institutions in the City. And now he was a process analyst, and concerned himself with business problems and their solutions. His embryonic career as a linguist with academic aspirations had been packed away in the box marked 'Ireland. Not to be disturbed.'

And apart from the dream, it rarely was disturbed. He finished his drink. He'd taken the morning off work for this appointment, and intended to get in a half day at the office. He could walk to the

City from here, along the embankment. He liked that walk and it was a beautiful day. The sun warmed his back as he strode by the river, admiring the view. He could see several cranes in action, and realised that ever since he could remember the cranes had been a part of the City of London skyline. He smiled to himself. Should be a nice town when it's finished, he thought.

'I had a mystical experience the other day.'

'Really Harry,' said Cindy. 'Is this a common occurrence?'

Dr. Lucinda Roberts was a psychotherapist with a practice in Chelsea. He'd been seeing her twice a month for the last year, albeit at first reluctantly. When Sophie had insisted he do something to address his drinking, which she thought was his way of 'self medicating' his anger at Natalie's death, he'd picked up on the unspoken implication that if he didn't agree his marriage might be headed for trouble. There were times, especially after a few glasses of wine, when he would snap at her irritably, which almost inevitably precipitated a shouting match, though he was the one doing most of the shouting. Sophie would rise to the bait for a short while, then she would sit quietly looking miserable till he shut up. He hated himself the next day, but it seemed a pattern had developed.

Sophie knew Lucinda, or Cindy as she preferred to be called, through Susanna, who had apparently consulted Cindy some years ago. Harry had never asked why, but he was almost certain Clive was the reason. Another man who drank too much, perhaps he was hell to live with too. So in the interests of marital harmony he had consented to meet Cindy.

She was in her mid 40's and rather too glamorous in his opinion for her profession. He had a pre-conception of a serious spinster type with horn rimmed glasses who spoke with perfectly received pronunciation, but Cindy was petite and well shaped, with a mane of shoulder length blonde hair, which tended to fall over her eyes on occasion. When this happened she would toss it back over her shoulders with a theatrical nod of the head, which always momentarily startled him. She had a penchant for short skirts and black stockings, and he often found himself distracted, especially when she crossed her perfect legs to reveal a generous expanse of thigh as the short skirt got even shorter. He was sure she did it to titillate him, and considered it to be rather unprofessional, but he thought what the hell, they were there to discuss his neurosis, not hers, he would put up with her quirks. And she was Australian, though the accent had been diluted after ten years in London. For some reason their shared Antipodean heritage gave him a sense of connection, and though he knew it was irrational, it helped to relax him nevertheless.

He realised he was staring at her legs again and had missed her last remark.

'Sorry, what was that?'

'Tell me about your mystical experience, Harry. You went quiet for a minute.'

'Sorry, lost in thought.' He described his meeting with the Beech trees. 'For a while it seemed I just forgot myself completely, it was actually quite beautiful. I don't remember ever feeling like that.'

'What do you think it means?'

'I have no idea. Maybe it means there are opportunities to transcend my mundane little world from time to time. Just thought I'd mention it to you.'

Her hair was getting unruly. Here it comes he thought, the toss of the head, but she didn't oblige. 'What else has happened since we last met?' she asked.

'Well, I've been diagnosed with a possibly fatal illness, otherwise nothing much.'

The head went back, and the mane was restored to order. He thought about suggesting an Alice band, but restrained himself.

'I'm sorry to hear that. What sort of illness?'

After he'd recounted his visit to Thomas's she asked him how he felt about it.

'Scared, worried.'

'Angry?'

'Yes, as it happens.'

'Perhaps your mystical experience and your illness have a connection,' mused Cindy.

'What do you mean?'

'Sometimes, when people have an existential crisis they start seeing the beauty in everyday things around them that they never noticed before. When they realise their time in this world is finite after all, they start paying attention to things that have always been there, but that they've never really seen, if that makes sense. As a culture we do a lot of looking without seeing.'

'Is that what I'm having – an existential crisis?'

Cindy smiled. 'I shouldn't be putting words into your mouth. Will you take the treatment?'

'I don't know yet. Maybe.'

'And how are you and Sophie doing?'

He thought for a bit. 'We're doing ok. I don't shout at her for no reason as much as I did.'

She smiled. 'Good. I'm pleased to hear that. Are you still angry about Natalie?'

He sighed. 'Yes, that never changes.'

A week later he was still undecided on what to do about his hepatitis. The research he'd done had not given him huge cause for optimism. The side effects of the drugs on offer ranged from mild itching and fatigue to full blown depression and psychosis. It was hardly an appealing treatment regime, but it seemed there was no alternative.

Sophie's reaction didn't help either.

'Is it contagious?' She looked slightly disgusted.

'I don't know. I don't think so. Transmitted blood to blood I think he said.' He realised with alarm that he hadn't considered the possible effects on people close to him. 'You can get tested, maybe you should.'

130

'What about sex, Harry?'

'We didn't discuss sex.'

'Well, find out please. I suppose I will have to get tested. How horrible.'

'I'm sure there's nothing to worry about.' She looked less than convinced. 'But yes, I'll find out for you.'

He couldn't swear to it, but he felt that for the rest of the evening she went out of her way to make sure he wasn't too close to her. And sex was most definitely off the agenda that night.

Chapter 11

The following evening found him in a wine bar near Brick Lane, with a friend from work. It was low lit and cosy, with candles burning on strategically placed wine barrels to enhance the ambience. A half full bottle of good claret stood between them. One bottle had already been disposed of.

'You know Neil, I've never been mad about financial services,' said Harry.

'Just mad about the money, Harry'. Neil was another contract analyst at the bank. He was 10 years younger than Harry, single, good looking, and he dressed the part of the City wide boy. He was also intelligent and funny, with a dry sense of humour that Harry found refreshing.

'Yes, it's always about the money, and then about more of the money. Non-stop really.'

'Very profound of you Harry. Have some more wine. I'm just going to powder my nose. Can I interest you?'

'Thanks Neil, but alcohol is my poison of preference. Go ahead mate'.

When Neil came back his eyes had that certain sparkle. Harry smiled in spite of himself.

'I was going to suggest a restaurant, but no doubt your appetite is non-existent now' he said.

'We should sustain ourselves on nothing but liquids and chemicals Harry. I swear by it.'

'Don't know how you do it, actually.'

'Listen Harry, the only really important thing in life is the pursuit of pleasure – women, drugs, money, that's my religion. Excess is the only rule I live by. Hell, you could be dead tomorrow.'

How very true, thought Harry.

Neil disappeared again to replenish his nose. Harry looked across the room at a group of young women laughing at something over their drinks. One of them, a dark haired Italian looking beauty, looked across at him briefly and flashed a smile. He smiled back. They look so beautiful and alive he thought. He felt a stab of anxiety. One day, this will all be gone, I'll be dead, and what the hell will it have all been about? Perhaps Neil has a point after all.

Feeling rather dispirited by this turn of thought, he reached for the claret and poured another glass. Nothing more wine wouldn't fix. His mobile rang. It was Sophie.

'Where are you?' she asked.

'With someone from work. Wine bar in Brick Lane.'

'Right.' There was a pause. 'I had a blood test today. It will take a week to come back.'

'Yes, sensible thing to do,' he began, but she cut in.

'I'm staying in Fulham for a while, Harry. There's so much to do at work and it's just easier than commuting every day. You'll be ok on your own for a bit, won't you?'

'How long is "a bit"'?'

'I don't know.' She sounded irritated. 'I'll call you when I do. Bye darling.'

'Sophie, hang on ..' She'd gone. He leaned back in his chair. Didn't see that coming. Was he becoming untouchable? No, she was just over reacting.

Meantime, Neil had reappeared.

'Everything ok, Harry? You look a bit pissed off.'

'Do I? Piece of advice, Neil. Don't get married, it's far too much like hard work.'

Neil grinned. 'I take it that was your wife. Well, if that's the effect she has then your advice is duly noted.' He looked at his watch. 'I've got to move. Meeting a lady for a late dinner. Sorry to leave you in the lurch, she's just texted me. I'd forgotten all about it.'

'That's fine, Neil. I need to get the train soon anyway.'

Neil departed, and Harry examined the wine bottle. One more glass in there he thought. I'll finish that and I'm out of here. He filled his glass, wondering whether he should call Sophie. He sat, mobile in hand, then returned it to his pocket. Can't reassure her without any facts to back me up he thought. And not until she has her test results. It will be ok.

He was aware of someone beside him. He looked up.

'Hello Harry.'

For a moment he was nonplussed. The man next to him was in late middle age, wearing a well cut pinstripe suit. Grey haired with almost feminine eyelashes, and smiling at Harry's obvious lack of recognition.

134

'It has been a while since we last met.'

'Christ, is it you Jack?'

'One and the same,' replied Jack Hudson. 'Mind if I join you?'

Harry stared back blankly. Then he found his voice. 'No, of course not. Can I get you a drink?'

'I'll get you one. Give you a chance to recover. I wonder if this place serves Irish whiskey.' He headed off in the direction of the bar.

Harry watched him go. Jack Hudson, who he hadn't seen for twenty years. What on earth was he doing here now? He took a few deep breaths. Maybe he'd had too much wine and was hallucinating. He suddenly felt as though the last twenty years had dropped away. Perhaps he should just nip outside and reassure himself that he was in Brick Lane and not Dublin. He decided against it. After all, if it did turn out to be Grafton Street out there, what would he do next?

Jack returned, pulling up a chair opposite.

'They do have whiskey.' He handed one to Harry, raising his own glass. 'Slainche.'

'Cheers. How did you find me?'

'I know where you work, Harry.'

'I see. It might have escaped your attention, but this isn't my place of work.'

Jack laughed. 'Things have moved on a lot since Dublin. I have your mobile number. And a little software that's programmed into my phone helped me track you down. Useful, don't you think?'

'Remind me to get one.'

'Not available to the general public yet. For a lapsed SIS employee though, I might be able to pull a few strings.'

'Lapsed. Right.' Harry took a sip of his whiskey. 'Think I might need another one of these. So, this isn't a happy co-incidence?'

'I don't know about the happy part, but no, this is not co-incidence. You could at least ask how I am.'

'How are you?'

'I'm well, thank you. You're not looking so bad yourself. I understand you re-married?'

Harry's mind went back to Dublin, an image of Natalie and Christmas in Harcourt Street. 'Yes, I did. A few years ago.' He sighed. 'Sorry Jack, you're turning back the clock for me right now.'

'Yes, I thought that might happen. Can't be helped though. Do you remember me saying you don't resign?'

'Do I even count as a current SIS employee? Our association didn't last very long, did it?'

'No, Harry. But we have been paying you regularly ever since.' He noted the flash of annoyance in Harry's eyes, but was unperturbed. 'Yes, perhaps you could call it a Death in Service Benefit for want of a better expression, but it is a payment nonetheless.'

'Which is your way of saying you have some entitlement to me, is that it? What exactly do you want, Jack?'

'We need your help. You remember Michael O'Reilly?'

Harry finished his whiskey. 'Get me another one please. This conversation is becoming distinctly unpleasant.'

136

Jack gave him a long look, but did as he was asked. When they were both refilled he continued. 'He disappeared as you know, quite effectively as it turned out. He was in Kilburn in London for a while in the 80's, but then the trail goes cold.'

'So why resurrect it now?'

'We think he may have information that will help us with a current investigation.' Harry raised his eyes in mock amazement. 'Yes, Harry. I know how long it's been. We want you to help us locate him.'

Now the amazement was real. 'What the hell can I do? Besides, if I find the bastard I may not be responsible for my actions.'

'You only need to pinpoint him, not go face to face. Now listen. What we do know is that he had a woman in Dublin, a German nurse. We think they are still in touch. We've located her, and through her you're going to locate him.'

Harry was finding this hard to take in. 'What am I going to say to her exactly? And why me, you could send someone more persuasive, couldn't you?'

'Think about it, Harry. You speak the language. And the bank you're currently working for has a branch in Frankfurt, which is only an hour away from Heidelberg, where she lives. You're not exactly seasoned intelligence material, so I doubt she'd suspect your motives, even if the thought crossed her mind. We'll get your contract transferred to Frankfurt and take it from there.'

'My God, you've already got this thing in motion haven't you? One thing you haven't told me is how I get this information out of her, assuming she has it.'

Jack smiled ever so slightly, then produced a photo from his inside pocket and passed it across. 'Her name is Sabine. She's attractive don't you think? Perhaps you can have an affair with her.'

The last train from Charing Cross rushed through Kent, as though impatient to reach its final destination and turn in for the night. All Harry could see was his own face and those of the other tired looking commuters reflected back from the windows.

He'd given Jack an email address, and Jack had promised to send a file on Sabine Maier the following day. His protestations on the feasibility of an affair with her had been batted to one side.

'I'm married Jack, you seem to have overlooked that little detail,' he'd objected.

'Think of it as an intimate friendship then,' was the rejoinder. 'You need to get close to her, but only for a short time. Full blown romance won't be necessary. We've arranged an introduction, it's all in the file. Read it and get back to me.'

Fine, he thought, I'll read it then tell him what to do with it. But even the claret and whiskey couldn't dull a growing sense of anticipation, the reason for which eluded him. He would wake up stone cold sober tomorrow and apply some objective thought to the matter then.

He printed Sabine's file when he got home the following evening. There'd been no word from Sophie all day, and although he'd been alone in the house many times before, tonight it seemed cold and lifeless without her. Perhaps the antidote was to eat out later, if only to be in the presence of other people. He sighed. He'd get the reading out of the way first, then formulate some appropriate response to Jack Hudson, detailing all the reasons why this proposed assignment was a total non-starter. He fixed a gin and tonic, made himself comfortable on the living room sofa, and began to read.

An hour later he'd learned that Sabine Maier had been born in Heidelberg in 1961 to a German father and Irish mother. She'd had one older sister named Monika, who had died age 20 (no reason given). Some details about education, including the fact that she'd done philosophy at Heidelberg University, then having decided not to enter academia (which might have been the logical next step), trained as an intensive care nurse. She spent 1981 in Dublin at St. James's hospital, where she met Michael O'Reilly when she nursed his sister Siobhan after a shooting incident. Returned to Heidelberg 1982, and since then had divided her time between nursing and a career as a jazz musician. Highly regarded as a leading female exponent of the alto saxophone on the contemporary European jazz scene.

How they'd made the connection between her and O'Reilly was not explained, nor was any reason given as to why they thought she might still be in touch with him. It seemed a little tenuous. A deliberate omission perhaps.

He read on. She had never married, no children from any relationship, and was currently single. Had an apartment in Panorama Strasse not far from the Old Town, drove a blue Golf, paid her taxes and was ostensibly a model citizen. But nothing about her personality. The photo was a full length shot of a slim dark haired woman standing outside a restaurant somewhere in Germany (the name 'Goldene Rose' clearly visible behind her). She wore a belted blue dress that clung enough to show a well defined figure, and she smiled into the camera, projecting a quiet self confidence that so many Germans he'd met seemed to share. There was mischief in that smile though. She was attractive, no doubt about that. Whether he'd still think that after they'd met and she'd opened her mouth was another matter. If they met.

Now came his cover story. Yes, he worked for a bank in Frankfurt, but was also a part time writer for 'Jazz Europe' magazine, who wanted to do a profile of Sabine Maier for their next monthly issue. She had been contacted by the magazine and had consented to an interview. He was to attend an upcoming gig in Heidelberg, then meet her the following day, at her apartment.

To assist in any gaps in his knowledge, a file of relevant interview questions and an electronic copy of 'The Jazz Saxophone – History and Players' had been thoughtfully attached. Any queries he might have after reading these should be listed and returned to Jack. He was advised not to present himself as an authority or critic, and just stick to the pre-prepared questions, one of which would raise the subject of her time in Ireland.

140

It was all rather speculative, he reflected. She was hardly likely to mention her affair with O'Reilly no matter what he asked her about Ireland. When was he supposed to be doing all this? He scanned the final page. His transfer to Frankfurt was effective in two weeks, and the gig was the week after that. How on earth had they arranged the transfer? And they'd done it in what seemed like the certain knowledge of his co-operation. It would seem that refusal on his part was not anticipated. Or simply not an option.

Jack had included a phone number, with the instruction to call once he was ready for the 'additional briefing.' No time like the present, he thought, reaching for his mobile.

Jack answered almost immediately. 'Well, Harry. What do you think?'

'Tell me the rest first.'

'Ok, it's simple enough. We want you to get a feel for this woman. Especially her political affiliations. I need to know why she would be happy sleeping with a terrorist, however long ago it was.'

'Fine, I'll make that an additional question, shall I? And how do you know she did sleep with him?'

'We tracked O'Reilly as far as Kilburn. But before we could move in, something spooked him and he left rather hurriedly. When we searched his flat we found letters between the two of them, with enough intimacy to conclude they were lovers. We dropped our pursuit shortly afterwards, because it became apparent that we weren't the only people looking for him. We thought if we left well alone the problem might be resolved without us. And then we got sidetracked onto more important things, so unfortunately we don't know what happened.'

'Who else was looking?'

'IRA colleagues. He was on their hit list apparently. We don't know why though.'

'Seems to be quite a lot you don't know.' Harry was intrigued, in spite of his earlier misgivings. 'He could be dead then. You're shooting in the dark Jack, it seems to me. Incidentally, why do you want him now?'

Jack gave a short laugh. 'You don't need to know that. Let me summarise it for you. Sabine Maier is the only link we have. O'Reilly may well be dead, and if that's the case it would be a good result for us, I can tell you that much. Just ask your questions, find a way of meeting her again, and see what you can find out.'

'I see. It seems harmless enough. Can't quite see her confessing all though.'

'To an extent I agree with you, Harry. So there's one last thing. We'll give you a key to her apartment. At some point you'll search it for any sign of contact between them. We'll also give you a couple of CDs with some pre-loaded software that will let you download the contents of her computer, assuming she has one. You'll probably need no more than an hour.'

It was Harry's turn to laugh, but it was devoid of mirth. 'Christ, that's all I need. And if she just happens to walk in?'

'She won't. You'll do it when she's in Munich. She has a gig there the week after the Heidelberg interview. There's no risk at all, Harry.'

What am I getting into, he wondered. Whatever it was, it didn't stop him from deciding there and then. 'Ok, Jack. I'll do it. And while I'm in Frankfurt, get me somewhere nice to stay. An apartment, not a hotel.'

'Already done. Welcome back, Harry.'

The day following his conversation with Jack he was summoned to a meeting with the head of the bank's Programme Office, who was responsible for overall management of resources and budgets for all the projects currently underway in London. Looking somewhat bemused, she informed him that the German branch wanted him to kick off a process initiative in Frankfurt.

'Totally out of the blue Harry. I know it's short notice, but can you do it?'

Harry looked suitably surprised. 'I think so, Gina. I'll need to discuss it with my wife of course.'

'Let me know as soon as you can. I've told them they can have you for a month, tops. You speak German, don't you?'

He nodded. 'Been a while, I'll be quite rusty to start with. I bet most of them speak better English than I do. Shouldn't be an issue.'

He spent the next fortnight at work ensuring that any outstanding processes and documentation were ready to be handed over to a temporary replacement. It was time consuming, and at home there was still no sign of Sophie, or even any sign that she'd been in the house. He called her mobile several times, but got only voicemail. He missed her.

He was due to fly out in two days. He would call her again this evening, and if it was still bloody voicemail he'd have no option but to leave a message, and hope she bothered to listen to it. Maybe he should just go round to Fulham and find out what was on her mind. No, she'd just use Clive and Susanna as reinforcements if it came to an argument. He could do without that.

That evening he left the office at a reasonable hour, politely declining Neil's invitation to join him for a drink. He wanted a clear head tonight. He arrived home around 8ish, and was surprised to see lights on as he pulled into the drive. He had a moment of doubt – hopefully that was his wife inside, and not a team of burglars turning the place over. Could be Sabine Maier of course, mounting a pre-emptive strike. Only one way to find out.

It was Sophie. She rose from the sofa as soon as she saw him, walked across the room and wrapped her arms around him, hugging him tight.

'Harry, I'm so sorry. I've been a bit of a bitch. Forgive me?'

For a quiet moment he revelled in the warmth and smell of her. 'I missed you. Are you ok?'

She raised her head and kissed him. 'Yes, you?'

'Sure. What about your test?'

'I'm clear Harry. I just freaked out when you told me, that's all. Needed time to think.'

'Thank God you're ok. And now you've had time to think, what's the verdict?'

She gently thumped his ribs. 'You're not on trial. I was worried that I wouldn't be able to make love to you. But I was being stupid. If we both had it, what difference would it make? And if you picked it up years ago, and I'm clear, then it amounts to the same thing. Apparently I'd have to be pretty rough with you in bed for the risk to be real.'

He smiled. 'How rough, exactly?'

'Rough enough to draw blood. Not exactly my style, is it?'

He moved his hands to caress her waist, and she pressed her body against him. 'I've forgotten your style, actually.'

She laughed. 'Time I refreshed your memory then. Let's go upstairs.'

They ordered a takeaway, Chicken Jalfrezi with dhaal and chapatties, washed down with a Chilean Sauvignon Blanc.

'Tesco's finest, quite nice too,' remarked Harry as he filled Sophie's glass.

She took a sip. 'Mmm, not bad. You know that people with hepatitis shouldn't drink, don't you?'

'Yes, I've had the lifestyle advice. No alcohol, but sex is ok in a monogamous relationship. I've told the other women it's over, so you've nothing to worry about in that department.'

She gave him a quizzical look, but didn't bite. 'Some changes might be a good idea, that's all I'm saying.'

'No, you're right. I'm not ignoring it. When I get back from Germany we'll organise a program of pure living, with minimal indulgence. They'll probably canonize me.'

'You didn't tell me you were going to Germany. When?'

'In two days. Which is one of the reasons I was trying to call you. They want me to do some work in the Frankfurt office. No more than a month. Sorry to spring it on you, but it was sprung on me too.'

She considered for a moment. 'Well I suppose I can spare you. I'll take a few days leave and come and see you. I'm sure there are lots of pretty German towns we can visit.'

'I'm sure there are.' His stomach flipped at this first unforeseen complication. 'That's a great idea. Let's drink to it. Prosit!'

Chapter 12

Harry stood on the Old Bridge spanning the Neckar river, looking up at Heidelberg Castle. It was dark now, but the famous old castle in its elevated position in the foothills above the town was clearly visible. Its fortifications and towers were illuminated by unseen spotlights, which imparted a soft golden glow to the aged brown stone. It formed a singular and imposing structure on this side of the river, with only the blackness of the surrounding forest for company.

The Old Town lay at its feet. He'd walked nearly a mile from the tram stop at Bismarckplatz, down a wide straight Main Street, or Hauptstrasse, to get to the bridge. The place was buzzing with tourists, snapping the sights and each other, before almost invariably ducking into one of the many bars or traditional sausage and sauerkraut restaurants. The day had been mild, but the night wind blowing across the river held a sharp chill, heralding the approach of Winter.

Maybe it's just normal October weather, he thought, wrapping his scarf a little tighter. He took a last look at the castle, then walked off the bridge and back into town. Turning left at the Hauptstrasse he continued on, scanning the side streets until he found the one he wanted. The Jazzhaus was halfway down.

He went down some stairs to what appeared to be a converted beer cellar. It was a narrow and intimate venue, with a stage at one end and groups of small tables filling the rest of the space, with a bar behind them. He decided to sit as far back from the stage as possible, and was glad he'd come early. The place probably couldn't hold much more than 50 people, and it was half full already. He checked his watch. Sabine was due on stage at 9pm, one hour to wait. He found an unoccupied table near the bar, and signalled the waitress.

She took his order. 'Are you alone?' she asked. He nodded. 'You won't be for long. We have a very good group tonight, and by 9 we will be full up. Hope you don't mind sharing.' She smiled and went off to fetch his beer.

She was right. By 9 it was standing room only. A couple who'd driven across from Mannheim had joined him, both jazz enthusiasts. When they found out he was from England they regaled him with tales of visits to Ronnie Scott's club in London, and some of the famous names they'd seen there. He was pleased that he actually knew some of the names, if not their music. He decided not to pretend he knew more than he did.

'I'm no expert, but tonight's group was recommended to me, especially the sax player.'

'Ah yes, Sabine Maier. That's why we are here. You will like her.'

The band's instruments were already on stage, all that was needed was the appearance of their owners. At the appointed hour three men rose from the table they'd been occupying closest to the stage and took their places – drummer, electric bassist and guitar player. He wondered where Sabine was. At that moment there was a round of

polite applause as a woman entered the room, straight from the

148

street he assumed. She lifted her hand briefly in acknowledgement. The sax diva had arrived.

She walked to the stage and faced the audience, smiling. 'Sorry, I'm a little late.'

Now he had a good chance to observe her. She didn't know he'd be here tonight, the magazine had simply arranged the interview and made no mention of attending gigs. He was to confirm their meeting tomorrow morning by phone from the hotel. From his perspective It gave him the advantage of sizing her up in advance, without her knowledge.

He watched as the band did some preliminary tuning of their instruments. She was prettier than the photo, he decided. Dressed quite casually in jeans, boots and white cotton blouse, she looked poised and relaxed as she exchanged a few words with the guitarist. The smile had that same element of mischief that he'd noticed in the photo.

Then they launched into their first number, a slow ballad that alternated the melody between guitar and saxophone. She played with a deep rich tone that filled the room, and he leaned back in his chair as the bitter sweet tonality of the piece caressed his senses. If this was modern jazz he was fast becoming a fan. He had a moment of alarm when he realised he might need to discuss this music with her tomorrow afternoon, and he didn't even know if this piece was a standard or an original composition. To hell with it, he thought. The die is cast, and the worst that could happen is that she would see him for the fraud he undoubtedly was, and he would slink back to Frankfurt a chastened man. Right now, he would enjoy himself.

They stopped for a break an hour later, leaving the stage and occupying a small table to one side of it. The waitress brought them a tray of drinks, and various members of the audience wandered over to exchange pleasantries. The couple he was sitting with, Gerhardt and Kristina, asked him to save their places while they went to have a word.

'We've been following her progress for many years,' announced Kristina. 'Back in a minute.'

Harry ordered another beer. While he waited he cast his glance around the room, checking out the clientele. There was an even mix of old and young. The groups of twenty something men scattered throughout were casually dressed and clean shaven with mostly shortish hair. Their girlfriends looked scrubbed and smart. Probably a lot of students, as this was a university town. In contrast, everyone over 45 of both sexes seemed underdressed and undergroomed – all beards, longish hair, the odd corduroy jacket and even a few colourful ankle length hippyish dresses in evidence. He grinned to himself. An eclectic mix, to say the least.

He returned his attention to Gerhardt and Kristina, who had now found Sabine. As there was nowhere else to sit at her table, Sabine had stood up to chat, and he had a good view of the three of them. Kristina was doing most of the talking. Suddenly she gesticulated towards the back of the room, looking directly at him. Sabine followed her gaze, and their eyes met. He swore inwardly, but nodded and smiled.

She smiled back for a moment, then as he watched he saw the smile replaced with surprise, quickly followed by perplexity. It was all over in a split second and then she turned away. He thought he'd imagined the whole thing, but as Gerhardt and Kristina made their way back she gave him another thoughtful look, before returning to her own table. He was as perplexed as she appeared to be.

The incident left him with a vague sense of unease, which he tried to ignore for the rest of the gig. The pace picked up for the second set, with a couple of frenetic solos that saw her playing phrases of harmonics that sent the audience into rapturous bursts of applause. The energy levels in the cellar went up a notch. The drummer rode on the buzz and contributed a five minute solo that pushed it up again. To bring everyone back to earth they finished the evening with something sedate and bluesey, the guitarist leading. Harry had thoroughly enjoyed it from start to finish.

He got up to leave, and threaded his way through the tables towards the door. There were a few people on the way out, but most of them seemed in no hurry to go anywhere, they were talking and drinking. Then suddenly she was in front of him.

'Hello,' she said.

He tried to look unconcerned. 'Hello. You're very good, I enjoyed it a lot.'

'Thank you.' They were close, and he became aware of what he thought of later as a still and serene quality about her. It was charismatic and a little unsettling. He extended his hand.

'Harry Ellis. I'm interviewing you tomorrow. Just thought I'd catch you in advance. I was going to call you tomorrow morning.'

She shook his hand. The thoughtful look was still there, and she didn't reply immediately. Then the penny seemed to drop. 'Of course, from "Jazz Europe." That explains it.'

'Explains what?'

'I thought I knew you from somewhere. But now I realise it was the photo of you that the magazine sent.' Her face relaxed into a smile. 'You should have told me you were coming tonight, we could have met up earlier.'

He felt an inexplicable surge of relief. 'Yes, you're right. Sorry if I alarmed you. Do you have time for a drink right now?'

'Unfortunately not, but I look forward to seeing you tomorrow. You have my address don't you? Is 2pm ok?'

'Perfect. Talk to you soon.' He made for the exit. On the way out he turned to get a last glimpse of her. She was looking right back at him with that thoughtful expression again. Then she smiled, raised her hand in farewell, and turned away.

The following afternoon was dry, bright and cold. He decided to walk to Sabine's apartment, it was only fifteen minutes away from the hotel. He set off down Rohrbacher Strasse, past a petrol station and a cemetery, then turned left. Another left found him in

152

Panorama Strasse, which climbed steeply into the Heidelberg hills. He arrived at her apartment block slightly out of breath, thinking a taxi might have been the smarter option. He rang the bell and waited.

She opened the door and ushered him in. She was on the top storey of a two storey block, and as he walked into the living room he saw that Panorama Strasse lived up to its name. There was an unobstructed view of the town for miles. Not of the Old Town or castle, which lay behind them, but of a sprawling carpet of houses, schools and shops, and one large area nearby that took his interest, which consisted of rows of grey institutional like buildings, and a number of flagpoles flying the U.S flag.

'What's that?' he asked.

'US Army barracks. They're still here. For our protection of course. There's a bigger one in Mannheim.'

'That one looks big enough. Great view from here.'

'Yes, I'm lucky to have this place. Let me get you a coffee.'

She disappeared into the kitchen. Harry looked around. The room was comfortably furnished and doubled as a dining area. Sabine's laptop was perched on the dining table. There were two saxophones on their stands in one corner, and some photos and pictures on one wall. One photo showed Sabine with an older bearded black man brandishing a saxophone of his own. The pictures consisted of what he thought looked like a Picasso print of a man and a guitar, and a large landscape of a lake surrounded by cloud covered mountains, which could have been anywhere, but looked to him to be reminiscent of the South Island of New Zealand. A well stocked

153

bookcase occupied the opposite wall. He stood inspecting the books, and wondered where she kept her letters.

Sabine reappeared, two cups of coffee in hand. 'Some of them are in English,' she remarked, nodding at the books. 'But your German is very good. Where did you learn?'

'At Uni. It was a long time ago. How's your English? It would be good if we could speak English for the interview. I brought a tape recorder with me.'

'That's fine,' she replied. 'Sit with me on the sofa and ask your questions.'

He sat, perusing the list. It was drawn up on a chronological basis – when had she first picked up the saxophone, how had her career unfolded, who were her influences? It was designed to let her do all the talking, and for him to simply record the answers without discussing things he knew little about. It worked well enough. He got through the early stages of her love affair with the instrument, then asked her when she first started playing professionally.

'Professionally? The first time I got paid was in Ireland actually. I was 20 and spent a year there visiting my relations and working. Nursing mostly. But I played some nights in Dublin and we were paid for that. Do you know Ireland?'

He decided to varnish the truth a little. 'I visited once, but no, not really. How was your time there?'

She didn't miss a beat. 'Nothing to tell. I didn't even get out of Dublin. But I enjoyed being there. It made a change from Germany for me back then.'

154

'So you didn't make any lasting connections while you were there?'

She looked at him sharply. 'Is that a pre-prepared question?'

'Sorry, no. Just curious. You were a young single woman. I'm just being nosey.'

She looked at the ceiling for a moment, thinking. 'I met one or two people. Nothing worth mentioning though.'

Pretty much as he'd expected. Perhaps he should just ask her if the name O'Reilly meant anything to her. That would spice things up a little. He restrained himself, and continued with the prepared format. They covered her rise in the German pantheon of jazz musicians, and he asked what her aspirations for the future might entail.

'I don't do this for the money, I just love playing. I'm hardly known outside of Europe, and I'm not bothered about fame and fortune. If it happens I won't complain of course.' She gave a short ironical laugh. 'Jazz musicians are like painters, no one appreciates them until they're long dead.'

'Maybe you'll be the exception to the rule. When's your next gig?'

'Munich, next Wednesday. You should come.'

'I will if I can make it. I think we're done now. This will appear in next month's issue. Is there a photo we can use?'

She smiled that mischievous smile. 'You didn't bring a camera? I have a photo I give to people sometimes. You can scan it. I'll just go and get one for you.'

Harry turned off the recorder and prepared to leave. Sabine returned from wherever she'd gone with a black and white image of herself. She was sitting on a chair in some club with the sax around her neck, looking at the camera with a steady gaze and just the hint of a smile on her lips.

'I like it,' he said. 'Captures you quite well. Thanks.'

'You're welcome.' She walked him to the door. 'Will there be any follow up questions?'

He paused in the act of putting on his coat. 'Follow up? I don't think so.' He thought he detected a hint of a challenge in her eyes, and reconsidered. 'Actually, there may well be follow up questions. Can I call you after Munich? I don't think I'll be free on Wednesday, so perhaps I can buy you dinner instead.'

'Yes, I'd like that. And then I can ask all the questions. Deal?'

He cursed himself inwardly. This was probably not a good idea. But he heard himself answering despite that. 'Deal. This is your town, so you can pick the restaurant. See you soon then.'

After she'd shut the door he took a few moments to scrutinise the lock and memorise the maker's name. Once Jack Hudson had that information he would courier a skeleton key post haste, and Harry could return next Wednesday to visit the apartment undisturbed. He felt a pang of guilt at what he was doing. But as he descended Panorama Strasse he knew he wanted to find out what had happened to O'Reilly as much as Jack did. If the answer was inside that apartment, then guilt was a price well worth paying for the deception involved. And Sabine would be none the wiser. Armed with this rationale, he sauntered back past the cemetery and into town. Everything would be just fine.

The key arrived at the Frankfurt office the following Monday. He now had everything he needed for Wednesday night. He had a small digital camera, and all he needed to do with the CDs was turn on Sabine's laptop and slot one into the drive. According to Jack one should be enough, but if he needed both he'd see a message telling him to load the second one. The pre-loaded software would do the rest, effectively cloning the contents of her hard drive.

He'd told his project leader in Frankfurt that his visits to Heidelberg were part of a brief given to him by the London office. The bank had targeted a private client there, with whom he was discussing the pros and cons of investing his considerable wealth. For reasons of confidentiality he couldn't identify the client either. As long as nobody talked to Gina in London that story should hold up. And after this week his 'client' would regrettably decline the opportunity, and Harry would have no further need to be out of the office.

He took the train late Wednesday afternoon, and at 6pm he was back once more at Heidelberg Central Station. It was a little early in his estimation to be carrying out a burglary, so he took a tram into Bismarckplatz. He would eat first, then when it was completely dark around 8pm, he could walk to the apartment. In and out, then back to Frankfurt, with no taxis or hotel stays to mark his presence. The meal would provide an opportunity to compose himself and calm the nerves, and a couple of glasses of wine should help too. He knew he was about to violate her space, and right now he didn't like himself too much for doing it.

It was quiet in Panorama Strasse. Sabine's apartment was in darkness, as was the one below it. The hedge bordering the block offered cover for his approach, but he was exposed on his way up the steps to her front door on the upper level. He paused when he got there and quickly surveyed the area. The nearest neighbouring building was some 20 metres away, and he saw nothing in that direction to concern him. Now, all he had to do was open the door.

The key fitted perfectly, and with a sigh of relief he was inside. Now, he thought, do everything as quickly and efficiently as possible. First the computer. He extracted a pencil torch from his coat and entered the living room. The laptop was as he'd last seen it on the dining room table. He turned it on and inserted the first CD as instructed. Apparently the computer would read the CD before doing anything else, and then the normal boot up sequence would be bypassed, which meant no log in and no password to worry about. Very clever, he hoped it worked. He'd been told to photograph as much of the apartment as possible, and he began to shoot the living room from all angles. No need for flash in the darkness with this camera either, it was equipped with an ultra sensitive lense for all but the most pitch black of conditions. He wasn't shooting completely blind, there was enough light from the street to assist his aim.

He photographed every room, including the bathroom, which struck him as overkill, but he might as well be thorough. The bedrooms, of which there were two, didn't seem to offer potential for any correspondence, but there was a study leading off the main bedroom. It was small, but there was enough space for a writing desk and chair, and a small filing cabinet. This room might yield something of interest. He closed the door, and as the room had no window, turned on the light. He began to investigate the contents of the desk drawers, taking care to replace everything as he'd found it. He'd been engaged in this task for a minute or two, his senses on high alert, when his mobile rang.

'Shit!' He almost leapt out of the chair. He quickly found his phone and glanced at the incoming number. It was Jack Hudson, who knew exactly where he was right now and what he was doing. Maybe it was a warning. He took the call.

'Harry, how are you getting on?'

'Is everything alright Jack? You do know where I am I assume.'

'I know where you should be. Are you there?'

'Yes, I'm here. I don't want to be here talking to you though, in fact I don't want to be here one second more than I need to be. What do you want?' This unwarranted interruption was not helpful.

'I won't keep you long, Harry. Tell me, did your interview reveal anything?'

'Nothing, as expected.'

'Ok, then it's absolutely necessary you get the contents of her computer and anything else you can find. She doesn't have any suspicions I take it?'

'No, I don't think so. I had a bad moment though when I went to her gig last week. She seemed to recognise me from somewhere, but when I told her I was from 'Jazz Europe' she realised she knew me from the photo they sent her. Unnerved me a bit.' There was a silence. 'You there Jack?'

'They didn't send her a photo, Harry.'

'What?' His mouth felt suddenly dry.

'I suggest you finish up as soon as possible and get out of there. Our best bet is her computer, so make sure the transfer finishes. You should get a message to that effect when it does. Call me when you're safely out. I'm hanging up now.'

Harry turned the phone off, trying not to panic. He concentrated on nothing but his breathing for ten seconds, slowing it down. He hadn't completed the inspection of the writing desk, but he decided it might be better if he finished up now and got the hell out. He turned out the study light and retraced his steps into the living room.

There was a message on the laptop requesting the insertion of the second disk. He quickly did so then fidgeted impatiently as another five minutes passed. Finally it was done. He extracted it from the machine, which he turned off, and took one last look around. He was pretty sure nothing had been disturbed. Then he quietly left Sabine's apartment and slipped into the night.

He had plenty of time to think on the train back to Frankfurt. She'd lied to him about the photo, obviously to cover the fact that she did recognise him from somewhere. And the only place that could be was St. James's hospital in Dublin. He didn't remember her, and even if she had seen him then, why would she recall it all these years later?

He called Jack on the journey to discuss this hypothesis. Jack was inclined to agree.

'She was nursing Siobhan O'Reilly at the same time you were admitted, so it's certainly possible. Both incidents were IRA related, so that may be the reason you stuck in her memory.'

'Can't be any other explanation. But why go through with the interview?'

'Curiosity perhaps, or just wanting to understand your motives. I think we can only assume you've been rumbled Harry. It won't be too hard to work out that O'Reilly is the common denominator in all this.'

Harry felt a twinge of regret at the prospect of foregoing another meeting with Sabine.

'Guess you're right. So Ms. Maier is off limits then?'

'Not necessarily. Wait till we've checked the data you downloaded. If there's nothing there to point her to O'Reilly you can simply come clean and ask her about him.'

'But if I mention the intelligence services she won't admit anything.'

'You don't know that. She knows already that you're not quite the man you appear to be. Whatever you tell her, I would be interested to know her reaction.'

Me too, thought Harry. He promised to get photos and CDs off to London first thing in the morning. If there was anything incriminating to be discovered, they'd know it by Saturday. Until then, nothing to do but wait.

Sophie flew in on the Friday, just for the weekend. He'd booked a hotel in Freiburg for the occasion, and they drove down on the Friday evening. The route took them right past Heidelberg.

'We could have gone there, Harry. I've heard it's gorgeous.'

'It is. But as you wanted picture postcard Germany I thought Freiburg was the better option. It's even more gorgeous, and right on the Black Forest. You won't be disappointed.'

They spent the next two days exploring this most picturesque of German towns, sauntering the streets enjoying the numerous examples of historical architecture. They took the longest cable car ride in the country, some two miles, up to the Schauinsland mountain in the Black Forest. The day was cold and clear, and the views spectacular.

'We should come back at Christmas, Harry. Do they have a Christmas market here?'

'Be surprised if they don't. They have one in Heidelberg, we can always go there.'

The hotel was close to the town centre, with easy access to restaurants. They succumbed to traditional German cuisine, dining on Bratwurst and Sauerkraut on Saturday evening. With so many different varieties of sausage on offer it was difficult to know where to start. They gave up and asked their waitress what she liked.

'This is rich food,' remarked Harry. 'It needs plenty of good German beer to wash it down.'

'Light or dark?' enquired the waitress.

They settled for light. Harry remembered the dark beer as being so dense he'd found it difficult to get past two pints in earlier encounters.

'They know how to make beer in this country.' Sophie, who to his knowledge drank nothing but wine, amazed him with her sudden capacity for Freiburg's finest ale. He found it hard to keep pace with her.

They returned to the hotel slightly the worse for drink, and decided to call it a night. Harry wanted to take a drive through the Black Forest the following morning, and wasn't going to oversleep if he could help it.

As he lay back in bed, waiting for Sophie to emerge from the bathroom, he reflected on the simple pleasure they had experienced together this weekend. No talk of babies or his drinking habits. But of course Freiburg was a complete distraction from their lives in London. And he hadn't thought about Sabine Maier once.

Sophie crept into bed. 'I think I had too much beer,' she whispered. 'I might just go to sleep now.' So saying, she proceeded to do just that.

He lay awake for a while, wondering what next week would bring. No more breaking and entering, which was just fine with him, and maybe even some answers. But how enlightening would they prove to be?

Chapter 13

He drove Sophie to Frankfurt Airport on Sunday evening.

'Two more weeks, then I'm back in London,' he told her. 'Where are you staying tonight?'

'I'll go to Fulham. Might as well stay there till you get back. But let me know when you're arriving and we can go back to our place that night.'

He kissed her. 'Give my best to Clive and Susanna.'

She went through to departures shortly afterwards. He dropped the car at the Avis collection point, then made his way back to the apartment. When he checked the fridge for some quick and easy dinner ingredients he found nothing but a half empty milk carton and an unopened but rather tired slab of cheese looking back at him. He couldn't remember the last time he did any shopping. Not a problem, there were plenty of restaurants nearby. But before going out he wanted an update. He didn't know what Jack did on a Sunday evening, but it was worth a phone call.

Jack answered, but it took a while.

'Am I disturbing you?' Harry enquired.

'Not at all. I would have called you earlier, but I remembered you were with your wife this weekend.'

'She's on her way back now. Is there anything to tell?'

'Unfortunately not, Harry. I thought if we'd find anything it would be in her emails. But there's nothing to or from O'Reilly, or anyone else who could be him under another name. It's a dead end I'm afraid. You found no written correspondence, did you?'

Harry grunted. 'I was checking her writing desk when the phone rang. And after that I thought it best to leave. So I did.'

Jack's sigh of exasperation was clearly audible. 'I suppose I can take some responsibility for that decision. The fact remains that if you're right about her reaction at your first meeting then she knows you from Dublin, and lied about it. Time to put your cards on the table I'd say.'

Harry felt a tiny butterfly of excitement spreading its wings. 'Ok, that's exactly what I'll do. And you'll be the first to know the outcome.'

If Sabine had any misgivings about meeting again, they weren't discernible on the phone. She suggested dinner at her place on Wednesday evening. She would cook something passable she hoped, and he could bring the wine. And he mustn't forget his follow up questions of course. He assured her he wouldn't. They just won't be the questions you might reasonably be expecting, he thought.

He arrived a little early, and she answered the door in a rush.

'I'm still preparing things. Go into the living room, I'll be there in a minute.'

Nice to be here with the lights on this time, he thought. No laptop on the dining room table either, instead it was set for the meal to come. He took off his coat and draped it over a chair.

'I brought red and white,' he half shouted in the direction of the kitchen.

'Bring the white in here, it can go in the fridge.'

She had her back to him. Her hair was up in a chignon, and she wore a pink t-shirt and jeans, with a long kitchen apron knotted around her neck and waist. She turned and smiled as he came in. 'Over there,' she said, nodding at the fridge.

'What are we having?'

'It's simple really. Chicken with asparagus, red onion, potatoes and carrots, with my secret herbs thrown in. All done in the oven for 45 minutes and served. The dessert is a secret too, so don't ask.'

He peeked over her shoulder. 'Looks good. Do you have a corkscrew?'

'Sure. Will you undo this knot round my neck please? I did it too tight.'

He stood close behind her, fiddling with the knot. She stood very still and appeared to stare straight ahead, but he was sure she was studying his reflection in the kitchen window. He took his time, letting his fingers brush against her neck. Then the knot was undone. Mustn't get distracted, he thought.

She put the baking dish in the oven. They returned to the living room and Harry opened the wine while Sabine selected a CD.

'More saxophone,' she explained. 'But not me – easy listening.'

'I thought you were easy listening last time I heard you.'

She laughed. 'You're too kind. So, let's get your follow up questions out of the way before we eat.' She sat on the sofa by the front window, and he moved his coat from the chair so he could sit facing her. They looked at each other.

'Sabine, there are some things I need to tell you. You may not want to eat with me once you've heard them. Can we wait till afterwards?'

She didn't seem worried. 'It's my turn to ask the questions as I recall. You may not want to eat with me either when I've finished.'

He felt the sudden tension between them. Show time. He tried to look cool.

'Ok, go ahead then.'

'Right.' She said nothing then, just looked out the window, and it was as if for a moment she had left the room entirely. He waited, and presently whatever memory had distracted her ran its course. She fixed him with a steady gaze.

'I remember you Harry. You were unconscious in a hospital bed at the time, with a bruised face and tubes in your nose. When I saw you at the Jazzhaus I couldn't figure out who you were at first. I almost lost my concentration during the second set trying to work it out.'

'How is it you remember me at all?'

She ignored him. 'Do you really work for "Jazz Europe"?'

He shifted uncomfortably. 'It's a part time thing – freelance. They're buying the interview, that's how it works.'

Her face was expressionless. 'Just tell me what you want from me Harry.'

There was no way to sugar coat it. 'We have a mutual friend in Michael O'Reilly.'

'I thought so.' She looked at the floor for a while this time. Then she got up. 'The subject is closed until we've eaten. I'm going to the kitchen now. You stay here.'

He heard her moving around. The oven door opened and closed. Then there was only the music, but he thought he heard her crying once or twice. Give her some space, he thought, she hasn't asked me to leave yet. He half expected her to emerge with a carving knife in her hand.

She stayed in the kitchen for what seemed an eternity. When she did come out it wasn't with a carving knife, but with an oven glove and a baking dish full of chicken and vegetables. She didn't say anything, just put the dish on the table and sat waiting for him.

He joined her. 'You ok?' Her eyes looked a little red.

'I think so. I want you to tell me everything please. How you knew about me, and what it is you want to know about Michael. Promise me you won't lie.'

He poured them both some wine. As they ate he told her about SIS, their renewed interest in Michael, and how her letters had been found in his Kilburn flat.

'And you work for these people?' she asked.

'I worked for them in Dublin, translating documents. Then after Ireland I heard nothing from them in twenty years, until a few weeks ago. They want Michael for some reason, I don't know why.'

She was calm and still again now, quietly assessing him. 'You don't know why, yet you came here and went through this ..' she paused, searching for the right word, 'this deception, yes? I don't understand Harry, why would you agree to do that?'

'Because Michael O'Reilly killed my wife.'

'I see.' She didn't seem alarmed, or indignant. She turned her full attention to the meal, and they both ate in silence until it was finished.

'Did you enjoy it?' she asked. He nodded. 'I have dessert.' She picked up the plates and cutlery and headed for the kitchen.

He wasn't sure he had the appetite for dessert right now. He sipped his wine and wondered how she maintained her cool demeanour, given the table talk. His cards were on the table, would she now follow suit?

She reappeared with dessert, and when he recognised the traditional New Zealand Pavlova, with its meringue base topped with whipped cream, strawberries and kiwi fruit, he did a double take.

Sabine seemed amused at his expression, in fact he could have sworn she was suppressing a smile. 'I tried to make this for the first time. I thought you might like it.'

The mood lifted a little. 'Did I tell you I was a Kiwi?' he asked.

She served him a generous portion. 'You have an accent, you know. Is it up to the right standard?'

He tried a piece, making appreciative noises. 'Very good. Delicious, actually.'

She resumed her place, watching him eat. 'Let me tell you about Michael and me,' she began. 'I remember you so well because it was a car bomb that injured you, and my first thought was it must be

170

IRA. I couldn't help wondering if Michael was involved. I was looking after his sister and your room was quite close, so I came and had a look at you. And it was all in the paper, they said your wife was from New Zealand.'

'I didn't read the paper.' Now he had definitely lost his appetite. He pushed the bowl away. 'And was Michael involved?'

The intensity between them was back. 'He said not. And I believed him. Yes, he spent a lot of time in my flat while I was at work, and he could have gone out at any time and done something, but I believed him. He had other things to worry about. His own people were looking for him, they thought he was an informer. He wouldn't tell me any more about that though. And he was worried sick about Siobhan. He felt responsible for what had happened to her.'

'An informer.' This was news. But of course, they were looking for him in Kilburn too. Yes, it made sense, but he knew better. He saw that Sabine was about to speak, and he silenced her with a gesture. 'Let me think a minute.' It was a long time ago, and he wanted to get the sequence of events right. She picked at her food while he thought it through.

'There was an incident on a beach in Cork that started all this,' he said after a long minute's silence. 'Several people were killed. There certainly was an informer, but his name was O'Riordan, not O'Reilly.' He realised suddenly that he'd never even stopped to consider why Siobhan O'Reilly had been shot in the first place. How could he have been so stupid? Too consumed with rage and grief, but now the scales were certainly falling from his eyes. He swore softly.

'What is it?' she asked.

'I don't know yet. Maybe I've been wrong about a few things. Do you know where Michael is now?'

She looked him straight in the eye. 'No, I don't. London was the last contact I had with him.'

He decided not to press the point. 'Tell me how you met then.'

He half listened as she told him about their first meeting in the hospital canteen. Whether she knew Michael's current whereabouts or not had become almost irrelevant to him personally. He believed her when she said Michael wasn't responsible for Nat's death, the whole idea seemed less and less feasible, but the question that really needed to be answered was why did SIS want him now? He suddenly became aware that she had stopped talking, and was looking at him expectantly.

'Sorry, I wasn't paying attention.'

'That's ok. I said, what will you do now? What will you tell your people?'

He considered for a few seconds. 'I'll tell them what you told me. You don't know where he is. That should be the end of it as far as you're concerned.'

She looked less than convinced. 'I hope so.'

They agreed to talk about something else, so he told her he really did like her music, he wasn't a complete fraud in that respect. She cheered up a little, telling him about the Munich gig. It had been a success by all accounts. She pointed at the photo on the wall.

'That's Sonny Rollins and me. Do you know who he is?'

'I know the name, so he must be famous if I've heard of him.'

She grinned. 'You're hopeless. He came to Berlin for a concert, must be five years ago now. I made sure I got a photo with him. He even knew who I was, so I was over the moon.'

She wanted to give him a CD or two, but confessed she had nothing in the apartment.

'Will you let me have your address? I'll send you a selection of my best bits.'

He wrote it down for her. Then he checked his watch.

'It's late. I need to go, not sure when the last train to Frankfurt is either.'

'Stay here tonight, Harry. Finish the wine with me, and you can sleep in the spare bedroom.'

'Well, I ..' No, surely after this rather painful exchange of confidences she wasn't thinking of seducing him. Trouble was, he knew he wouldn't resist too much if she tried. It wasn't about to happen though. 'Alright, thank you.'

It was past midnight when she showed him to the second bedroom. And I was here just the other night photographing it, he thought. If that ever comes out she will use the carving knife. He lay in bed, thinking about their conversation and the questions it had raised. If not Michael, who? And why was he still holding on to this after twenty years? It had bubbled away sub-consciously all that time, quietly fucking him up. Was it resolved now? He didn't know.

He was still trying not to think about any of it, when there was a tap on the door.

'Harry, are you awake?'

'Yes, come in.'

'I can't sleep, I keep thinking about Ireland. Can I come in with you please?'

He hesitated. 'Is that a good idea?'

She slipped under the covers. 'I'm not going to make love to you. You're married.'

His fingers strayed to his wedding ring. 'Alright then, as long as we've got that straight.'

'Just hold me, then I'll go to sleep.' She snuggled up to him.

He drew her close. She had a dressing gown on, and pyjamas. He was down to his boxers so at least there was something between them. Just. He would lie back, think of New Zealand, and do absolutely nothing. That would work.

And after a while fatigue and shared warmth did the trick, and they both slept.

He woke early, alone. He had to be at work, so he dressed quickly and found Sabine in the kitchen making coffee. She asked him how he had slept and if he wanted breakfast. He said he'd settle for coffee. She seemed a bit distant, almost formal.

'Are you angry with me?' he asked.

'Just with myself. I don't like being deceived. You used me to get to Michael, and I let you do it.'

He had nothing to say to that, other than 'Sorry.' She said she'd call him a taxi, so he finished his coffee as fast as he could, and said he'd wait in the street. She didn't dissuade him.

As he put on his coat he asked if he could call her again, just to assure her there would be no further questions from anybody.

'I think that's the least you can do, Harry. It was nice to meet you. Take care.'

Then he was in the street and he saw the taxi ascending the hill to meet him.

Chapter 14

Sophie wasn't at Heathrow to meet him the day he flew back. It was a Saturday morning, and she'd told him she wanted to go down to the house in Tunbridge Wells on the Friday night to fill the fridge and warm the place up. If the temperature in London was anything to go by, that was probably a wise move. He sat idly thumbing the in flight magazine as the Heathrow Express train rumbled its way to Paddington. He still needed to negotiate the Circle Line to Charing Cross, but engineering works notwithstanding, he should make it home by mid-afternoon.

The German 'mission', if he could call it that, was done. He'd reported back to Jack a day after returning to Frankfurt. Yes, she had remembered him from the hospital, and no she didn't know where O'Reilly was. Could he resume normal life now, and for that matter, could Sabine?

'Was she telling the truth Harry?'

'If she wasn't then she's a pretty good liar. Will you leave her alone now?'

'No need for you to get protective. There's no point in pursuing that line of enquiry any further. It could get a little messy if we were to put a German National under duress.'

Anger and relief vied for supremacy. Relief won by a short head, and Harry kept his voice level. 'Good, she had enough duress from yours truly. I'll let her know. What will you do now?'

'We'll try O'Reilly's father. Mother's dead I think. He's in Belfast, so we can take a more official line with him. Depends how stubborn he is I suppose.'

'Right. Well, do you need anything more from me?'

'Not right now Harry. If I find out anything that throws light on Natalie's death in the course of my enquiries I'll let you know. But for now, thanks for your help.'

And that was that. He'd phoned Sabine and relayed the good news. She didn't sound particularly reassured.

'I hope you're right Harry. Are you finished with your part in this now?'

'Nothing more for me to do. I'm sorry I lied to you. But I'm glad we met. You told me enough for me to think Michael wasn't involved after all, and maybe after all this time I can start to move on. So it wasn't all bad, for me at least.'

'I'm glad, Harry. I apologise for being so rude the morning you left, but it was a bit disturbing having the past dragged up like that. Anyway, if you're ever near Heidelberg again, let me know. I'll make another Pavlova.'

He laughed, suddenly happy. 'Sure, you can depend on it.'

He made it back to Tunbridge Wells without delays. He phoned Sophie on the way and she picked him up from the station. He slung his two cases in the boot and claimed the driver's seat.

'Nice to drive on the right side of the road again,' he said.

'This is the left, darling,' replied Sophie with a straight face.

He placed his hand on the back of her neck, as if to throttle her. 'Thank you for that.'

'Any time.' She grinned. 'Good flight?'

He looked at her. 'You look gorgeous. I think I should exercise my conjugal rites when we get in. Last time you slept with me you were incapable.'

She cast him a sideways glance. 'Laying down the law now? I had too much beer last time. But if you're patient and very nice to me ..'

'I'll see what I can do.' It was good to be back. No more cloak and dagger, and maybe no more dreams about Ireland either. He felt a cautious optimism emerging as they pulled into the drive. It became so pervasive that as soon as they got inside he found himself casting patience aside as he reached for his only slightly protesting wife, and took her straight to the bedroom.

They emerged a couple of hours later, and it was already dark.

'I get first shower,' said Sophie. 'There's mail for you downstairs.'

He went down to the lounge in his dressing gown and turned on the lights. It was getting dark so early already, he thought, and the temperature outside was no doubt plummeting. The lounge was warm. His mail lay on the coffee table, and he sorted the envelopes. Statements and bills mostly, but there was also something from St. Thomas's. He opened it and skimmed the contents.

They wanted him to have a biopsy. An appointment had been made for the 15th November. It was all explained. Someone would
slide a needle between his ribs under local anaesthetic and take a

178

small liver sample for analysis. He should be prepared to stay in for 6 hours afterwards just to ensure there was no internal bleeding following the procedure. Apparently this was the best way of ascertaining just how damaged his liver might be. Please direct any questions he might have to Dr. Ashe on the following extension. And so on.

He sat down, placing the letter on the table as he did so. While he'd been away he'd completely forgotten he had this bloody condition. And of course he'd pledged to become the new improved Harry, who would henceforth subsist on only lentils and pomegranate juice, and no doubt live to be 100 years old. Or perhaps it would only seem that long.

Sophie came down the stairs, scrubbed and dressed. 'All yours,' she said. 'I'm going to cook something.'

'Ok. See you in a minute.' He went back upstairs to the bathroom and stood under the shower. He put his left hand on the right side of his body, over his ribs. Before he discovered hep C he didn't even know where his liver was. We take so much for granted, he reflected, certainly feels the same as ever. And they want to stick a needle in there. Well I suppose there are worse places to put it.

The shower was refreshing after so much travelling. He got dressed, then took the letter into the kitchen for a second opinion. Sophie took it with an enquiring look and started to read. 'Stir that for me, will you?' she said. There was what looked like a casserole simmering on the stove. He stirred as instructed, and waited.

'This doesn't seem like much fun,' she remarked, after reading it twice. 'You should go though.'

'Yes, you're right. At least afterwards I'll know what I'm up against.'

'And they can treat it?'

'Mmm. The drugs sound horrendous, and not too effective either. I'll need to weigh up the pros and cons first.'

'I think we should worry about it tomorrow.' She looked worried nonetheless.

'Don't be too concerned, I'll work something out.'

'I know. Right now I'm more concerned about the casserole. Keep stirring.'

'Yes Miss.' He smiled to himself, and did as he was told.

Work assumed its normal routine once the inevitable jibes on his time away had been delivered. Certain colleagues felt obliged to let him know that now he was back the German economy could resume its normal upwards trajectory in spite of his best efforts to derail it, and that the women of Frankfurt would once again feel free to go out unaccompanied, as reported by the Frankfurter Allgemeine Zeitung only that morning, should he require confirmation.

Bloody wits, he thought without rancour. Gina wanted a run down of his time in the Frankfurt office and a discussion of what he needed to do now he was back. They went out for a lunch meeting, at which she made it clear that she was satisfied with what her

German counterpart had told her about him. No mention was

made of private clients in Heidelberg, for which he breathed a silent sigh of relief. Neil dragged him out for a drink that evening, but he cut it short after two beers. He was mindful that he needed to cut back on the booze, and that it wasn't going to be a trivial undertaking given his liking for it. His willpower was about to be tested.

The 15th arrived, and having booked the entire day off he arrived as scheduled at St. Thomas's. A doctor he'd never met before escorted him to a cubicle, where he removed his shirt and lay on a hospital trolley while the needle was inserted. Even with the local it was an uncomfortable sensation, and then they wheeled him off to a recovery area, where his blood pressure was taken at hourly intervals. His shoulder hurt, which he thought was strange, and they told him it was referred pain and nothing to worry about. After six hours they discharged him, saying that in two weeks Dr. Ashe would have the results. And would he make sure he had someone in the house with him tonight, just in case. He assured them that he'd find someone and left feeling glad it was all over. He went straight to the station, just in time for the 4.15 train. The Mercedes was in the station car park and he was back in the house by 5.30.

There was a jiffy bag on the hall floor when he opened the door. He picked it up and saw that it was postmarked Heidelberg. Must be the CD's Sabine promised, he thought. What he really wanted at that moment was a gin and tonic, so he made one and sat down at the kitchen table with it. Should I do this after a biopsy? he wondered. Probably not. He opened the envelope and two CD's slid out.

The first one had a cover showing her and the group he'd seen at the Jazzhaus, clearly a studio recording, with a list of tracks and some blurb in German on the back. The second was a plain CD, no cover. And there was a letter, also in German. He began to read it.

'Dear Harry, the first disk is an album I recorded in 1998. The second is a mix of tracks I played on over several years, and that I like the most. I hope you will too. Let me know what you think. On a separate subject - the phone number below is a public call box in Universitätsplatz. I will be there on Monday 19th November at 11am. There is something I want to discuss with you privately. Do not call me from your mobile please, but either from a call box or your office. When you get this either text me with "Thank you for the CD's", meaning yes I will call you at 11am, or "Where are my CD's?" for no, not available. Love, Sabine.'

He was intrigued, she didn't want to chance being overheard, that much was clear. Whatever it was it must be important if she'd gone to all this trouble. He texted her the 'yes' message, then decided it might be a good idea to dispose of her letter. He went upstairs to the little study, where he copied the phone number on to a post it note, then used the paper shredder. His mobile bleeped, he had an incoming text. It was her. 'You're welcome, speak soon x.' He wondered what the hell it was about. Roll on Monday.

He realised when he got back to the kitchen and retrieved his neglected drink, that Sophie knew nothing about his forays into the German jazz scene, and would wonder about the CD's if he started playing them in the house. He could invent some story

182

explaining their arrival he supposed, but he didn't want to do that. No, he'd keep them in the car, or play them when she stayed in Fulham, as she did at least one night a week, purely for the convenience of being close to work. He took them upstairs and found a drawer for them in the study. She would be home soon, and he was supposed to be resting. He'd wait for her call, then collect her from the station, and they would spend a normal evening together doing what married couples do. Which wasn't always a hell of a lot admittedly, he thought, but I'd rather do that with her than without.

As if on cue his mobile rang.

'Hi, I'll be there in ten minutes,' she said. 'How did it go today?'

'It was fine. I don't like hospitals that much though. I'm supposed to be taking it easy, and if I bleed to death in the night you need to be here to call someone.'

'Harry! Can you drive? I can always get a taxi.'

'No, I'm ok. I'm leaving now.'

'Ok, see you soon.'

He found his overcoat and car keys, then made for the car. He dumped the jiffy bag in the rubbish bin on his way past. It was only sensible to remove all incriminating evidence he figured. They'd make a spy out of him yet.

There was a tiny meeting room on the 6th floor of the bank, big enough for two people and a phone. Harry booked it and made his way there just before 11am on Monday. Before going in he had a quick look around. There were dozens of people sat at neat rows of desks, staring at computer screens and tapping at keyboards. He had a fleeting vision of battery hens, then he stepped inside and closed the door.

He could dial Germany without going through the operator, which was convenient. He just hoped someone else hadn't reached the call box in Heidelberg ahead of Sabine, but the number wasn't engaged, and she answered straight away.

'Harry?'

'Yes, it's me. I'm at the office. This is all very mysterious, Sabine. What's going on?'

'Before I tell you, I need your promise that this conversation stays between you and me. It's not to go any further. Can you do that?'

'Yes, of course.' There was a short silence. 'Did you hear me?'

'Yes, I heard.' He could sense the reluctance in her manner as she continued. 'After you left Heidelberg I had a conversation about your visit with someone. That person asked me to contact you with a suggestion.' Another pause.

'What suggestion? And who was it?'

She didn't answer directly. 'I think this is unwise, but I agreed to talk to you. The suggestion is that if you still want to know who killed Natalie, he may be able to help. He thinks the same man is responsible for the death of his sister.'

'I see. And how can he help, exactly?'

'He wants to meet you, Harry. I told him about your involvement with certain people, but he wasn't put off. I still think it's stupid, and the best thing for you to do is say no. But it's your decision.'

184

He thought for a moment. She was right, it was certainly risky on O'Reilly's part. He could have no assurance that Harry wouldn't simply turn up accompanied by Jack Hudson and anyone else from SIS he might care to bring along. So why do it?

'Where do we meet?' he asked.

'You come to my place. You'll need to arrange a week's holiday, because we will be taking a long drive. And Harry – this concerns you and you only. Give me your word on that.'

'You have my word. When do you want to go?'

'In the next two weeks if possible. Let me know when you want to come, and I will fit it in with my schedule.'

He wasn't sure if he could take leave at such short notice. He'd just have to be creative about it. 'Ok, I'll get back to you. Tell him I agree to the meeting.'

'Fine, see you soon then. Bye.' She was gone.

He wondered if he looked as furtive as he felt, and he was glad to have the privacy of the meeting room and the thinking space it offered. There was no reason for Jack to know about this, and if O'Reilly was right about Nat's killer it was surely a step in the right direction. He must be pretty sure of himself on that score to reveal himself like this. Or was there another motive?

He quietly exited the room and made his way to his next meeting, thinking that it might just be better to let sleeping dogs lie. But it seemed it was already too late, this one was wide awake, and ready to bark. And he wanted to be there when it did.

He told Gina he was feeling run down and needed a week somewhere warm to recuperate, the Canary Islands perhaps. He was sorry for the short notice. She was less than pleased, but conceded that she would prefer him not to be working if he didn't feel 100%. And he wouldn't be paid for his absence.

'Is Sophie going with you?'

'No, just me. She's busy at work.'

'Everything alright at home?'

'Fine, Gina. I just want to eat, sleep and see Lanzarote. Sophie can do without me for a week.'

Gina didn't press it. He told Sophie he was needed for a week in Frankfurt, which was almost the truth. Sophie and Gina had never met, and as he wasn't expecting that to change anytime soon if ever, he thought he should be covered. He texted Sabine to say he could make it first week of December, which she confirmed, and he was ready to go.

The last thing he had to do prior to leaving, apart from cancelling his next appointment with Cindy, was to discuss his biopsy results. Two weeks after the event he found himself once more in Dr. Ashe's office at St. Thomas's, apprehensively awaiting the findings. The doctor came straight to the point.

'Mr. Ellis, your biopsy shows that your liver has stage 3 fibrosis, which is in the severe range. Given that ..'

'What does that mean?' interjected Harry.

'Sorry,' replied Dr. Ashe, shuffling Harry's notes to one side. He leaned forward slightly, placing his elbows on the desk and clasping his hands together, as if in prayer. 'Fibrosis is scarring essentially, and too much scarring impairs liver function. Which eventually leads to cirrhosis and other complications. My recommendation is that you start treatment as soon as possible.'

Perhaps I should be doing the praying, thought Harry. 'Or what?'

'Or you increase the risk of developing cirrhosis and liver failure. It could happen quite quickly, or it could be some years away. That's what we're looking at.'

'I see.' This was not what he wanted to hear. 'Tell me about the treatment then.'

The treatment consisted of one self administered weekly injection of interferon combined with ribavirin tablets, ideally over a 12 month period. If he didn't respond after 3 months they might consider stopping it. These were powerful drugs, and he might suffer side effects like fatigue, itching, hair loss, possible thyroid problems and depression. People responded differently to treatment, and there was no way to predict how things would progress.

'I know it sounds a bit daunting,' said Dr. Ashe, 'but you may sail through the treatment with very few problems.'

'Let me think for a minute.'

'Of course. You might want to consider this – it's estimated that there are 100,000 people undiagnosed in this country, and by the time a lot of them find out about it, it will be very difficult to help them. You have an opportunity to catch it early, so to speak.'

Harry considered. If he did nothing he would have to live with the uncertainty of never knowing when this thing might actually do some serious damage. Fatal damage. And there was another thing. After 20 years he had a golden chance to find out who really did kill Natalie. It would be just his luck to be struck down on the verge of discovering the answer to the question that had been gnawing away at him for so long. He wasn't going to let that happen. And then there was the bleeding obvious. He wanted to live. 'Alright. Let's give it a try.'

'Good. I'll see if the practice nurse is available. She will give you the drugs and tell you how to use them. And she's there for any support you need while on the treatment.'

Harry sighed. He hoped he'd made the right decision. The nurse was able to see him, so he found his way to her office. She was a bubbly Scottish woman named Isobel, in her mid twenties. She took some blood, then weighed him and did some calculations. She asked him to wait while she collected the drugs from Pharmacy. The ribavirin was in tablet form, and the interferon came in a pre-loaded syringe, all he had to do was attach the needle and inject himself once a week.

'Are you comfortable doing that?' she asked.

'I'm sure I'll manage,' he replied.

'You may feel as though you're getting the flu the first time you inject. It's actually your immune system making itself felt. Nothing to worry about, your body will soon adjust.'

She gave him her card and said he must feel free to call her with any queries, and that they would see him again after the first month, to monitor progress. He thanked her and left. He had a month's supply of drugs. Apparently the stuff was expensive, so they doled it out only as and when it was required.

He would be flying to Frankfurt the following day so he decided to have his first injection that evening. That would last him a week, but to be on the safe side he'd take another syringe with him and leave it at Sabine's apartment. You were supposed to keep it refrigerated, so no doubt he'd need to explain why he wanted to use her fridge to store drugs. She was a nurse, he was sure she would raise no objections once he'd told her about his condition.

Sophie was in Fulham that evening, and he was relieved that he wouldn't have an audience for his first injection. Not ever having stuck a needle into himself, he was a little apprehensive. But after dinner he summoned up his courage and injected the first dose into his left thigh, just below the hip. Once he got the needle in it was easy enough. Sure enough, an hour later he had a slight headache and aching joints. He took his tablets and decided to have an early night. Last thing he wanted to do was oversleep and miss his flight.

Chapter 15

When Sabine opened the door to him she seemed happy and apprehensive in equal measure. She kissed him on the cheek, and when she withdrew he was sure she paused long enough to get a good look at the street over his shoulder.

'I'm all alone you know.'

'Are you sure? I hope so.'

They moved through to the lounge, Harry manoeuvering his one large suitcase on wheels awkwardly as they went.

'I hope you brought some warm clothes,' said Sabine, smiling at his efforts to avoid ruining her paintwork.

'Germany in Winter – you bet I did.'

'Where we're going, it's very cold,' she replied. 'Perhaps I should take you shopping later.' She motioned towards the sofa, and after removing his coat he sat down.

'You lied to me about Michael then,' he stated in what he hoped was a neutral voice. 'You told me you lost contact with him after London.'

She sat next to him. 'You're not really in a position to judge me Harry. Do you know yet why they're looking for him?'

He shook his head. 'No, I've been told nothing.'

'I did lose contact actually, for almost ten years. Then one day I got a letter from him. He was living in Sweden, he married a

Swedish girl. And he changed his name of course. He's not Michael O'Reilly any more.' Her face became suddenly wistful.

'Are you still in love with him?'

'What?' The wistfulness passed. 'After all this time? No, I think I'm sometimes in love with the memory of him. I loved him in Dublin, but that was a long time ago and I haven't seen him since. We talk on the phone maybe once a year, if that.' She laughed. 'And I have had one or two relationships since then.'

'Sorry, none of my business really. Have you ever been married?'

'No, I haven't. I like my independence. Any more questions?'

'All finished.'

'Good.' She got up, and before he could make a move she had grabbed the handle of his suitcase and was wheeling it towards the spare bedroom. He looked at the view as he waited for her to come back. The US Army hadn't gone anywhere in his absence he noticed. It was dusk, and as he looked a carpet of twinkling lights unrolled below him, greeting the night. He was suddenly hungry.

'Can I buy you dinner?' he asked the vacant space.

Sabine reappeared. 'Yes please. We won't go shopping here, we'll wait till we get to Stockholm. But I can show you the Christmas market if you like. It's very pretty.'

'Ok, sounds good. And when do we leave for Stockholm?'

'Tomorrow morning. Let's go and eat now, we can walk to town from here.'

There was no wind as they walked down Panorama Strasse, the air was crisp and cold and still, and he thought if it wasn't freezing yet it was near as damn it. He wondered how long it would be until it snowed. Tomorrow they would go North and it would get even colder. He should have gone to Lanzarote after all.

The Hauptstrasse was packed with tourists and locals. They sauntered with the humming crowd, encountering the first real evidence of the market at Universitätsplatz. The square was filled with brightly lit wooden huts selling all manner of Christmas paraphernalia. Local liqueur sellers competed with candle sellers, traditional wood carvers, and others offering an array of Christmas cards, books and decorations. One hut contained a nativity scene, with carved life size representations of the players. Sabine bought a huge red candle and a silver hanging Star of Bethlehem.

There was music in the air, courtesy of random groups of musicians with guitars and violins, who were playing what to Harry's ears sounded like traditional folk tunes. And of course there was plenty of Bratwurst and Glühwein on offer. He bought two mugs of the warm steaming wine, and they found a relatively quiet spot on the corner of the square to sample it.

'It's sweet,' he intoned, screwing up his face in mock horror.

'What did you expect?' laughed Sabine. 'Don't forget to take the mug back when you've finished if you want your deposit back.'

His mug was bright red, with a painted scene of the market encircling it. It would make a nice souvenir. Then he thought of Sophie's disappointment on seeing it, and changed his mind.

'Where can we eat?' he asked.

192

'I know a place close to the river, come on.'

The crowd thinned as they made their way down a side street. The restaurant served mostly traditional German fare, and Harry settled for a schnitzel, while Sabine ordered pasta. The place was half full, and service was quick and efficient. He chose a local Riesling, which initially came as a shock to the palate after the sweetness of the Glühwein, so he ordered some water to compensate.

'It will be strange seeing Michael again after so long,' Sabine remarked, as he poured water for them both.

'What I don't understand is why we need to see him at all. If he has something to tell me what's wrong with the phone?'

She shrugged. 'There is something he wants to show you, I don't know what. So we must go to him.'

'So you're prepared to drop everything and drive me to Stockholm. That's a lot to do for a man you haven't seen for twenty years.'

He thought he caught a flash of annoyance in her eyes, but she answered calmly. 'It is a debt of friendship, Harry. Perhaps you don't understand these things.'

Perhaps I don't, he thought. He raised an apologetic hand. 'Sorry, I'm worried that we'll go all that way for nothing.'

'Are you changing your mind?' He shook his head. 'We're going further than Stockholm,' she continued, 'to a place called Kiruna, which is in the north of Sweden. It's inside the Arctic circle, that's why you need the warm clothes.'

'Will that Golf of yours make it that far?'

'We can fly from Stockholm if we need to. But Michael thinks it's better if we drive. He thinks it's more secure that way.'

The timely arrival of the food gave him some thinking space. He had to admit it was a sensible precaution. Better not to show up on a flight manifest if it could be avoided. Not that anyone should have reason to check of course, because no one knew what he was doing.

'We should start early tomorrow. Perhaps we can share the driving,' he said.

'Yes, I agree. We can have an early night.' She indicated his wine glass. 'Don't drink too much.'

Shades of Sophie, he thought. He took her advice nonetheless, and poured himself another glass of water.

When they got back to the apartment Sabine produced a Road Atlas, and Harry sat at the dining room table studying the map of Sweden. Stockholm to Kiruna was a distance of some 1200 kilometers.

'How long do you expect this journey to take?' he asked.

'I was thinking three days,' came the reply. 'Tomorrow we drive to Hamburg then take the ferry to Denmark, and spend the night in Copenhagen. The next day we can make Stockholm in about six hours. I think that's around 1500 kilometers. Then after that, Kiruna.'

'Yes, but Kiruna is almost two days drive away from Stockholm, maybe we should fly after all. I only have a week you know.'

'Let me see.' Sabine emerged from her bedroom, where she was packing, and peered over his shoulder. 'My God, you're right. We'll be exhausted if we drive the whole way.' She thought for a moment. 'I have a travel guide for Sweden, let me just check something.' She went back to the bedroom, and reappeared a minute later, guide in hand. 'I thought so. There is a night train from Stockholm. If we take the 8pm train we can be there about 14 hours later. And they have sleeper berths. How does that sound?'

'Much better. We can pay in cash, and we won't leave a trace that way.'

Sabine tapped on his bedroom door the next morning.

'Harry, are you awake?'

He grunted something in response, then checked his watch. It was 6am.

'The shower is free, I'm going to make some breakfast,' she said.

He was half asleep as he found his way to the bathroom, where he briefly toyed with the idea of a cold shower as a form of instant rejuvenation, but rejected it as too Spartan an act at this hour of the day. Warm water revived him, and he was dressed and in the kitchen 15 minutes later, wide awake.

Sabine had prepared sausages, fried eggs and toast, with cuts of ham and cheese on the side. 'Eat plenty Harry, I don't know when we will stop for lunch.'

He took her advice, and after breakfast he took their cases down to the car. Sabine locked up and followed. He was curious to see her come down the stairs with her saxophone in its case.

'I might be able to sit in on a gig in Stockholm on the way back, if we have time,' she explained, laying the case across the back seat.

They were ready to go. 'One last thing before we leave,' said Harry. 'Turn off your phone. From now on we use public call boxes unless it's an emergency.'

Sabine muttered something about 'damned secrecy' but did as she was asked. She took the driver's seat, handing the road atlas to Harry as he made himself comfortable next to her. 'I'll tell you when I need you to start navigating,' she said.

She pulled out into the empty street, and they were underway.

It was a clear sunny morning, and they were soon on the A5 going north. The Autobahn was congested as they approached Frankfurt, but once the rush hour traffic thinned out the pace picked up, and Sabine cruised the Golf around 110kph. It seemed a rather average speed to Harry, if the numerous other cars overtaking them was any yardstick.

'Can't you drive faster?' he enquired.

'This isn't a Porsche. We're doing fine, thank you.'

He laughed. The Autobahn wasn't totally without speed limits, so they were slowed down occasionally in certain areas, but there was plenty of unrestricted road, and he made a mental note to return with the Mercedes at some point and see how it performed.

Hamburg was their first target, some six hours away, then he'd
agreed to swop driving duties from there to Copenhagen, which
would take a further four hours, including a ferry trip. So he had the
unusual luxury of doing nothing for a while.

He looked at Sabine, who was deep in her own thoughts with her
eyes on the road. He was aware once again of the quietly intense
energy she exuded, and the way her face wore just the hint of a smile
in its natural repose. She had a way of retreating into some kind of
untroubled solitude deep inside, and for a moment he envied her.
Apart from the jazz and their common interest in Michael O'Reilly,
he knew little about her.

'Tell me about your nursing career,' he said.

'What do you want to know?'

'Everything of course.'

She smiled, eyes still on the road. 'Well, nowadays I look after
terminally ill people who are mostly in the last stages of cancer. At
that point they need someone to support them emotionally, and also
help them with practical arrangements. It can be quite demanding on
both sides.'

'Know anything about hepatitis c?'

'A little, why do you ask?'

He told her about his diagnosis and the treatment regime. 'I've
started the drugs, as of yesterday. I left a syringe in your fridge by
the way.'

'Yes, I saw that – interferon. I was wondering when you might tell me why it was there. How do you feel?'

'Ok at the moment. I just hope it's effective.'

Sabine gave him a look of concern. 'I'll need to keep a professional eye on you. If you find it all too much then there are alternative approaches you could consider, like Chinese or Indian medicine. I can make some enquiries when we get back if you like.'

'Let's see how it goes. The disturbing thing about all this is that I find myself thinking about death a lot lately.'

He was surprised to hear her laugh. 'That might be a good thing, Harry.'

'What the hell do you mean by that?'

'Did you think before your hepatitis that you were going to live forever? Of course not, you're a rational man. But in our culture we prefer not to think about it, we push it away. So when it becomes a real possibility we aren't ready. We take life for granted.'

She paused for a minute to concentrate on the traffic, which was slowing down for no particular reason. Harry didn't want to break her train of thought and stayed silent.

'I didn't mean to laugh', she continued. 'You've realised that you aren't immortal after all, and that is a good thing to realise. I've had plenty of time to think about this issue in my professional and private life, so I think I know what I'm talking about.'

'What, you mean you've lost parents?'

She had her profile to him, but he could see the sadness in her expression.

198

'No, not my parents, my sister. She died young, and I was even younger when it happened. I thought about it a lot at the time and ever since.'

'Sorry, shall we talk about something else?'

She reached out a hand from the steering wheel and half unsightedly finding his hand, squeezed it quickly. 'It's ok Harry. Let me explain. I did philosophy at university, and in Heidelberg we're quite famous for our philosophy. I had good teachers. As we were all so busy trying to define the meaning of life we sometimes tried to understand the meaning of death too. Have you heard of Nietszche?'

'Can't say I have,' replied Harry.

'A very famous German philosopher. He wrote like a poet. He said that "the certain prospect of death could sweeten every life with a precious and fragrant drop of levity." What I think he meant was that the awareness of certain death could encourage us to live with a much fuller appreciation of life. So I try to live with a little levity every day.'

'I see.' He considered her words. 'Not sure if that helps or not. So you're a philosopher too – did you find the meaning of life?'

She grinned. 'Perhaps there isn't one. You need to find your own meaning. I find it mostly in my music. For you, it will be something different I guess.'

Yes, he thought, that makes a kind of sense. Where was the meaning in his existence? Not in his work, that was for sure.

'I'm sorry about your hepatitis, Harry. Didn't mean to lecture you with philosophy.'

'That's ok. It's funny, I thought so much about Nat's death and the meaninglessness of it, and never stopped to think about my own. Stupid of me.'

The traffic was speeding up again, the unseen obstacle restraining it now gone. Sabine accelerated through the gears and they were soon back at cruising speed.

'My turn,' said Sabine. 'Tell me about your wife. What's her name, what does she do?'

Harry was happy enough to change the subject, for now at least.

Near Hamburg they found an Autobahn service area and stopped for lunch. The opportunity to move around was a welcome relief after nearly six straight hours of driving. After lunch Sabine squeezed the saxophone into the boot and stretched out on the back seat for a cat nap. Harry took the wheel, heading for Puttgarden and the ferry to Denmark, and less than two hours later he was queuing to load the car on for the 4pm crossing. Sabine woke up as the Golf rumbled into the hold to take its place in the neat line of vehicles ahead.

'Here already?' She yawned and sat up.

'Yes. It only takes 45 minutes to get across. Want to go up on deck?'

As the ferry pulled away they made their way to the stern. Puttgarden was part of the German island of Fehmarn, and the receding landscape behind the port was completely flat and covered with a dusting of snow over what looked like nothing but

200

farmland as far as the eye could see. Day was giving way to dusk in an overcast sky, and a crisp breeze grazed their faces as they stared into the fading light.

'Snow at last,' said Harry. Until he'd driven across the bridge connecting Fehmarn to the mainland it had been snowless. 'Wonder how long it's been here.'

'Let's go back down,' said Sabine, 'it's freezing. There will be plenty of snow for you to look at later.'

They spent the remainder of the crossing in the car, as did most other people. An announcement 15 minutes away from Denmark ordered all drivers to their vehicles, then the next significant sound was the powerful reverse thrust of the engines as they manoeuvered into port.

It was dark as they exited the hold and followed the other cars out of the harbour area. Copenhagen was clearly signposted and the traffic on the E47 flowed smoothly. Harry was about to resume Autobahn speed when he realised he was in the wrong country. He eased off the accelerator, looking for signs.

'It's 80kph,' said Sabine, reading his mind.

Two hours later they were approaching Copenhagen.

'Now all we need is a hotel,' he said.

They found one in the Vesterbro district, 'the coolest part of town' according to the receptionist, who looked surprised when Harry asked for two single rooms. He recovered sufficiently to suggest two with an adjoining door, which Sabine pronounced as perfect, and having settled that they took the lift to the third floor, trailing one suitcase each plus a saxophone.

His room was large and furnished in solid Scandinavian wood, with a big free standing wardrobe he thought he might get lost in, a comfortable armchair, a writing desk and a king size double bed. Tall french doors led on to a small balcony overlooking a side street. He took a shower under an enormous showerhead set directly overhead, which completely enveloped him in a luxurious steaming downpour. He liked Denmark already.

Emerging refreshed, he dressed and sat at the desk, contemplating his mobile. He wondered if he was being paranoid in wanting it switched off. Would Jack Hudson be interested in his movements now that attention had moved away from Sabine? And if Sophie tried to call she would worry if he didn't answer or return her messages. He turned it on, and received an immediate text message welcoming him to Denmark, followed by two missed call notifications, both from Sophie.

'As I thought,' he muttered, hitting the call back option.

'Sorry I missed your calls,' he began when she picked up. 'You ok?'

'Is there anything I should know?' Her tone was icy.

'Like what?'

'What you're doing in Lanzarote would be a good start.'

He felt a stab of apprehension. 'What makes you think I'm in Lanzarote?'

'I wanted to talk to you about coming over to Frankfurt on Friday night, I thought we could go to the Christmas market there. When I couldn't get you I rang your London office to get the Frankfurt number. And guess what? They told me you were on holiday. I felt like a first class idiot when I heard that.'

Much the same as I feel now, he thought. 'I'm in Copenhagen, actually.' It seemed pointless to maintain the fiction any further. 'I didn't want the office to know what I was up to, that's all.'

Now she was hurt. 'Or me. What are you up to?'

He sighed. 'It's about Ireland. I got some information and I'm checking it out. I didn't want to worry you with it either. In fact I'll be back in Frankfurt this weekend, we can still ..'

'Not Ireland, Harry,' she interjected. 'Can't you just let that go? What is there possibly left to find out about twenty years later? And in Denmark?'

Her exasperation was completely understandable, he had no ready answer. Before he could think of one he was interrupted.

'Harry?' Sabine had come into the room. If she'd knocked on the connecting door he hadn't heard her. Sophie heard her clearly enough.

'Who's that?' she demanded, and in the short pause that followed she reached her own conclusion. 'You bastard.' She hung up.

Harry sat, head in hands. 'Oh shit,' he murmured. Then he rounded on Sabine. 'Can't you knock first?' he said, in a steadily rising voice.

'I did.' She was clearly upset. 'I thought we weren't using our phones.'

'What? Well it was definitely a bloody stupid idea for me to use mine. That was my wife. Do you know what she thinks now?'

Sabine didn't reply, and he glared at her from his seat at the desk. She stood just a few steps into the room, and he saw the hurt on her face. His anger evaporated.

'I'm sorry,' he said.

'I'm going back to my room now. When you calm down I would like to go out to dinner with you. If you don't come and get me in 20 minutes I'll go without you.' With her poise and some semblance of dignity restored, she gave him a last cool look of dismissal and left the room.

He slumped back in the chair feeling somewhat chastened. He spent the next ten minutes wondering how on earth he could explain all this to Sophie, but came up short. There was too much he hadn't told her already, and she wouldn't be in the mood to discuss it rationally right now anyway. He decided to put it on hold for 24 hours. In the meantime there was someone next door he needed to pacify.

He knocked gently on the connecting door and waited for an answer. When she responded he went in, apologised once more and suggested to her that he was feeling a little stressed, and if she would forgive him and let him take her out to dinner he would behave like a grown up for the rest of the evening. She smiled a little at the last part, and to his relief allowed herself to be persuaded.

There was no shortage of restaurants nearby. The district was obviously popular with students and artistic types, and a few ladies in thigh high boots and tight short skirts graced the odd street corner. Over dinner he told Sabine of Sophie's ignorance about this trip and its purpose, hence her less than gracious reaction to Sabine's presence. She agreed that he had a lot of fences to mend, and was sorry Sophie had misunderstood.

'Whatever Michael wants to show me better be worth all this grief,' he said.

'We'll know soon enough. This time tomorrow we will be on the train to Kiruna. Not long to wait.'

Back at the hotel he lay in bed wondering what he would do once he knew the identity of Nat's killer. Shoot him? He'd already had occasion to point a gun at the man he thought responsible twenty years ago, and he'd not pulled the trigger. He put it out of his mind and sent Sophie a text, saying they needed to talk. An hour later there was no answer forthcoming, and he fell into a restless sleep.

Denmark to Sweden proved a welcome diversion. From the Danish side they entered a 4 kilometer tunnel and emerged on to the Öresund Bridge, which extended across the Öresund Strait for a further 8 kilometers into Malmö in Sweden. It was a spectacular feat of engineering, and a pleasure to drive across once Harry had paid the expensive toll charge. The sun played across the strait below them, and he found the glittering water a calming antidote to the angst of the previous evening.

They arrived in Stockholm six hours later, and made straight for the Central Station, where Harry bought two sleeper tickets for the 6pm train, while Sabine parked the car. They had a couple of hours to kill and Sabine consulted the travel guide, looking for a jazz club she thought was nearby.

'Yes, about ten minutes walk from here,' she said, pinpointing the address on the city map. 'It's called "Fasching". I think they have jam sessions quite regularly, so when we get back I want to visit it.'

'I though "Fasching" was a carnival.'

'Now it's a jazz club too.'

With the help of the guide they found the place, which was closed, and then retired to a nearby bistro for an hour before doing some quick shopping for thermal underwear, snow boots and a thick Winter jacket for Harry. Sabine had come pre-equipped. With a detour to the car park to retrieve their cases, they made it back to Stockholm Central with 15 minutes to spare, and boarded the train.

Harry checked the tickets. 'We're sharing one compartment, hope you don't mind. It was cheaper that way.'

She was unruffled. 'No, does it have two beds?'

He laughed. 'Of course. And a shower and toilet.'

'That could be a little tricky.'

'We'll work something out. Follow me.'

It had been dark for three hours already when the train pulled out.

'Is Michael expecting us?' asked Harry.

'Yes, I texted him while you were buying the tickets. He will meet us. I'd like to take a shower now.'

206

'Ok, I'll get out of your way for a while. Meet me in the bar if you like when you're ready.'

'Don't drink too much, Harry. It won't mix with your drugs.'

He walked down the corridor to the bar, the lights of the city flashing past the windows like shooting stars. He pulled out his phone looking for a response from Sophie, but there were no incoming messages. Not a good sign, he thought. When he found the bar he ordered a large lemonade although a Scotch was his preferred choice. He'd hoped that one or two drinks would help anaesthetize the culpability he felt, deserved or otherwise. Anaesthetised or not, there was nothing he could do about the situation until later. Right now he had a reunion to look forward to.

Chapter 16

It was still dark when they arrived. The train pulled in at 8am, and when they stepped on to the platform the world had turned white. Thick snow covered the station roof, and the platform itself was one long white carpet. Beyond the confines of the station lights it was still too dark to see anything else. The wheels of Harry's case jammed with clinging snow as he dragged it determinedly towards the station entrance. He left it just outside then went back to help Sabine, whose case was somewhat larger and was resisting her best efforts to shift it.

They stood in the ticket office while the other passengers swept by, and ten minutes later they were in sole possession of the place.

'Has he forgotten us?' said Harry.

Sabine didn't answer. She must feel nervous he thought, meeting him again after all this time. He stamped his feet, now firmly encased in snow boots and thermal socks, and walked back out to the platform. The train had gone and it was eerily quiet. He went back inside, wondering what the temperature was, and when the sun would rise.

Sabine had company. They were sitting together on a bench close to the exit. He had his arm around her and Harry thought she might have been crying. He felt loth to intrude, but then Michael looked up and saw him. They locked eyes, and for a moment Harry was transported back to a Belfast church, and the rage of that day touched him fleetingly, then flickered out. He crossed the floor and extended his gloved hand. 'Hello Michael.'

Michael stood up. The pale blue eyes hadn't changed, the black hair was flecked with gray, and he was still a well built man, his bulk perhaps exaggerated by the thick jacket and trousers. His face had acquired a few lines, but it was unmistakeably the face of the man Harry had met so many years ago.

They shook. 'Welcome to Sweden, Harry.'

Then they were all lost for words for a while. Sabine wiped her eyes and Michael took her case and led them out to the car, a Volvo Estate. Sabine took the front seat and Harry settled himself in back behind her. They drove down a snow laden road, the headlights sweeping past fir trees on either side, their branches frosty and white. There was no breeze, and the stillness of the quiet frozen landscape was spellbinding. Harry broke the spell.

'How on earth did you end up here?'

Michael laughed. 'It's a long story. I came to Stockholm in the mid-eighties, and met Ingrid. We got married a year later, and we stayed in Stockholm for a while. But she has family here in Kiruna, and we decided to move up here in 1990. I got a job as a shift supervisor at the mine. It has the advantage of being remote, and I thought I could live here undisturbed.'

'And so you have,' said Harry.

'Until now. I think that may be changing.'

'What's she like?' asked Sabine.

'Ingrid? Blonde, Swedish, happy. I'm lucky.'

'No children?'

'No, she didn't want kids. I didn't mind too much.'

They drove on for another fifteen minutes, then Michael turned down a side road and five minutes later they arrived at a two storey wooden house painted a deep red, and fronted with a white verandah. It was surrounded by trees, and if there were neighbours they weren't close by. Michael turned into a small driveway, and cut the engine.

'Before we go in, there are a few things you should know. First, I'm Michael Sullivan now, just for the record. Second, Ingrid knows everything – the IRA, Siobhan, the lot. She married me in spite of all that. And she knows you're here because of my past, but that's all. Just be discreet about what you say in front of her, I don't want her upset.'

'Right, will do,' replied Harry.

'I forgot something.' Michael looked at Sabine. 'She knows about you too.' He smiled at Sabine's obvious concern. 'It's ok, she isn't the jealous type.'

'Really,' replied Sabine, with a quick smile of her own. 'How do you know?'

Ingrid was certainly blonde and happy, and probably in her mid to late thirties thought Harry. She was well built like her husband, tall and broad shouldered, and she moved with an athlete's confident grace. Her blue eyes fixed the new arrivals with a quiet curiosity, and she seemed genuinely pleased to see them. She'd even made them breakfast.

'Please,' she said, gesturing to the dining table. 'It's typical Swedish food, hope you don't mind that.'

There was cereal and dark bread, to be topped with pickles, tomatoes, cucumber, cheese, cuts of ham and slices of fish, and a large glass of Lingonberry juice. And plenty of coffee. Harry was ravenous, he attacked the meal with gusto. Ingrid excused herself as she'd already eaten, and the three of them were left alone.

'When does it get light around here?' asked Sabine.

'At this time of year we get light between 10am and 1pm. It's a strange kind of light, the sun doesn't get above the horizon, and the light comes from reflections in the air and from the snow. You'll see for yourself soon.'

'Not sure I could live in perpetual darkness,' said Harry.

'You get used to it. It's completely dark in January. But then in June and July the sun doesn't set and you get the other extreme. How long are you here for?'

'Two days at most.'

Michael thought for a bit. 'Better make the most of it then. I have a plan of sorts. Today I'd like some time to talk to you privately Harry.'

'Fine with me. What about Sabine?'

'Ingrid wants to take Sabine to the Ice Hotel, it's not far from here.'

'That would be nice,' said Sabine. 'I hope you two won't lock yourselves away all day though.'

'We just need a few hours, we'll be done by the time you get back. Then we can have an evening eating and drinking like normal people.'

Breakfast was done. Michael began clearing away, and Ingrid reappeared to show her guests where they'd be sleeping. She took them upstairs.

'We only have two bedrooms,' she said. 'Can you share?'

'We seem to manage,' replied Sabine. Harry made no comment.

Ingrid left them to unpack. The room was ensuite, but contained only one double bed.

'Perhaps he's got a camp bed I can use,' said Harry.

'You can always ask. I don't mind sharing with you, Harry. I'll wear something if that helps.'

He laughed. 'Ok, it's only for two nights at most I guess.'

Ingrid came back with a fur lined hat and a thick pair of gloves for Sabine to try on.

'You need to make sure your ears are covered,' she said. 'You need a warmer jacket?'

Sabine thought the jacket she already had would suffice. The hat fitted perfectly, and the two women disappeared downstairs. Shortly afterwards he heard the Volvo start up, and they were gone.

He went back to the dining room, where Michael sat waiting.

'Fancy a drive?'

'In what exactly?' asked Harry. 'You have another car hidden away?'

'Follow me.'

Harry grabbed his jacket and boots, and they headed towards the back door. Michael produced another ear covering hat for him, then took a coat from its hook by the door.

'Try this Harry. It's reindeer.'

Harry dropped his jacket and put on the reindeer replacement. The fur lined exterior was further insulated on the inside by a thick woollen lining. It was a good fit.

'They're perfect for this climate,' said Michael. 'We get them from the Sami people up here. They herd reindeer all over the Arctic Circle.'

Now identically attired, they stepped outside. There was a thermometer tacked to the wall, and Michael stopped to take a look.

'Minus 12 today. Not too cold.'

Harry followed in his footsteps through the fir trees into a cleared area with what looked like a small garage. Michael opened the door to reveal two snowmobiles inside.

'Ever driven one of these?' he enquired.

'Never.'

'Throttle on the right, brake on the left. It's a bit like riding a motorbike. I'll get them out.'

Harry mounted his snowmobile, then gingerly engaging the throttle he followed Michael along a path to the road. They went away from the direction of the main road into a forest of white firs, then they took another turn and the road became a track through the wilderness. After five minutes of this the track wound down a slight incline, till there were no more trees, just a vast flat expanse of snow ahead.

'Frozen lake,' explained Michael, as Harry pulled up level.

'Wow.' The day had arrived, with a grey subdued twilight that divided the clear dark sky and the pristine white earth. Like something out of a fairy tale he thought. If the Snow Queen should appear now he'd be totally unfazed.

Michael moved out on to the lake and picked up his speed, Harry doing likewise. The cold air brought tears to his eyes, but in his sheer exhilaration he hardly noticed. He could get used to this. After ten minutes of this high speed pursuit Michael slowed down, then came to a halt. Harry pulled up close by, and they cut their engines. It was vast and very quiet, and for a minute so were they.

'This is as private as it gets,' said Michael.

'Yes,' agreed Harry. 'So, where do you want to start?'

'First, do you accept that I'm not the person who planted the bomb that killed your wife?'

'Yes. Who was it?'

'We'll get to that. I know from Sabine that you work for British Intelligence, though according to her there was a twenty year gap in your employment. Is that true?'

Harry nodded. 'Till a few weeks ago. They wanted to use me to find you. No reason given.' He was curious. 'Why invite me here? I could have led them right to you.'

214

Michael dismounted his snowmobile, and paced the snow while he thought. Then he turned to face Harry. 'I've lived in Sweden for more than 15 years now. No one came looking for me. After Sabine called me though I began to worry. Soon after that I called my father in Ireland, the housekeeper answered. Dad had been arrested was all she could tell me, and I haven't dared call back since. I hope they don't keep him in too long, he's past 80 now.' He paused, clearly concerned about his father.

'Does he know you're here?' asked Harry.

'He knows I'm in Sweden, just not exactly where. It won't be hard to intimidate a man of his age to reveal that much. And I called from the landline, so I expect that to be traceable. I got careless Harry. Thought I was home free.'

'But why do they want you now?'

'I have a theory about that, which is why I asked you here. If my theory is right then your people will catch up with me sooner rather than later. But you and I have a common interest. The man responsible for Siobhan is the same man who ordered the bombing of your vehicle. And he wanted me out of the way too. I was labelled an informer, but over the years it's become increasingly obvious to me that he was protecting himself. There's no other explanation that makes sense.'

Harry felt confused. 'Yes, but that was all a long time ago. Why worry about it now?'

'Good question. He's in politics now, a Republican Sinn Fein man. Not exactly a friend of England you would think. He's becoming influential though, and I think your friends in SIS would like me out of the way because my theory is correct. He's working for the Brits.'

It's plausible, thought Harry. And not something Jack Hudson would want to tell him about either, they wanted him focused on Michael. Still, he wasn't totally in agreement.

'I don't see why you should be such a threat even if you're right about all this,' he said.

Michael remounted the snowmobile. 'I could expose him for what he is. I have motive after all. It didn't matter though until he got where he is today.' He flexed his gloved hands. 'That's my theory. And I figure that if I'm not in a position to do anything about it in the near future you might be.'

They looked at each other for a long moment. 'Christ,' said Harry. 'Who is this man?'

'Let's go back to the house, there's something I want you to see.'

They made their way back. Ingrid and Sabine were still out, and Harry was glad to get inside the house again, his feet were cold in spite of the boots and thermal socks. They went into the living room where it was reassuringly warm.

He looked around. There were some photos on top of a bookcase against one wall, and he wandered over to take a look. A couple of Ingrid and Michael together, both wearing t-shirts. Obviously taken in the Summer, though he couldn't imagine this place having a

Summer if this was the Winter. And another of a younger Ingrid,

216

in a tracksuit bottom and a vest, standing facing the camera and holding what looked like a javelin. He picked it up for a closer look.

'She was a javelin thrower when I met her,' said Michael. 'Even had a trial for the Swedish Olympic team. She still throws sometimes, not competitively though.'

'I see.' Harry replaced the photo. Explains those wide shoulders, he thought.

Michael was kneeling in front of the TV. There was a VHS player next to it, and he inserted a video. 'Sit down and watch this,' he said.

The picture flickered for a few seconds, then they were looking at what Harry supposed was a church hall, the pews filled with people listening to a speaker on a raised platform at the front. It was shot from the back of the hall, and the camera zoomed in towards the speaker, giving a clear shot of his face.

'His name is Colin Fitzpatrick,' said Michael, 'and this is a Republican Sinn Fein rally from about five years ago now.'

Harry watched closely. Fitzpatrick was a slim middle aged man with a full head of swept back grey hair and a ruddy complexioned weather beaten face. He was saying something about the continued need to work for a re-unified Ireland, and to support his party in making that a reality.

'He's ex IRA,' Michael explained, 'my Battalion Commander in 1981. This is the man I'm talking about, Harry. Seen him before?'

Harry shook his head. 'No, means nothing to me.' There was a pause in the speech now, and Fitzpatrick was taking questions. He had a strong Belfast accent and a resonant tone that Harry thought would easily fill a large public space. A useful attribute if you were an up and coming politician. 'Never seen him.'

Michael reached for the remote and paused the tape. 'Remember that face. He's the man responsible for killing my sister and your wife. I'm certain of it.'

Harry stared at the still image on the screen. Something was tugging at his memory.

'Run it on,' he said.

He watched and listened for a little longer, then he had it.

'I've never seen him, but I've heard him. That's Sean O'Riordan.'

Ingrid did Reindeer steak for the evening meal. Sabine helped her in the kitchen, and it was clear the two women liked each other. They had developed an easy rapport, and the conversation drifting through to the living room was punctuated by quiet laughter. The two men, who were still digesting the implications of Harry's earlier revelation, were muted by comparison.

'I suppose I should be pleased I got it right,' said Michael, looking anything but.

'They knew all along,' Harry muttered.

'Who?'

'Hudson and Litchfield, my SIS colleagues in Dublin. That O'Riordan and Fitzpatrick were one and the same person. And they must have known your relationship with him. Yet still we were targeted by your people. Why?'

218

Michael's expression darkened. 'Fitzpatrick would need to be seen to be doing something after we lost all those guns. They knew the vehicle they wanted to target, but not who would be in it. Unless ..'

'Unless what?'

'Perhaps they did know.'

Harry waved a dismissive hand. 'Meaning I was to be the sacrificial lamb? That's ridiculous.'

Michael smiled without mirth. 'You think so?'

Dinner was served. Sabine did most of the talking, describing their visit to the Ice Hotel, and the ice sculptures she'd seen.

'There's a lovely ice chandelier, and they have a wedding chapel. And an Ice Bar. You really should go and take a look Harry.'

'Sounds great,' he said, his mind elsewhere.

She caught his mood and decided not to distract him.

The meal was conducted mostly in silence, then Ingrid suggested they go back to the Ice Bar after dinner for a couple of quick drinks.

'Actually that's a good idea,' said Harry, snapping out of his reverie. 'Let's do that.'

The Ice Bar was a welcome diversion, with its hewn columns of pale blue ice supporting the ceiling, and semi circular sculpted booths with reindeer skins covering the ice seats. The glasses were ice tumblers, and the drink of choice was vodka, served by barmen in fur hats and padded jackets and thick gloves. The place maintained a constant -5 degree temperature, which while tolerable wasn't conducive to a long stay no matter how well you insulated yourself. Harry thought that after a couple of drinks the novelty might lose out to hypothermia, or maybe after sufficient vodka he wouldn't notice.

'Why don't you take a look around now you're here,' said Sabine. 'It's a lovely place.'

'I'll come with you,' said Michael.

They made their way down the arched corridors, pausing to peek inside bedrooms as yet unoccupied. The basic arrangement consisted of a bed made with two huge slabs of ice pushed together, topped with a mattress and reindeer skins. The more elaborate rooms had carved ice headboards, chairs and animal sculptures.

'People actually sleep here?' asked Harry

'For one night usually, then they put you in warm accommodation.'

In the chapel they took a seat on one of the pews, admiring the altar and huge white cross behind it. The floor level lighting bathed the equally white walls in a subtle glow, giving the place an intimate feel. Harry looked behind, but there were no other churchgoers sharing their intimacy. He turned to Michael.

'What are we going to do? We can't prove anything we might accuse Fitzpatrick of.'

Michael pursed his lips and stared straight ahead. 'I'm going to write a press release naming him as a British agent. I'll reveal my credentials as the only survivor of the gun running incident in Cork, and I'll accuse him of trying to protect himself by killing me. All of the background to this will be on record – the guns, Siobhan's shooting. I'll say I'm breaking cover because I have reason to believe my life is being threatened by the Secret Intelligence Service, and that I want some kind of justice for my sister. It's all rather circumstantial, but I think I can find an Irish journalist who will run with it.'

'But there's still no proof.'

'We just need to sow the seeds of doubt at this point. If we can get people asking questions we will have achieved something. And it might keep SIS away from me too. If I were to disappear suddenly that would only strengthen the case against Fitzpatrick.'

'What do you want me to do?'

Michael stood up. 'Nothing, Harry. You've confirmed something I thought was true for a long time now. No point in putting you at risk too. I'm already at risk so I have no choice in the matter.'

'Alright. One thing though. Even if we were to expose him he'd still be running round free. The worst you can do is bring a case against him for Siobhan's murder.'

'Yes,' agreed Michael. 'But if he was known to be a British Agent there'd be plenty of people willing to put a bullet in him for it. That's what I'm counting on.'

They left the chapel and returned to the Ice Bar.

'Did you get lost?' said Sabine. 'You were away for ages.'

Harry gave a wry smile. 'We stopped in the chapel. Praying for guidance.'

They had another drink and decided it was time to leave. When they stepped outside Sabine grabbed his arm and pointed upwards. 'Look at that,' she said in awe.

The sky was clear and no snow had fallen in the short time they'd been here. And tonight the aurora was weaving its magic in the heavens, its swirling violet and green rays criss crossing the sky. It was heartstoppingly beautiful, and both he and Sabine stood transfixed.

'You're lucky,' said Ingrid. 'A lot of people come here just to see that and they never do.'

They spent most of the trip back looking at it from the the car. When they were inside the house Sabine was drawn to the window at regular intervals to look again.

'I think I'll go to bed,' announced Harry. 'It's been a long day.'

In the bedroom he checked his phone for messages and found nothing. Sabine came up shortly afterwards and rummaged in her luggage, then retired to the bathroom. She emerged ten minutes later wearing track suit bottoms and a t-shirt. She had brushed her dark hair and it was loose now and down around her shoulders.

'Am I acceptable?'

He was under the covers clad in t-shirt and boxer shorts. 'Perhaps you should wear a jacket.'

He was treated to a look of incredulity, then she got into bed. 'It's big enough for both of us. What did you talk about today?'

He filled her in on the day's events. She listened quietly without interruption and with increasing concern as he told her about the arrest of Michael's father, the video session, and the press release. When he'd finished she put her hands behind her head and stared at the ceiling for a while.

222

'This is not a good situation for any of us, is it?' she said.

'No, but officially you and I know nothing. And if Michael gets his story out it should make him safe too.'

She wasn't reassured. 'Turn off the light please.' She turned to him and gave him a quick hug. 'Sleep well Harry.'

The next day Michael locked himself away to draft his statement. Ingrid was in an angry and tearful mood, and managed to break a glass and a plate while doing the dishes after breakfast. The sound of breakage and what could only be cursing in Swedish drew Sabine to the kitchen, and after a while she returned with her arm around a clearly upset woman.

'Michael told her everything,' she explained.

'I'm sorry Ingrid,' said Harry.

'I don't blame you, and I'm scared for him.' She sat at the dining room table with the anger etched on her face. 'Can't he be left alone, after all this time?'

Harry had no answer. Ingrid took a few deep breaths to compose herself. 'We talked last night, and we think you should take the train back to Stockholm tonight. Michael will try to find a journalist that he can email today with his statement. After that we will wait here for maybe two days so he can answer any questions that come up. Then we're going to disappear until we know the story has been released.'

'Right,' said Harry. It all seemed to be moving rather fast. 'But how will I contact Michael if you disappear?'

'You won't be able to. I have Sami friends here, and they will take us reindeer herding for a while. We can get lost up here for months.'

That should keep Michael out of harm's way, thought Harry. 'Ok, we'll go back to Stockholm as you suggest.'

As the morning passed Harry found it increasingly difficult to relax. Michael could be vaguely heard talking on the phone, but he didn't emerge from his study. Sabine was quiet and calmer and exchanging small talk with Ingrid in the kitchen. Harry had an idea.

'Can I borrow the snowmobile? I'll go back to the lake.'

Ingrid managed a smile. 'Yes, of course. Go with him, Sabine.'

They took the one snowmobile and she rode pillion with her arms around him. The lake was deserted and they spent the best part of an hour traversing it in what remained of the daylight, stopping occasionally just to absorb the stillness and seemingly infinite whiteness. There was no need for conversation. The sky was overcast, and as they turned for home fat flakes of snow began to fall. Sabine tightened her hold around him and he could feel her breasts against his back. 'It's wonderful, Harry. Thank you.'

Michael was out of seclusion when they got back, and Ingrid was making lunch. Michael had found a bottle of whisky, and poured Harry a glass.

'Swedish malt,' he said. 'Forgot I had it till now.' He passed Harry a sheet of paper.

'This is my statement, as we discussed. I've emailed a copy to a journalist on the Irish Times, his name and contact details are all

there. And I've talked to him. He wants to run a few checks, and

224

if he's satisfied he'll publish. He said if that happens I should prepare for a "shitstorm", and I should be prepared to do an interview if necessary.'

'In Ireland? Is that wise?'

'No, here in Sweden.' He sighed. 'Done all I can I think. Now we wait.'

'Yes, but don't wait around here too long.'

'I don't intend to. Keep that copy Harry. I'd rather you have it printed and not emailed to you. There's one last thing. My father's address is on that sheet. If anything should happen to me I want you to go and see him, and tell him the whole story. Will you do that?'

'Sure. But I hope I don't have to.'

Michael made inroads into the malt after lunch, but Harry declined to join him, muttering something about one glass being his limit. Michael became somewhat melancholic and started reminiscing about the greenness and beauty of Ireland, and the character of its people, all of which he missed. Harry responded with a sermon on the wonders of his own homeland, citing its rainforests, fiords and mountains. All of which he had to admit he didn't miss as much as he should.

Michael turned to Sabine. 'You didn't bring your saxophone. We don't get much jazz in Kiruna, you know.'

Sabine looked thoughtful for a moment. 'Mmm, it's in a car park in Stockholm right now. I should have brought it really, it would have sounded amazing played on the lake. Next time.'

Ingrid took away the bottle shortly afterwards, and made Michael drink some coffee.

As they drove to the station the Volvo's headlights cut a swathe of brilliance through the lightly falling snow, and the trees on either side of the main road drooped even further under their new blanket. Ingrid drove steadily and not too fast with the restricted visibility, but they still made it with time to spare.

The train arrived on time and they had five minutes to say their goodbyes. The two women hugged each other, then Ingrid kissed Harry on both cheeks, telling him to come back any time. Sabine gave Michael a long embrace, then stepped back and gave him a longer look as though she was burning him into her memory.

'Before you go reindeer herding you are to ring me and let me know everything is ok, yes? If I haven't heard anything from you in three days from now I'm coming back.'

'I will, don't worry,' he replied. 'And when the story comes out in the Irish Times you'll be the first to know. Now go.'

He turned to Harry. 'Thank you for coming, Harry. I'm sorry about the circumstances that brought you here. I'm glad we met though.' The two men shook hands.

Then they were on the train, and it was pulling away, and all they could see through the frosted windows were two blurry figures waving in the snow.

Chapter 17

They had separate sleeping compartments for the return trip. After agreeing to meet for dinner Harry found his compartment and slept for an hour. He woke and showered, then feeling warmer and cleaner he sat cross legged on the fold down bed and stared at the blackness rushing past the window.

He checked his phone again for messages but there were none, and he turned it off, wondering if the act of turning it on for even a short time was enough to pinpoint his location, and if so whether Jack Hudson was checking on him. If they now knew where Michael was they would certainly wonder what Harry Ellis was doing there too. He groaned inwardly at his own stupidity, he should just have left the bloody thing off. And he wondered what would happen when SIS found Michael. Would they involve the Swedish authorities and have him arrested, or did they have something more permanent in mind?

There was a knock at the door, and he let Sabine in.

'Shall we go to the dining car?' she asked.

'Sure, sit with me for a minute first.'

They sat together on the bed. She looked at him expectantly.

'What is it, Harry?'

'How was it, seeing him again?'

'It was nice.' She paused. 'It's like he's just the same, but of course we're all older now and we aren't the same people anymore. The anger has gone though, I noticed that. Why do you ask?'

Harry shrugged. 'Curious I guess. I like him, never thought I'd say that of an ex-terrorist.'

'He never considered himself a terrorist.'

'Let's not get bogged down in semantics. I should have asked him what his politics were these days.' He laughed. 'I'm sure he's still staunch Republican though.'

Sabine smiled. 'Yes, but without the sub-machine guns. Or maybe he just doesn't think about it now.'

Harry got up. 'Come on, let's eat.'

The dining car was filling up fast but they got a small table to themselves. They decided on reindeer with mashed potatoes and lingonberry chutney with half a bottle of house red, and nibbled peanuts while they waited.

'It'll be morning when we get back to Stockholm,' said Harry. 'Still want to play at that club in the evening?'

'I suppose we need to get back to Heidelberg as quickly as possible. You're running out of holiday aren't you?'

'Yes, but I think I can extend my time off. Let's stay in Stockholm tomorrow night then I'll call the office when we get to Copenhagen.'

'I won't be bothered if I don't play the club. There's no guarantee of being able to fit in with whoever is there anyway. I'm just speculating really.'

228

'No, let's stay over. Ring Michael tomorrow night, I want to make sure he got the press release finalised before we leave Sweden.'

'Ok, but what will we do all day tomorrow?'

He grinned. 'We'll be tourists of course. You can get out your travel guide after dinner and work out our itinerary.'

'Is that so? In that case you're buying dinner somewhere expensive tomorrow night. I'll list if for you so there will be no mistake. Deal?'

He nodded. 'Deal.'

Stockholm seemed almost warm after the sub-zero temperatures in Kiruna. Once their luggage was back in the car they walked to Gamla Stan, the original medieval city centre. There they found churches and museums to saunter through, and after a break for lunch the itinerary moved on to the Royal Palace with its endless richly decorated reception rooms and Royal Armoury. By mid afternoon Harry was pleading culture fatigue and was more interested in finding somewhere to stay for the night. They tried three hotels in the area before striking lucky, then it was back to the car to retrieve their cases.

There were no adjoining rooms this time, they were separated by the length of a corridor. As they parted company Sabine said she'd meet him again in an hour, and then he could take her to her chosen restaurant. In the meantime she would ring Michael for an update. After a shower Harry changed into some fresh clothes and channel surfed the TV, searching unsuccessfully for something in

English. He settled instead for reading several of the many pamphlets on the attractions of Stockholm that had been thoughtfully left for him by the management.

'We missed the Vasa Museum,' he said, when Sabine arrived.

'Show me.' She took the pamphlet and glanced at it. 'I'm sure it's very nice, but you said you'd had enough for one day.'

'Yes I did, I'm kidding you. Did you reach Michael?'

'Yes, and the story goes to print in 3 days at most. They are leaving Kiruna tomorrow morning for at least a week, he said.'

'Good. I hope this story has the desired impact. We'll just have to wait and see.'

The restaurant Sabine had picked was expensive even by Scandinavian standards, but she wasn't drinking prior to playing, and Harry restricted himself to one glass of wine. By the time they'd collected the saxophone and walked to the club it was 10pm. Inside it was relatively quiet, and although there was a trio consisting of piano, bass and drums performing, the mood of the audience was one of distraction. The music wasn't grabbing them, not just yet anyway. It wasn't grabbing Sabine either.

'This is a little too traditional for my taste,' she said. 'I won't ask them if I can sit in. Let's have a drink and see if it improves.'

They stayed for an hour and she didn't hear anything to change her mind. 'We picked the wrong night, that's all,' she said as they made their way back to the hotel. 'And to be honest I don't feel much like playing tonight anyway.'

230

That surprised him. 'Why should you not want to play?'

'I don't know Harry, for me it's most unusual. Maybe I'm just tired.'

The next evening they were back in the same hotel in Vesterbro. The receptionist was the same too.

'Ah,' he exclaimed. 'The adjoining roommates. Same again?'

Sabine knocked very loudly before coming into his room this time.

'I didn't want to interrupt,' she said half in jest.

'I've left the phone off,' he replied. 'I'll explain everything to Sophie when I get back.'

Now that it was all done he felt an impatience to be back in London. Since their departure from Heidelberg his existence had assumed an air of increasing unreality, a bubble of the surreal which was now deflating like a tyre with a slow puncture. He was feeling flat and it didn't help that he had no idea what would happen once Michael's story got out. Maybe nothing. He tried to snap out of it.

'Let's go for a walk and find somewhere to eat. It's an interesting neighbourhood around here, the people are quite exotic.'

Sabine was momentarily puzzled. 'Exotic? Oh, you mean the people on the corners in their tight skirts.' She laughed. 'Shall I enquire about price for you Harry?'

He grinned back. 'That won't be necessary. I'll do it myself.'

It was too late to call the office and extend his break, so he made a mental note to do that on the drive back tomorrow, and they went out into the buzzing Vesterbro evening. She put her arm through his and smiled her mischievous smile and he felt good. They ate fish and chips and drank beer in a crowded café which appeared to have been taken over by good natured Danish Hell's Angels, then on the way back they tried to figure out which tight skirted lady would be the most expensive. The criteria were less than scientific, length of leg and brunettes versus blondes were the vital factors. They were still undecided when they got back to the hotel and went into the bar for a nightcap.

'Will you drive to the ferry, Harry? Then I'll do the Autobahn.'

'Yes, no problem.'

'Thanks. Would you believe I'm still hungry? I'm just going to the bar to see if they have any peanuts.'

Less than ten seconds later he heard her shout. 'Harry, quick!'

He rushed over to the bar. She was staring at the TV mounted on the wall. 'It was Michael,' she almost sobbed, 'his picture …'

A police official was talking to the camera. In the background he could see the flashing red lights of what looked like an ambulance. Then the camera panned across to the deep red painted house with the white verandah, and he frantically gestured at the barman to join them.

'Can you translate what's going on for me?'

The barman, who was a young man in his twenties, gave Harry a curious look and then turned to the screen. Michael's face appeared once more, then after another half minute of commentary it was over.

'That was in Kiruna in Sweden, last evening,' the barman began. 'You know Kiruna?'

Harry nodded furiously. Sabine clung to his arm, and he could feel her nails digging in to him.

'The policeman said that the man you saw in the picture was shot dead late last night by someone when he answered the door. His wife is unharmed.'

'Jesus Christ,' breathed Harry. 'And this bastard just walked away no doubt.'

'No, this is the amazing thing.' The young man seemed slightly in awe. 'When he went into the house she threw a javelin from the top of the stairs. Straight through his chest but he's still alive! They took him to Kiruna hospital. They had to trim the javelin first to get him into the ambulance.' He almost laughed until he saw Harry's face.

'Thanks,' said Harry. 'Come on Sabine, upstairs.'

He had to almost drag her through the reception area, she was clinging to him and stumbling with the shock and crying almost soundlessly. In the end he picked her up and carried her into the elevator, and kept her that way while they went up, then the door opened and he got down the corridor to his room.

He put her down on the bed but she refused to let go of him, so he lay down next to her, and she buried her face in his neck. He could feel the heat of her tears on him and he put his arms round her, pulling her close. He held her like that for he didn't know how long, until the tears subsided and his heart rate returned to something close to normal.

'Don't let go of me.' Her voice was toneless and far away.

'I won't.' He tried to think rationally. Michael was dead, it must have been the phone call to Ireland that led them to him. They hadn't succeeded in silencing him, the story was out there and they would be helpless to prevent it running, they knew nothing about it. But Michael couldn't substantiate any of it personally now. Would that matter? And the man they'd sent to do the job had bungled it. If he was questioned by Swedish police would he embarrass SIS with his answers?

If they even suspected Harry and Sabine of being in Kiruna that could have unpleasant consequences. The conversation he'd had with Michael about the night of Natalie's death flashed through his mind. Had he been the 'sacrificial lamb' that night? He couldn't understand the callousness required to set him up like that, but it made perfect sense if you were a callous bastard like Litchfield, and given what he knew now it was the only logical explanation. He'd been used as a pawn, both then and now. He wondered if Jack Hudson had been in on the decision, and assumed he must have been. These people are so cold blooded they won't mind sacrificing me a second time, he thought.

He prised Sabine's arms from around his neck and gently lay her back on the bed. She looked blankly at the ceiling. 'I loved him, Harry.'

'I know.'

'And Ingrid, what must she be feeling? We should go back.'

'No, that's exactly what we mustn't do. Look at me.' She turned her head slightly and they locked eyes. 'We need to get you back to Germany as soon as possible. Heidelberg is probably the safest place for you now. Do you understand?'

'How can you be so calm about this?'

'I don't feel calm. I think we should assume that SIS knows we've been in Kiruna talking to Michael. At the moment I don't know what that means for us, but I just want you back in your own country.'

She nodded, her eyes still on his. 'Sure.'

'It's late. Go next door and have a shower. We're leaving early. Do you want to sleep with me tonight? I don't want you alone even if you are next door.'

'Yes, I don't want to be alone.'

'Ok, go and shower. I'll bring your things in here.'

He gave her five minutes to get into the shower then transferred everything to his room. He put the 'do not disturb' sign outside her door and fixed the chain on the inside. Then he went to his own bathroom and took a shower. As the water cascaded over him he thought of Ingrid, and felt a surge of vicious satisfaction at the image of her impaling the man they'd sent to kill her husband.

Sabine was in bed when he came out of the bathroom. He went over to the adjoining door and made sure it was locked, and gave his own entrance door the same treatment he'd given hers. He rang down to reception and asked for a wake up call at 6am, then he joined her.

'Try to sleep,' he said, turning off the lights.

'I want you to hold me.'

She cried softly for a while and he stroked her back through her t-shirt as she lay with her head on his chest. He found the action strangely calming, and thought she did too as he felt her breathing gradually deepen into sleep. He was still stroking her back at intervals and staring at the ceiling an hour later, but soon after that his racing mind decelerated, called time, and let him drift into a dreamless slumber.

They had no appetite for breakfast the following morning and could stomach only coffee, and by 7am they were on the road. It was late afternoon when they arrived back at Panorama Strasse. Sabine had spent the first part of the journey to the ferry silently staring out the window, and Harry was too preoccupied dealing with the shock he'd suppressed the previous evening to make a sensible attempt at conversation. When they swopped the driving duties near Hamburg he felt edgy and realised he was becoming paranoid. He was checking the occupants of every car that overtook them and turning around at frequent intervals to see what was behind. Sabine caught the tension in him and when he did try to talk she snapped at him in irritation. As a consequence they both arrived feeling exhausted.

'I'll see what's in the fridge,' she said, once the car was unloaded and they were back inside the flat.

'Do you have anything to drink?'

She looked at him for a second, but made no comment. 'Wait,' she said.

She brought him a bottle of wine and a corkscrew. 'I'm going to cook. Open that for me please.' She went back into the kitchen and a minute later he could hear the sound of vegetables being chopped. He opened the bottle then joined her. She gestured at the two wine glasses she had ready on the worktop, and he poured.

'You need to relax Harry, you're making me nervous.'

'Yes I know, sorry.' He took a large sip of wine. 'Damn, I forgot to call the office. Oh, the hell with it.' He topped up his glass. 'Can I put some music on?'

'Help yourself.'

He took the bottle with him, and after a cursory look through the CDs settled for Miles Davis. He retreated to the sofa and let the music and the wine slowly unwind his tension. After ten minutes Sabine came in.

'Vegetable stew, it will take an hour or so.' She looked at the wine bottle. 'You're getting through that quickly.'

'I'd like another if you don't mind. Don't worry, I'm a happy drunk.'

'Take it slowly then. You can be happy, just not speechless.'

The wine was making itself felt, no doubt due to the fact they hadn't stopped for lunch, or bothered with breakfast. Sabine found a second bottle and kept it within easy reach.

'I'm rationing you till the meal is ready.' She poured herself a glass.

'Who's rationing you?'

'I don't need rationing, I have perfect self control.' For the first time that day he saw a hint of a smile.

When the meal was served they both found their appetites had returned with a vengeance. 'I should have made more,' said Sabine. She brought in the casserole pot and spooned the remainder on to Harry's plate. 'Finish it.' He held up the empty wine bottle enquiringly. She said nothing, just took it from him and went back to the kitchen, returning with a fresh one.

'You know I have no idea where to get a copy of the Irish Times in London,' he said. 'Must be somewhere in the City that sells it.'

'When are you going back?'

'I should really go to Frankfurt and get a flight tomorrow.'

'Are we safe, Harry?'

'I think you are. Where I'm concerned I'm not sure what to think. Theoretically I'm no threat to anyone. Just over reaction on my part, that's all.'

'Keep in contact with me won't you?'

'I will, don't worry. Once this story has broken we will have a better idea of where we stand. I'll be calling you every day.'

'I'm going to wash up.'

He finished the dregs of the wine while she was away.

'I'm tired,' she said on her return. 'Are you?'

'Yes, now you mention it.'

'You take the first shower then.'

He set the water to as hot as he could stand, then let it wash over his head and back and chest, easing away the last remnants of tension. He put his hands high on the wall and raised his face to the oncoming water, and tried to think of nothing at all. He didn't hear the shower door open, then Sabine had her arms around him from behind, and he could feel her breasts pressing against him as she tightened her grip.

He gasped. 'Sabine, what the ..'

'Don't stop me,' she whispered.

She kept one arm tight around him and began exploring his body with her free hand. He felt himself responding straight away and realised he had no intention of stopping her. He freed himself from her grasp, spun around and kissed her long and hard.

'Take me to the bedroom,' she said.

Their passion was brief but intense. Then they lay quietly together, absorbing the implications of what they'd done.

'I think I had too much wine,' she said. 'Don't be mad.'

'I'm not.' He ran his hand over the curve of her hip. 'You're still wet from the shower. I'll get a towel.'

He dried her, taking his time. Then he dried himself, kissed her and pulled the covers over both of them.

'I thought you were tired,' he said.

'I am, I just got tired of waiting for the shower, that's all.'

'Of course, how stupid of me.'

'Will you be ok, Harry?'

'I think so. Sleep now. Or are you going to attack me again?'

'No, I'll ask your permission next time. Good night.'

The next morning he woke with a headache and a raging thirst. Sabine was fast asleep beside him. Being careful not to disturb her he got out of bed and went back to his room to find some clothes. Once dressed he went to the kitchen and drank two glasses of water, staring absent mindedly at the view from the kitchen window.

'Hallo.' She stood in the doorway, looking uncertain. 'Could I have some water?'

She drained the glass he passed her then came over to the sink and refilled it. 'I'm sorry about last night Harry, I wasn't thinking. Can we just forget about it?'

'Don't apologise, I didn't exactly resist. I think I've been wanting that to happen for a while now. But yes, we should try to forget about it.'

'Ok,' she said, with a rueful smile. 'Would you like some breakfast?'

'Yes, and will you drive me to the station later? I need to get back home.'

'Sure. Don't forget you've got the syringe in the fridge.'

'No. I'd better use that before I go.' He felt a bit nauseous. 'Drank too much last night.'

'The drugs and the wine don't mix, Harry. If you want your treatment to work you need to drink as little alcohol as possible – preferably none.'

He knew she was right, and he was surprised at how difficult it was to break the drinking habit, even when his health depended on it. That would have to change.

Around mid-morning Sabine brought the Golf to a stop directly outside the station entrance. They got out and she watched as he unloaded his case and stood it on the pavement.

'I want you to text me every evening from now on,' he said. 'I need to know you're ok. I'll try to call you, but it may not always be … convenient.'

'I understand. When will I see you again?'

'I really don't know if that's wise.'

Her face was inscrutable. 'Good journey then.' She hugged him. 'Kiss me please.'

He kissed her for what seemed like minutes but was just a long moment, then he turned away and went in to the station. When he looked back she was getting into the car. He knew that not seeing her again was a difficult choice to make, but it was the only one. He found a ticket machine and fed it with notes, then armed with his ticket to Frankfurt he marched on to the platform and turned his thoughts towards London.

Chapter 18

Sophie had bought a Christmas tree. It stood in the far corner of the living room, reaching almost to the ceiling. He smelled it first, the sweet woody scent clearly discernible as he shut the front door. A large box full of baubles had been left next to it, and the lights were laying in a knotted heap at its base. There were a few strings of silver tinsel wound through the lower branches, and he had the impression of something abandoned, as though the decorator had been unavoidably interrupted, or had simply lost interest.

He had texted Sophie on his way back from Heathrow to let her know he was back, and this time he'd got a reply, saying she would see him later. He'd also rung the office to let them know he'd be in the next day, and they'd put him straight through to Gina.

'You're three days overdue, Harry. Out of simple courtesy you could have let us know earlier, couldn't you?'

'I'm sorry about that Gina, something came up and I was – delayed.'

'I see. I don't know what's going on in your private life, but I can't have it affecting my professional life. I expect to see you tomorrow, and if I don't I'll be thinking about terminating your contract and getting someone who will turn up on a daily basis.'

'I'll be there.' He'd winced at the tone of their exchange, then found himself feeling surprisingly laissez faire about it.

He turned on the heating and shuffled through the mail. Nothing that looked worth opening right now. He decided to have a drink and think about what he was going to say to Sophie when she got back in a couple of hours. He settled reluctantly for tonic without the gin, as there was no other soft drink in the house, then wondered what to do next.

He had the lights working and on the tree when Sophie rang.

'I'll be at the station in ten minutes, come and get me please.' Her tone was neutral, as though she might be reserving judgement on him. Soon find out.

She gave him a perfunctory kiss on the cheek and said nothing on the journey from the station. When they got in she asked him to fix her a drink, then went upstairs to change. He was in the kitchen when she returned. She came straight to the point.

'Who is she and what were you doing in Copenhagen?'

'Her name is Sabine. You need to hear the whole story and then you'll understand why she was there.'

Sophie sighed. 'Yes, something about Ireland wasn't it? Tell me then.'

He started with Jack Hudson's appearance at the wine bar. She looked incredulous.

'But you haven't heard from these people for years. Why now?'

It was hardly a smooth narrative. There were further interruptions:

'You pretended to be a music journalist?' with a wide eyed shake of the head.

'This was all happening while we were together in Freiburg?' with a pointed look condemning his deception.

He was glad he'd left out the break in at Sabine's apartment. He stopped and made them both another drink prior to the Swedish instalment. Sophie raised her eyes in surprise.

'You're drinking tonic without gin?'

'I started medication just over a week ago. I'm trying to cut down.'

'You never said …'

'I was going to, but we got onto this subject.'

They were sat at the kitchen table and she stayed quiet when he resumed, staring at the full glass in front of her with an air of almost fatalistic detachment, as though she was being told something she knew she should hear but didn't really want to know about. When he got to Michael's shooting there was a sharp intake of breath, then she looked confused and horrified in equal measure.

'My God, what have you done?'

'Nothing. I was in Denmark when I heard. They found him and they killed him. End of story.'

'And the press release?'

'In the Irish Times any day now.'

She slammed her glass down, sending a spurt of gin and tonic across the table.

'Why couldn't you just leave it all alone? You should have told that man Hudson to go to hell. What do you think you're going to achieve anyway?' She stood up. 'I hope you're satisfied, whatever it is.' She moved to the sink and began rinsing the spilt drink off her hands.

What I'd really like, he thought, is for someone to realise Fitzpatrick is the informer and murderer I know he is, and then put a bullet in him. He decided to keep this sentiment to himself.

'I'm sorry, and you're right, I should have told him to go to hell. Once it started though I needed to see it through, and now it's over. There's nothing more I can do or need to do. Let's draw a line under it and move on.'

'Have you told me everything?'

He wondered what his face was saying, and was glad she had her back to him. 'Yes, I've told you everything.' He got up and moved to the lounge, where he busied himself with opening the mail and pretending to be interested in the contents.

She came in. 'There's some Lasagne in the freezer. Is that ok?'

'Yes, that would be great.'

'Tell me about these drugs you're taking.'

She seemed to be distracting herself from any doubts she might have about what he'd just told her, and he seized on the respite. He filled her in on the treatment regime.

'Any side effects yet?' she asked.

'Nothing to speak of. It's early days though.'

His phone beeped, he had a text. Sabine – 'Still here, Love S x'

He sent off a quick acknowledgement, then discarding the half read mail he decided it was time to embrace the Christmas spirit. He went back to the tree and began festooning it with glittering glass stars and multi-coloured baubles, making sure the dancing fairy had pride of place as close to the top as he could get it.

He returned to work the following day, but found it hard to concentrate. He went out at lunch time and found a newsagent near Cannon Street who sold the Irish Times, but even after scanning it from front to back he could find nothing about a former IRA man accusing another of being a British informer. The afternoon passed slowly, and just as he decided he'd done enough for one day and was ready to leave, he had a call from Sabine.

'I thought you should know,' she said. 'I've been in touch with Ingrid. The man she injured with the javelin died yesterday. Never regained consciousness apparently.'

'You called her? I thought we agreed to leave her alone.'

'I couldn't. She's expecting to be charged with manslaughter, but we think she'll get bail. Anyway, I'm going back to help organise the funeral. It's next week.'

He knew then that he didn't want to try and change her mind. 'Give her my condolences. Just take care of yourself.'

'If anything happens to me there'll be a diplomatic incident. I'm leaving a letter with my lawyer before I go to Sweden. It has enough information in it to embarrass your intelligence services I think. Maybe even your Prime Minister.'

He was impressed. 'Good idea, maybe I should do something similar.'

'Anything in the papers yet?'

'No, I'll let you know when there is.'

'Ok. I'm taking a flight from Frankfurt tomorrow. And the phone will stay on this time.'

It was the following day, the Friday before Christmas, when the story broke. And it made the front page, or to be more precise, the lower half of the front page.

Former IRA Man Says Republican Sinn Fein Treasurer Colin Fitzpatrick is British Informer.

Michael O'Reilly, who was a member of the IRA from 1972 until he was forced to leave Ireland in 1982, was the sole survivor of the ambush at Ballyrisode Beach in County Cork in 1981 that left eight men dead at the hands of the SAS and deprived the IRA of a large arms shipment. There was widespread speculation at the time as to how the SAS knew where the arms would be delivered.

According to O'Reilly, he was on the run and staying with his sister in Dublin only a day or two later when he was targeted by a hitman representing his own organisation. The man told him he had been labelled an informer, and in the scuffle that followed O'Reilly's sister Siobhan was shot and the hitman fatally wounded. Siobhan O'Reilly later died of her injuries. Ambulance men, who acted as witnesses in the subsequent inquest, placed a man answering O'Reilly's description at the scene, who referred to her as his sister.

O'Reilly states that Colin Fitzpatrick, now a prominent member of Republican Sinn Fein, was his battalion commander, and that he was protecting his own role as an informer by attempting to silence O'Reilly. He had no hard evidence to support this conclusion, and since leaving Ireland has lived quietly for the last 15 years in Sweden, where he had no further reason to revive his past.

When it came to his recent attention that British Intelligence were showing an interest in his whereabouts, and that his father was helping Belfast police with unspecified enquiries, he began to worry for his own safety, and contacted this newspaper with what he considered to be 'the only insurance policy I may have.' It was his assertion that he was to be silenced to ensure that Fitzpatrick's continuing role as an informer, who could inflict significant damage on RSF, would never be revealed. O'Reilly hoped that by bringing the issue into the open he might forestall any action contemplated against him.

Mr. O'Reilly knew that his evidence was at best circumstantial, and accordingly this newspaper was dubious about the merits of publishing the story. It now transpires however that Michael O'Reilly's fears for his safety were well founded. Two days after he spoke to the Irish Times he was shot dead at his home in Sweden by an unknown assailant. That assailant was seriously injured during the incident and has since died.

It is on record that Mr. Fitzpatrick was a member of the IRA prior to entering politics. We contacted the RSF office in Dublin to solicit a reaction from him, but he has so far declined to comment.

Was it enough to sow the seeds of doubt, he wondered. The next week should bring an answer. He'd bought two copies of the newspaper, and he cut the front page from the second copy and stuffed it into an envelope which he addressed to Sabine. He texted her to let her know it was on its way and tried to focus his mind once again on his work.

They buried Michael in Kiruna on Christmas Eve. Sabine called to tell him it had been a low key affair, with about a dozen mourners, none of whom were Irish. Ingrid had indeed made bail on a manslaughter charge, and her lawyer was confident of getting her off on a plea of self defence. Sabine would stay for a few more days, and be home before New Year.

Harry spent Christmas Day with his in laws. They were no doubt briefed in advance by Sophie, as they took a softy-softly approach to the occasion. The chatter was constant as ever but it was conducted at a lower decibel level, and the word 'Ireland' had been erased from the lexicon. If Clive had been to Dublin on business since their last meeting he was making a distinct effort not to mention it. Harry restricted himself to two glasses of wine the whole day. Clive was concerned.

'You alright Harry? No shortage of booze if you want it.'

Harry said he was feeling rather tired, which in fact he was, and two glasses had been plenty, he had no appetite for more. He spent the latter part of the day in what he liked to think of later as a 'thoughtful stupor' in front of the television.

There was a riposte to Michael's accusations in the New Years Eve edition of the Irish Times, this time on the inside front page. Fitzpatrick refuted Michael's assertion, saying that the accusation was one of a bitter man who blamed the IRA for the death of his sister, which while regrettable had never been specifically linked to the IRA. He had not been Michael's battalion commander in 1981 and knew nothing of hitmen, and was not and had never been in the pay of British Intelligence. Nor was he in any way connected to the ambush on the beach. He was shocked at Michael's death in mysterious circumstances and concluded that under the circumstances he had no case to answer.

How very convenient, thought Harry. He read the article again, sat at his desk at work. He was due to finish early and have a quick drink with some of his team as a run up to whatever festivities one might have planned for later. The day had been relatively quiet, with a lot of the people he would normally speak to out of the office, and no one took any notice of his absorption in what might have been labelled 'frivolous activity' on a normal business day.

He thought back on all that had happened since he and Sabine had left Heidelberg only a few weeks ago. Was he now looking at the final outcome of that journey and the revelations it had produced, all summarised in a few words in a broadsheet – no case to answer?

He picked up the desk phone and dialled Gina. He hadn't seen her all day but he thought she was in. She was, and he said he needed a word in person. A minute later he was in her office.

'What is it Harry?' She'd been a little brusque since his return.

'It's short notice I know, but I won't be back next year. If you don't mind I'd like to terminate the contract right now.'

She was momentarily shocked, then perplexed. 'Harry, what the hell is going on with you?'

'You were right about my private life, that's all. It's screwing up both our professional lives. There's something I need to do, and I'm afraid it takes priority over everything else. Sorry, but there it is.'

She looked at him in silence for a while, then shrugged. 'Ok, if that's how it is. Find someone to hand over to before you go. And leave your pass at reception on the way out.'

Sophie had invited some of the neighbours around for New Years Eve, and they stayed up past midnight to welcome in 2002. He didn't mention his intentions till the afternoon of New Years Day.

'I quit the bank.'

'What?' She'd been nursing a mild hangover and was stretched out on the sofa. 'Did you say you'd quit?'

'Yes, I'm flying to Belfast on Thursday.'

He had her full attention as she sat bolt upright. 'I don't understand. Why?'

'I have some calls to make. Then it's over.'

She considered this for a moment, then laughed derisively. 'I thought it was already over. How many more times do I have to listen to this? Will you never stop?'

'Try and understand Sophie, I ..'

She cut him off. 'Understand? What do you think I've been trying to do? Are you really going to Ireland? Or is it Lanzarote, or Copenhagen, or is it Heidelberg maybe?'

'What do you mean?'

'Did you sleep with her, Harry?'

She caught him totally off guard with that, and his face was answer enough.

'I thought so. You do whatever you like, but when you get back don't expect to find me here, and you can start thinking about finding somewhere else to live while you're at it.'

She walked calmly up the stairs to the bedroom, then slammed the bedroom door violently. This was not the start to the New Year he'd envisaged.

Chapter 19

He landed in Belfast just after 1pm, then took a taxi straight to the address Michael had given him. He hadn't rung in advance, on the assumption that the call might be recorded. It was a small terraced house in a street of small terraced houses, and he could see the peace wall that still divided the two communities rearing up two streets behind it. He rang the bell and waited. Presently the door was answered by a grey haired middle aged woman wearing a dirt smudged blue apron over a brown cotton blouse and loose fitting jeans.

'What can I do for you?' She was business like but not unfriendly.

'I'm here to see Mr. O'Reilly. I'm a friend of his son.'

She looked at him impassively for a moment, then waved him in. 'Just a minute, I'll tell him you're here.'

He stood in the hall. Directly ahead there were stairs against the adjoining wall, leading up to the second level, and to his right there were what he took to be two reception rooms though both doors were shut. The woman, who he thought must be the housekeeper, had walked directly down the hallway into the kitchen area and was talking quietly to someone out of view. He heard the squeak of a chair being pulled back, then she came out and beckoned him in.

Michael Senior was standing at the kitchen table with a look both curious and sad clouding his features. His hair, still abundant, was white and close cut, and for a man of eighty something he retained an impressive bulk, reminiscent of his son. The eyes were the giveaway though, the same pale blue. His voice when it came was soft but still deep and clear, and heavily Belfast accented.

'You say you know my son?'

'Yes,' said Harry, extending his hand. 'We met in Sweden recently. He asked me to come and see you.'

There was a slight hesitation in the grip, but the older man's handshake was firm. 'You know he's dead, don't you?' he said, almost diffidently Harry thought.

Harry nodded. 'Yes, he wanted me to talk to you if anything happened to him.'

'What's your name?'

Harry introduced himself, and after Michael Senior bid the housekeeper, who identified herself as Mrs McDonald, to make some tea, he was ushered through to the sitting room.

There were two large armchairs and a sofa arranged around a fireplace, in which an artificial fire was burning. His eye was caught by two photos on the mantelpiece, one of Michael in earlier years and another of a red headed woman.

'Is that Siobhan?' he asked. Michael Senior nodded. It was a simple head and shoulders portrait which must have been taken when she was around 20 years old. The fiery red hair and the blue eyes were the first thing to hit you, then the sheer energy of her youth in her smile and radiant complexion. She had very clear skin for a redhead, he thought, and she was pretty.

'I thought you might be another of those bastards from the intelligence community,' said Michael Senior. 'But there'd be no point in them coming back. They found him, didn't they?'

'Yes, I'm pretty sure that's what happened. I'm sorry for your loss. But I want to tell you how I met Michael, and what we found out together.'

The tea arrived. Mrs McDonald showed no sign of leaving the room, and seeing Harry's hesitation Michael Senior assured him that he could talk without reservation in front of her. Harry told them the whole story, from his arrival in Ireland and his part time job with SIS, through Nat's death and the twenty year gap right to the events in Sweden and directly afterwards.

'So you do work for British Intelligence then', said Michael Senior, looking slightly bewildered.

Harry smiled. 'When it suits them I think. I've been used rather than employed, if that makes sense. It's personal now.'

'That's some story, Harry. And you believe this Fitzpatrick man to be a British informer then?' Michael Senior had listened almost without interruption and with deep concentration. His age hadn't as yet dimmed his powers of comprehension as far as Harry could tell. 'There was a Fitzpatrick Carpentry here in Belfast way back,' he continued. 'I remember him. Didn't know he'd gone into politics though. To be honest Harry I pay no attention to it now. I've lost two children to the Republican cause, which is ironic as I'm one myself. Anyone who still espouses the politics of violence is a bloody fool for my money. But revenge I do understand.'

'Yes, I suppose when it comes down to it, revenge is what we're talking about. Or justice if you're being charitable.'

Mrs. McDonald went out to brew a fresh pot. 'Have you come equipped for justice, Harry?'

Harry was momentarily perplexed, then he clicked. 'No, you don't understand. I have no intention of shooting anyone. I'll tell you what I plan to do.'

He explained his intentions to the older man, who regarded him dispassionately as he did so. When he'd finished Michael Senior thought about it for a while, then rose from his armchair and walked across to a sideboard on the far side of the room. He opened a drawer, his back to Harry.

'I've outlived two children and a wife, Harry. It's unnatural and it makes me sad. We've only just met but I'd like to think I won't have to outlive you too. If you're going to do what you say you are you should think about self protection while you're here.'

He came back carrying a shoe box, which he placed on the coffee table. 'Open that.'

Harry lifted the lid. Inside, on a bed of coarse white cloth, lay a Walther PPK, with several clips of ammunition.

'They used to be very popular with the Ulster Defence Regiment,' said Michael Senior.

'Someone told me that once. Aren't you being a little melodramatic?'

'Just take it. If you don't use it return it to me on your way home. But frankly, at my time of life I don't care if they trace it to me or not.'

Harry took a long look at the gun, thinking the last time he'd held one of these he'd pointed it at this man's son. He shook his head in wonder. 'Alright, I'll take it. Do you have a holster?'

'Mrs. McDonald, do we have a holster for the gun?' shouted Michael Senior.

Mrs. McDonald popped her head round the door and spotted the open shoe box. 'Sure we do Michael, I'll fetch it. And keep your voice down, do you want the whole street to know we're armed?'

Harry made some space for the gun in his suitcase. He drank another cup of tea then asked Mrs. McDonald to ring for a taxi.

'Where to, Harry?'

'The nearest bus station. I'm going to Dublin.'

He assured Michael Senior that he'd call again on his way back.

'Watch the newspapers over the next few days,' he said. 'It might get interesting.'

The older man seemed rather detached. He shook Harry's hand as they parted. 'Whatever happens it won't bring my children or your wife back. Don't let your anger cloud your judgement Harry. We've been doing that here for years and it's done us no good whatsoever.'

He thought about that parting remark as he watched the peace wall dividing Catholics and Protestants pass him by in the taxi. The division seemed to him to be more tribal than religious, and rooted in so much history that any attempt to dismantle it would require a shift in hearts and minds that would make the fall of the Berlin Wall look like a walk in the park.

He turned his mind to his own problems. A wife on the verge of leaving and an illness as yet unmanifested. And soon his credibility would be tested too. All much easier to solve than the issue of Northern Ireland, he thought, and laughed quietly to himself.

The taxi driver gave him a queer look. 'Something I said?'

'No, sorry. Just thinking out loud I guess.'

The bus station came into sight. 'We're here,' said the driver.

Harry paid the man and got out. Next stop, Dublin.

He got off the bus at Grafton Street. Dublin didn't seem that much different, not around here anyway, though he noticed Grafton Street had been pedestrianised since his last visit. The revitalisation of the Republic's economy was more evident in the shiny office blocks in the financial district on the other side of the river. He walked up Grafton Street and past St. Stephen's Green till he got to Harcourt Street. He tried to remember where the flat had been and was shocked to find he wasn't sure anymore. The Harcourt Hotel hadn't moved, and he took a room for a week, unaware that twenty years before Siobhan had also been here.

He could have stayed elsewhere, but right now he wanted to remember how it had been and how it had felt, to revisit the Harry Ellis who was an Irish student and had a career lined up as a language scholar. And how that ambition had been irrevocably extinguished one Christmas Eve so long ago. It could be seen as

258

a masochistic indulgence if you were a critical observer, but to him it was a necessary part of preparing himself for what was to come. He had a pint of Guinness in the bar downstairs, then after a room service meal got an early night.

He phoned the Irish Times the following morning and asked for the journalist whose name Michael had left him. He wasn't available, so he left a message to the effect that he had information he wanted to share on the Colin Fitzpatrick story, and would Mr. O'Neill kindly return his call.

He spent the morning at Trinity college, this time as a tourist. He took a tour through the Old Library, which contained the Book of Kells, and although he'd seen the manuscript before he couldn't help but be captured anew by the ornate beauty of the pages on display. He was on the way out of the college when the phone rang. It was David O'Neill.

'Where did you get my name, Mr. Ellis?'

'From Michael O'Reilly, or Sullivan if you prefer.'

'I see. What's your interest in this story then?'

'I want to make a statement that you can use as an addition to your story. I met Michael shortly before he died. We had a common interest in Colin Fitzpatrick.'

O'Neill sounded cautious. 'That's interesting of course, but to be honest Mr. Ellis it looks as though the story really doesn't have much life left in it. As Fitzpatrick says, he has no case to answer. It will be difficult to prove otherwise.'

Harry had wondered if this might be the first reaction. 'Before you kill it then, will you do me the courtesy of listening to what I have to say?'

There was a pause, then O'Neill made up his mind. 'Ok, do you know where the offices are?'

'D'Ollier Street?'

'Yes. Come by at 2pm and ask for me at reception.'

O'Neill was in his forties, Harry guessed, a tall slim and vibrant man with a shock of curly black hair and a beard shot through with grey. He collected Harry from reception and led him to a meeting room two floors above.

'We won't be disturbed here,' he said. He placed a pocket tape machine on the table between them. 'Do you mind if I record this?'

'Be my guest.'

O'Neill switched the tape on and sat back, crossing his arms. 'What have you got for me then?'

Harry took a deep breath. 'You need to hear it from the beginning. In 1981 I was living here in Dublin with my wife Natalie and studying Irish at Trinity College. I had a part time job doing translation work ...'

Throughout the narrative O'Neill's reaction veered from initial incredulity through amazement and finally to barely contained excitement. He didn't interrupt, and when Harry had finished he leaned forward to switch off the tape. 'Jesus wept.' He thought for a moment. 'Did you bring any ID?'

260

Harry reached into his jacket pocket, and pulled out his British and New Zealand passports. 'Will this do?'

O'Neill checked the documents and pushed them back across the table. 'I'll need to run my standard checks on dates and places. Normally I'd ask you for a photograph, but that might not be a good idea just yet.'

'What do you think will happen?'

'With you being the second person to name Fitzpatrick, and being the victim of a bombing that was so close to Siobhan O'Reilly being shot ..' He thought some more. 'And you've named names. We will lobby for a public enquiry, though to be honest the chances of getting one are slim. But this will certainly put more pressure on him.'

'Good.'

'If there was an enquiry your testimony would be vital. Unless of course ..' He stopped and looked at Harry with real concern.

'Unless I don't get to testify, is that what you're thinking?'

'To put it bluntly, yes. I don't want you on my conscience too. Where are you staying?'

Harry told him. O'Neill stared at the table, and Harry could almost see the cogs turning as he considered the implications. He finally looked up. 'Ok, if we go public with this I want to do two things – first, get you out of sight, and second line you up for a television interview. Are you prepared to do that?'

'Whatever it takes.'

'Alright. Go back to the Harcourt now and stay by the phone. I may ring you to clarify some things. I'll work on this for the rest of the day, and if we're going to publish it will come out tomorrow. Then over the weekend we can gauge the reaction. I'll be in touch later.'

Harry left, feeling both trepidation and a lightness of spirit he'd forgotten he possessed. It looked like the 'shitstorm' might be unleashed after all. And all he had to do was stay out of harm's way when it was. At least there'd be no miffed Republicans to contend with this time, he reflected. But considering who he might have to contend with instead brought him precious little consolation.

When O'Neill began to call at regular half hourly intervals asking for more details on various parts of his story he knew it would all go ahead, and it was confirmed later that evening. He was advised to leave Dublin and find a quiet spot in the country.

'Don't tell me where, Harry. Keep your receipts for car hire and accommodation. We will reimburse you, and over the weekend I'm going to see about getting you a slot on the TV news. In the meantime keep a low profile.'

He told the girl on hotel reception that this would be his last night, then arranged a car for the following morning.

The Friday dawned cold and overcast, with a bitter gusting breeze that made him bow his head as he wheeled his case out of the Harcourt and set a vigorous pace to the Avis pick up point ten minutes walk away. He stopped briefly to pick up a copy of the

Times, and there it was – 'Second Man Names Fitzpatrick as British Informer.' There was a paragraph on the front page with his name and a mention of his association with SIS, then the reader was directed to 'the full and comprehensive story' on page 5.

I'll read it later, he thought, stuffing the paper into the zip pocket on the side of his case. He found the Avis office and after browsing the cars on offer settled for a Peugeot 307. He pored over the map in the glovebox and decided to try Kilkenny, about an hour and a half away. He would have liked to go further, but if they needed him for TV he should stay reasonably close to Dublin.

He switched off the phone. This time he'd pick up a cheap Pay as you go model and use that to talk to O'Neill. He still had no idea if his indiscretions with his phone in Sweden had been noticed by Jack Hudson, but he wasn't going to chance it a second time in Kilkenny, where he definitely wanted to stay 'out of sight'.

Being a popular tourist destination meant Kilkenny did not lack for hotels, and with it being the off season he had no trouble getting a room right in the centre of town. He had a late lunch in a nearby pub, made his phone purchase, then retired to review O'Neill's article.

It was all there much as he'd recounted it on tape. The full story, from his employment with SIS (naming Litchfield but not Jack), their suspicions of O'Reilly, Nat's death, and right up to the point where he identified O'Riordan and Fitzpatrick as the same man in Sweden. He used the new phone to call O'Neill.

'Harry, I've been trying to call you.'

'I've switched phones. Use this number from now on if you don't mind.'

'What do you think of the article?'

'Very good, certainly accurate. What now?'

'There will be a TV crew trying to get a reaction from Fitzpatrick over the weekend. And I'd like you to come back to Dublin on Sunday afternoon. We want to record some footage with you that we'll release on Monday.'

They agreed a time and place. On the Sunday at the Dublin studio O'Neill showed him a clip of Fitzpatrick, who had been ambushed by the news team outside his home the previous evening. He continued to deny the allegations against him, but Harry thought he looked shaken nonetheless. In the end he'd pushed the camera away and climbed into a car, which rapidly pulled out of camera shot.

'He's reeling I think,' O'Neill pronounced.

Harry's own interview was condensed into a two minute soundbite, which consisted of him essentially stating his allegations and saying that he was quite willing to repeat them in a court of law or at a public enquiry if necessary.

'Are we done now?' he asked O'Neill.

'Yes. Your face will be known after tomorrow, remember that. I don't know where you're staying, but I recommend getting right out of circulation now. How long can you stay in Ireland?'

Harry considered. He had money in the bank and no gainful employment. 'For as long as I need to.'

'I have a suggestion then.' He passed Harry a sheet of paper. 'This is the address of a cottage friends of mine own on the Dingle Peninsula. There's no one around for miles. You can have it for a nominal charge for the next month if you need it. If you want it let me know and they'll fix it up with fuel and food for you.'

'Ok, thanks. I'll take it. Tell them I'll be arriving Monday night.'

Chapter 20

In the final hour of his journey rain and wind lashed the car incessantly. It was dark now, and even with the wipers on top speed the sheets of water clinging to the windscreen would only clear for a split second at a time. He slowed right down and was glad that traffic was light tonight. O'Neill had given him a phone number and a name, Deirdre Brennan. He was to meet her at 7pm at a bar in Dingle and then follow her to the cottage.

The rain eased off as he reached the town. He found a place to stop and phoned Deirdre to find out exactly where the bar was. He was half an hour early so he found 'The Shamrock' and settled down with a pint of Lemonade to await her arrival. The place was quiet, perhaps the weather was keeping everyone indoors tonight. Or perhaps this assortment of elderly men sitting alone reading newspapers, and the odd groups of younger people chatting and laughing in a convivial yet almost circumspect manner were a typical Monday evening crowd.

She'd given him a brief description of herself on the phone, so when he saw a blonde wearing a grey windbreaker come in he raised his hand. She spotted him, walked across and introduced herself. She was in her mid thirties and tall, when he stood up to greet her they were almost eye to eye. Her hair fell in tangled waves to her shoulders around a narrow face with strong cheekbones and a prominent nose, and her eyes were brown and steady.

'You found your way then?' Her voice had a soft Southern accent that was easy on the ear.

'When I could see the road. Does it always rain here?'

She laughed. 'Quite often. This is the West Coast you know.'

She accepted his offer of a drink and they chatted. She lived with an older sister in the town, and worked at a crafts shop. She knew David O'Neill through her brother in Dublin. The cottage belonged to the family and was let out in the tourist season.

'It's quite remote, almost on a cliff top,' she said. 'There's a little beach within walking distance, which you'll probably have all to yourself.'

He followed her car as they drove out of town along the coast. She turned on to a single lane unmarked road about 20 minutes later, which wound up a steep hill then dropped down to a plateau on the other side. The stone built cottage had been constructed on this flat area and was bordered by a stone wall. Deirdre opened a wide farmyard style gate and they drove in, parking at the rear. Sighing gusts of wind blew in from the sea, and he could hear the rumble of waves breaking in the distance. He got out of the car and followed her inside.

She showed him around. There was a kitchen, dining room and a living room with a large fireplace downstairs, and two bedrooms and a bathroom upstairs. The fireplace had been cleaned and stocked with logs, and Deirdre talked as she kneeled in front of it and struck a match to coax it into life.

'We have electric storage heaters which come on at night. They're ok but you need the fire really at this time of year. There's plenty of wood in the outbuilding. The fridge is full, there's some booze in the cupboard if you want it, and the TV works.'

'No internet?'

'No, sorry about that. And the phone signal can be erratic too. There's a landline here though. Call me if you need anything.'

He thanked her and shortly afterwards she left, saying she'd drop in one evening during the week to see how he was doing. She'd shown no curiosity about his visit and he wondered what O'Neill had said about him, if anything.

The fire was burning nicely now and he pulled up a chair, warming his hands. The heat soon permeated the room and he found himself drifting off as he gazed into the flames. He shook himself awake and went into the kitchen to investigate the contents of the fridge. It was well stocked with frozen meat and a selection of vegetables and juices, with plenty of milk and eggs. He found a tin of vegetable soup and heated that up, then followed it with an omelette. There was a cupboard with bottles of red wine and even a bottle of Jameson's Whiskey, which he looked at longingly. Tea would have to suffice. He thought about ringing O'Neill but when he checked the phone there was no signal and he didn't want to use the landline. He decided to simply sit in front of the fire for a while, then have an early night.

He'd been sitting about 15 minutes, enjoying the heat and the play of the flames, when he began to feel an unaccountable sadness creeping over him. It started as an ache in his gut, then spread to his chest, and for a moment he thought he might be sick. Then suddenly he was crying. What the hell? he thought. He realised that a split second ago he'd been thinking about the night Natalie was killed, and then the dam had burst, releasing the guilt he'd always felt but never allowed himself to express. He put his head in his hands and let the tears flow. The intensity and unexpectedness of it all surprised him. Then he found he was berating himself: - he should have been driving, he should never have been so stupid as to accept the loan of the vehicle in the first place, he should never have accepted the job with SIS. He was a fool and he was responsible for Nat's death, what gave him the right to go on living when he'd effectively murdered his own wife?

In spite of the fire he was shivering, and now he felt a deep self loathing and disgust displacing his guilt. He went upstairs to the bedroom and retrieved the shoebox from his luggage, then sat again in front of the fire, cradling the Walther in one hand. Perhaps he could play a little Russian Roulette to pass the time. He laughed, and there was a touch of hysteria in it. Difficult to play Russian Roulette with a semi automatic, the next bullet was always available. Made it easier really.

The landline rang and he jerked upright in his chair. It was Deirdre.

'Sorry Harry. I forgot to tell you, the switch for hot water is under the sink. Put it on for an hour or so before you want a bath or whatever.'

He mumbled his thanks and hung up. He was breathing heavily, and his body felt heavy, almost immobile. He stumbled back to the chair. The phone call had interrupted the emotional turmoil, snapping him out of what he realised had been a frightening downwards spiral that could have proved fatal. For a moment there he'd lost all control. He'd never felt suicidal before, but he realised now that over the past few days he'd been a little depressed. He could only put it down to the medication. If that was the case then giving a gun to a depressed man was a recipe for disaster. He'd need to be very careful about his moods while he was here if he wanted to avoid a repetition of what had just happened. At least he knew the warning signs now.

He shook his head. How ironic. The drugs that were supposed to cure him might kill him instead, however indirectly. No, sod it, he thought. He hadn't come all this way for nothing, whatever he was or wasn't responsible for, he knew he wanted to go on living. There was too much left to be done.

He replaced the Walther in it's shoebox and stashed it in a kitchen cupboard, thinking that if he woke up in the night determined to top himself he might regain his senses on the way downstairs. The whole episode had frightened him, but he seemed to have his sanity back, at least for the moment. He sighed loudly. He'd had enough excitement for one night, it was time to get some sleep.

There was still no signal in the morning. The heating had come on so the upper part of the cottage was a lot warmer now. The

270

curtains in his bedroom had been partially drawn when he went to bed, and it wasn't until he parted them to let in the morning light that he first saw the sea.

The land around the house was green and treeless, dropping away from the plateau on which the cottage stood in a gentle slope that extended for some 300 metres before levelling out again near the cliff edge. The coast on both sides stretched in long jagged curves into the distance, with no houses in sight. He could see a few sheep faraway to the right, otherwise the place was deserted.

Straight ahead was the Atlantic, looking grey and ominous under the black clouded sky, filling his eyes and his mind with its sheer size and majesty. Now that the wind had subsided the sound of the waves was constant, and he realised that even as he'd slept he'd been aware of that sound. He stood and watched for a while, letting the sight and sound heighten his senses and clear his head. Then it started to rain, and he yawned and came out of his meditation. He was hungry.

He knew he couldn't stay here much longer, he needed to get back to London to collect his next batch of drugs. His thought processes had become a little muddled, he'd blithely told O'Neill he could stay as long as he needed to. He was becoming absent minded as well as depressed. Well, for as long as he was here he needed a routine. He would visit Dingle town once a day and pick up reading material, and call O'Neill for an update. Then whatever the weather he would get some exercise walking the clifftops. Maybe Deirdre would consent to have dinner with him, he wasn't accustomed to a solitary existence and would welcome the company. He could hardly have stayed indefinitely anyway. If there was a public enquiry it might not get underway for months. And bringing a civil case against Fitzpatrick for murder would come down to Harry's word against his. There was no prospect of a conviction.

He had a week to play with. He wondered if Sabine was ok, she didn't as yet know where he was and what he was doing. And since turning off the phone three days ago he hadn't seen her daily texts. He wanted to know how she was.

He had breakfast, then rummaged through his luggage for the same jacket he'd worn in Sweden. It had a hood and should keep out the Irish weather. The rain had stopped so he ventured outside. He checked the outbuilding, which was full of logs, then walked directly down from the cottage to the cliff, looking for the beach Deirdre had told him about. He could see it easily enough, and the cliff wasn't sheer. At this point it was more of a steep sided hill, and someone had dug out a pathway, with a handrail arrangement made up of posts hammered into the ground and joined with rope. The beach itself, a sandy cove about 200 metres wide, was about 50 metres below him. He wasn't sure if the tide was in or out, so decided to pick up a tide table when he got to town, then wandered along the cliff top for an hour until the rain returned and drove him back to the cottage.

It was late afternoon when he got into Dingle. He called O'Neill first.

'There is a development,' said O'Neill. 'Fitzpatrick has been suspended from his position while RSF hold some sort of internal enquiry.'

'Is that good?'

'It means that your story has got them wondering. They will ask him a lot of difficult questions about his past, and if they start believing he might even conceivably be working for British Intelligence he'll never be trusted again.'

So the best I can do is ruin him politically Harry thought. Still, it was never going to get any better than that.

'Oh, and I have a message for you,' O'Neill continued, 'Someone called me trying to get hold of you, wants you to call him.'

'Really – who?'

'A Jack Hudson, said you had his number.'

Harry felt a stab of alarm. 'Did you tell him where I was?'

'Course not, you do know him I take it.'

Harry suddenly felt unexpectedly calm. 'Yes, I know him. Tell me, did he call you on your mobile?'

'Yes he did actually.'

After mentioning his phone signal problems and promising to call again same time the next day, Harry rang off. Then he tried Sabine, but got her voicemail. He left a long message bringing her right up to date with his activities, and said he'd try to call again tomorrow. Then he picked up a tide table, a couple of books and some assorted newspapers, and went back to the cottage.

The next day the rain had gone. The sea had transformed from grey to blue, and the white billowy clouds parted, allowing a sprinkling of sunshine which brought a sparkle to the water. It was still cold though, and Harry made his way down the track to the beach with his jacket zipped tightly around him. He walked the length of the tiny inlet, watching the surf breaking on the rocks offshore or swirling in little pools of white foam at the waters edge. The only company came from the seagulls crying and circling overhead.

He'd brought a cardboard box from the cottage and he rigged it up with a broom so the brush end supported the box at chest height, with the handle dug into the sand. Then he stepped back ten metres and took the Walther from his jacket. He'd decided to use one clip of ammunition on target practice, and he took his time, remembering the stance, the two handed grip and the sighting before squeezing off the first shot. It was loud, but not loud enough to worry about in this remote location, and he discharged the rest of the magazine in quick succession. The box had been blowing sideways a little in the wind, but most of the bullet holes were close to centre, with two bullets going into the wood of the brush. He grimaced and hoped Deirdre wouldn't notice the damage next time she swept the place. He had satisfied himself that he could still fire a gun and probably hit what he was aiming at should it become absolutely necessary.

He retrieved the spent cartridges, and broke up the box so he could flatten it out and use it as a cushion on the damp sand. He sat cross legged with the gun still in his hands, watching the sea rise and

274

fall and wondering about Jack's intentions. It made no sense for SIS to harm him, after Michael's death a repeat performance would only cement any doubts anyone might have about Fitzpatrick. Still, if anyone other than Deirdre knocked on the door he wanted to be ready.

Sabine answered the phone that evening, and he felt a rush of relief when he heard her voice.

'Did you understand my message?' he asked.

'Yes, I got it all. I admire what you're doing, but will it make any difference?'

'It won't send him to jail, if that's what you mean.'

'Then you've done all you can. Go home. You can't hide in Ireland forever.'

That evening, after he'd eaten and stoked the fire, he thought over her words. Dingle was a way to avoid dealing with his issues and nothing more. A probable divorce, and the twenty years of unresolved guilt and anger could all be conveniently shelved while he played at discrediting a murderous Irish politician. He was marking time, and time was not a commodity that he could take for granted anymore. In fact it was foolish to think that he'd ever taken it for granted. It was time to stop procrastinating and get on with the rest of his life, however long that might be.

He stayed two more days. The space and the sea calmed him, and he felt the clean coastal air charging him with energy on his walks along the cliff top. On the Thursday night he called Deirdre and told her he'd be leaving the next day, and asked how she wanted to be paid.

'David will pay,' she replied. 'Hope you enjoyed it for the short time you were here.'

'I did. I just need to get home now, that's all.'

'I've been reading your story Harry. Good luck, and come back again some time.'

When he arrived back in Dublin he returned the car and took a room for one night at the Harcourt. He would catch the bus to Belfast in the morning and call in on Michael Senior, then fly out that evening. He rang O'Neill to say he was back in town and to find out if he had time to meet. The newspaper man was surprised to learn he'd left Dingle, and agreed to call in at the Harcourt after work. When he arrived that evening he was excited.

'Fitzpatrick will be on TV at 7.30, you might want to watch it.'

He wouldn't reveal anything else, but by his demeanour Harry knew it must be important. He played along, and they had an early dinner in the hotel restaurant before going up to his room and tuning in to the news.

Fitzpatrick was the leading item. It was a live broadcast, and he was shown sitting at a kitchen table in what must have been his home. Two grim faced men in suits, presumably RSF members, stood behind him, but the camera focused exclusively on Fitzpatrick as he read from a prepared statement.

'After recent newspaper reports and an internal investigation by my own party, I would like to state that I have been working as

276

an agent for the British Intelligence Services since 1979. This is a role I took up after being compromised in a manner I do not wish to disclose. I would also like to state that I did not knowingly conspire in the murders of Siobhan O'Reilly and Natalie Ellis in 1981, as reported in the Irish Times, and accept no responsibility for these regrettable deaths. I am resigning from my position of Treasurer with the Republican Sinn Fein party, effective immediately.'

He looked haggard and uncomfortable throughout, and refused to take any follow up questions. O'Neill was jubilant, thumping Harry on the back and thrusting his fist in the air.

'Bloody fantastic – the best result we could have hoped for.'

'I wonder how they found out,' mused Harry. He felt decidedly underwhelmed even though his efforts in the press had just been vindicated.

'They must have gone over that period with a fine tooth comb,' said O'Neill, 'and somewhere along the line he gave the game away. We'll never know in all probability.' He gave Harry a curious glance. 'You seem less than pleased, Harry.'

Harry forced a smile. 'I am pleased, of course I am. And a bit shocked, I didn't expect this kind of revelation, and so fast too. But he lied about one thing as far as I'm concerned.'

'You mean Siobhan and your wife? You're being a little optimistic to expect a murder confession on national television.' He grabbed Harry's hand and shook it enthusiastically. 'But you've won Harry. Come on, let's go downstairs and have a drink on it.'

O'Neill had several drinks before saying his goodbyes. He assured Harry that the story would be all over Ireland, North and South by tomorrow morning, and wished him well for the future. Harry went back to his room in a ruminative mood. Fitzpatrick had been ruined politically, and no doubt his personal life would be miserable from now on too, and that was as much as he, Harry Ellis, could do to hurt the man. Time now to bring down the curtain and make his exit. His thoughts strayed to the shoebox in his suitcase, and he had to resist the urge to entertain fantasies of bringing a more permanent end to proceedings. The man wasn't worth going to jail for.

The story had certainly reached the O'Reilly household by the time he got to the West Belfast address on Saturday. Mrs. McDonald smiled broadly when she opened the door.

'Harry, you've been busy.' She made tea once again while Harry joined Michael Senior in the living room. He extracted the shoebox from his case and handed it over.

'Surplus to requirements after all, was it?' said the old man, who to Harry looked happier than the last time they'd met.

'I've fired one clip, actually. Just to see if I could still hit anything.'

'Indulging in a bit of nostalgia by the sound of it.' Michael Senior cradled the gun between his hands and looked relieved to have it back.

'More like wishful thinking,' replied Harry, and they both laughed.

'As a Republican I have to say you've done a good thing, exposing that bastard. I hope your Intelligence colleagues don't take it too badly.'

'I hope so too.'

He couldn't stay long, the flight was due to leave in two hours, so he cut his visit short and promised to stay in touch. The taxi had an unimpeded run to the airport, and he checked in then went straight through to departures. When the plane finally left the runway and began its steep ascent into the overcast sky he felt an inexplicable sense of loss. Perhaps he wouldn't see Ireland again. The beauty of the country and the warmth of its people were something to remember with pleasure, but they might never be enough to offset the bitter memories of 1981, and the anguish he'd carried with him ever since. Still, after all that had happened this time the scales of justice had undoubtedly moved towards equilibrium. Whether that would be enough to satisfy him remained to be seen.

The house was cold and musty, and the Christmas tree was still where he'd last seen it, looking distinctly threadbare and tired. He opened a window to get some fresh if cold air into the place, and the neat piles of needles underneath the tree began to stir and blow across the room, so he shut it again. Judging by the stack of unopened mail inside the door he could be pretty sure that Sophie hadn't been here in his absence.

There was a letter from her solicitor in Fulham. Mrs. Ellis was starting a divorce action, and she was offering a clean break, which meant selling the house and splitting the proceeds, with no further claims by one against the other. He wondered if the situation could be retrieved, but felt that he had betrayed her even though he loved her or thought he loved her. And he also knew how bloody minded she could be. He wouldn't try to change her mind, the truth was he didn't want to.

A clean break makes it relatively easy he thought. There were no children to complicate matters, and on the upside this was a chance for him to downsize and cut back on expenses. He would accept her offer. Of course this meant he'd need to start looking at flats or smaller houses and get this one on the market. He would spend the next week organising estate agents and scouting locations for his next address, and looking for his next contract.

He went upstairs to the bedroom. The gaping space in the wardrobe told him Sophie had taken her clothes, and when he went to the bathroom it looked distinctly empty without her array of toiletries in it. He wondered if she would conduct the whole divorce action through her solicitor, and if so whether he would see her again. Perhaps she'll appear for the ceremonial distribution of the CD collection, he thought. The prospect was farcical, but he wasn't laughing. He decided to draft a reply to the letter after dinner, and get things moving as quickly as possible.

The next week went by in a haze of activity. He spent the mornings letting in estate agents to value the place and listening to them enthuse about the wonderful job they would do in selling such a desirable residence, and how delighted they would be to send him details of houses and flats in his price range. He rang job agencies and checked the job sites on the web between these morning appointments, and spent the afternoon driving around Kent wondering where to live next.

By the end of the week he could put it off no longer. He needed to know what Jack Hudson had to say, and was perturbed by the fact Jack hadn't tried to call since leaving his message with O'Neill. Perhaps Harry's fait accompli had taken the wind out of his sails and he had no reason left to talk, but until Harry knew the other man's mind on the matter he would remain uncertain of Jack's ultimate intentions. There were no estate agents scheduled that morning, so he did his best to put his worries about the call to one side, and dialled the number.

'Hello, Harry. Good of you to get back to me.' His tone of voice seemed restrained, almost flat.

'I was busy, but I'm sure you know that.'

'Are you calling to resign?'

'I wasn't, but it seems an appropriate thing to do. Yes, I resign.'

'Accepted. You've cost us a great deal in time and effort, not to mention the fact our operation against dissident Republicanism has been set back several years. You should have considered your loyalties before talking to the press.'

Harry was incensed. 'The same way you did when you set me up to be murdered by a car bomb up in 1981? You bloody hypocrite.'

He thought he must have touched a nerve if the slight tone of apology in the reply was any indicator. 'That was Litchfield's decision. I wasn't consulted.'

'Then tell Litchfield he's a bloody hypocrite.'

'I would, but he died of a heart attack a few years ago.'

Harry took a calming breath. 'Look Jack, I had my motives and I think you understand them. I want to know now that I'll be left alone, and that I'll have nothing further to do with you or SIS. Can you give me that assurance?'

'Yes, you'll be left alone. We're not vindictive people. Your payments have been stopped and as far as we're concerned you don't exist. I hope you're satisfied with the outcome of your meddling in all this.'

Harry felt a weight lift. 'Thank you. I did as much as I could to discredit the man who killed my wife. I'll have to settle for that.'

'You mean you don't know?'

'Know what?'

Jack laughed, but it was an ugly sound. 'Colin Fitzpatrick was shot dead two nights ago outside his home in Dublin. By Michael O'Reilly the elder, two in the chest and one in the head. Got quite a steady hand for a man of his age.'

Harry was speechless for a moment.

'Do you want me to repeat that?' asked Jack.

'What happened to him?'

282

'O'Reilly? He's been arrested of course. He'll spend the rest of his life in jail.'

Harry couldn't quite take it in. He mumbled a 'Goodbye' and ended the call. He wondered if Jack was lying to him and why he hadn't heard it from O'Neill, so he called the Irish Times for confirmation. O'Neill wasn't there but the journalist who answered the phone assured him it was just as Jack had said.

Michael Senior had done what Harry couldn't bring himself to do. He went straight to the kitchen and found the best whisky he could lay his hands on. He raised a glass in a silent salute to the octogenarian who had dispensed direct justice for the murder of his two children, and by proxy had avenged Natalie too.

Later that day he emailed Sabine, not only to tell her about Fitzpatrick but to let her know he was being divorced on the grounds of adultery, and that he was busy looking for a new house and a new job. He promised to call her when he had all that sorted out.

In the following days he looked at houses for sale and showed people around his own home. But it all felt like it was happening to someone else, and he was only mildly interested.

He dreamed one night that he was on the boat again with Nat in her long clinging dress, but this time when she turned around she smiled and took his hand. Then she looked into his eyes as if to say 'it's done now' before her image dimmed and faded from view. He woke feeling refreshed and unaccountably happy. If Fitzpatrick's death was the catalyst for this transformation then he knew it wasn't quite right, but he didn't care. Natalie had been exorcised and allowed to rest, and that was all that mattered.

It had been several weeks since he'd last seen Cindy, and although he often wondered if their sessions were actually helping him, he had to admit he felt better for talking to her. Her consulting room was his Confessional without the accompanying absolution. He'd never thought of Catholic priests as unpaid psychotherapists, but there were certainly parallels. Who needed Freud or Jung when 100 Hail Marys would do the job? He called her office and made an appointment.

This time he was shocked to see her in a very smart black trouser suit. It was a first as far as he could recall, and it must have showed on his face.

'I'm taking a more conservative approach,' she said by way of explanation.

'Whatever for?'

'Well,' she began, looking a tiny bit embarrassed. 'One of my male clients said he found my normal attire distracting, and he wouldn't talk to me until I changed it.'

He felt a touch of empathy with his mysterious fellow patient. 'You look very nice.'

'Thank you Harry. I must say there's a change in you too.'

That surprised him. 'What do you mean?'

'Your whole demeanour seems lighter somehow. What have you been up to?'

'A few things. First of all, the man who killed Natalie, or at least ordered the killing, is dead. It feels like some sort of debt has been paid.'

'Did he die naturally?'

He smiled, a little grimly. 'No, that wouldn't pay any kind of debt.'

'And this payment of debt – has it relieved your anger?'

'I think so.'

'You said "a few things." What else is there?'

'Sophie is divorcing me.'

Cindy tossed her head back, probably more in surprise than by habit, but it startled him anyway. 'What did you do to deserve that?'

'I slept with another woman.'

'You wouldn't be the first man to do that, Harry. Can't you do anything to get her to reconsider?'

'I don't think I really want to.'

'I see.' Cindy crossed her legs and he thought she looked just as distracting in trousers. 'And is this other woman married?'

'No, she isn't.' He smiled to himself. 'She likes her independence.'

'What about your illness?'

'I've started the treatment. They've given me some anti-depressants too, I was feeling rather low for a while. It's a common side effect apparently. I'm feeling much more positive than I was though.'

'You have been busy. Anything else I should know?'

'I'm de-cluttering my life. Harry Ellis is going to live the simple life and stop helping investment banks enrich themselves and their clients.'

She smiled. 'That's interesting. Perhaps you should take up psychotherapy. It has it's fulfilling moments.'

He laughed. 'Don't think I've got the legs for it.'

She looked mildly amused. 'Well, that aside, I think we're finally making progress.'

Sabine didn't reply to his email, he knew she was working a lot after the breaks she'd taken, and she had a series of gigs lined up again in Heidelberg and Munich in February, so he wasn't immediately concerned. He was confident now for her safety and no longer expected daily texts.

The sale of the house was progressing rather slowly. There'd been two offers but far lower than the asking price, and he'd rejected both of them. In the meantime he'd agreed with Sophie, through the medium of her solicitor of course, that he would stay until a sale had been confirmed.

He continued with his medication, and although some days he felt tired and irritable, his body seemed to have adapted. The anti-depressants had stabilized his moods and he was sure there would be no repetition of that suicidal moment in Ireland. There was enough money in his account to keep him going for a year if necessary, so he decided to rest as much as possible and give the therapy the best chance of working. The odd prospective buyer would call in, but apart from that he either spent time sorting his possessions in advance of moving, or simply lazing around the house. It was strange to have so much time to himself, he was used to the 9 to 5 commute cycle and the pressure of a City job, so having so much leisure time brought him face to face with himself. Strangely enough he found he wasn't bored. He wondered what on else he could possibly do for a living other than what he already did, and came up with a blank. But now the thought had been planted it wouldn't leave him alone, and he knew that it would be only a matter of time before something realistic occurred to him. The money, of course, would doubtless be much less than he was used to, but he told himself that money wasn't everything. Until you had none, that is.

Finally the day arrived for his three month hospital check up. At Thomas's he sat once more awaiting an audience with Dr. Ashe. He felt nervous, and hoped that the tablets and injections, which had left him feeling like something of a human pin cushion, had had the desired affect. After the customary wait he was called in.

Dr. Ashe was studying his file, drumming his fingers on the desk. Harry thought it looked ominous. The doctor looked up.

'Mr. Ellis, take a seat.'

He sat and waited. Dr. Ashe spent another half minute reading, then finally spoke.

'Your blood test reveals no trace of your virus, Mr. Ellis.' He was smiling.

'Really? You mean I'm cured?' He felt like leaping up and down, and only just stopped himself.

'It means you're clear at the moment. That's very good news of course. But to ensure the best possible outcome you should continue the treatment for another 9 months. You were told that at the outset weren't you?'

Yes, thought Harry, I was. 'That's a long time. But as we've come this far I can't see any alternative.'

'We need to be sure. I recommend another 3 months at the least. If you feel it's all too much after that we can stop, but our best bet is to go the full year. It is my opinion,' and here he held up a cautionary finger, 'that you are on course to make a full recovery.'

'Alright then,' concurred Harry, 'as long as it takes.'

'Good. I'm very pleased for you. Go and see Isobel now and get next month's supply.'

Isobel grinned when he appeared, saying how excellent it all was, and actually gave him a hug. When he left Thomas's and walked back across Westminster Bridge, he was grinning too.

A week later a buyer finally made a realistic offer. He realised with a start that it was finally time to move. He'd had all this leisure time and been so lazy he still hadn't bothered to look for his next home. He thought he would rent somewhere near the station until he found the right property. He ordered some boxes from a local removal company and began packing as much as was practicable himself. The solicitor doing the conveyancing contacted him to

288

let him know contracts would be exchanged in two weeks, so he redoubled his efforts and found a two bedroom flat only ten minutes walk from the station, and paid a deposit.

Sabine had been on his mind every day. It had been almost two months since his last email to her, and although he'd wanted to call her way before now, he had deliberately refrained from doing so until he knew what the outcome of his treatment was likely to be. That evening he picked up the phone and dialled her number. It rang for so long that he was about to give up, when suddenly she picked up.

'Harry?' She sounded hesitant.

'Am I disturbing you?'

'No, of course not.'

'I thought I might have heard from you, that's all.'

'I thought you might be mad with me, you know, with the divorce. I feel responsible.'

He cursed himself for his insensitivity. 'It's me that's responsible. Don't feel bad on my account.'

'I still feel responsible. How's your treatment going?'

'I'm clear. Well, for now. I need to keep going, but they have high hopes for me.'

'Harry, that's wonderful. What will you do now? Go back to work?'

'I don't know exactly. What I would like to do is see you again.'

'I see.' He could hear the smile in her voice. 'I thought you said that was unwise.'

'Yes, well I was wrong about that.'

She laughed softly and he knew she was happy. 'I'm quite busy right now. But if you should find your way to Heidelberg in the near future, you know where I am.'

8287886R00170

Printed in Great Britain
by Amazon.co.uk, Ltd.,
Marston Gate.